The Hanging of Betsey Reed

A Wabash River Tragedy on the Illinois Frontier

To Eric
Best Wishes
Rick Kelsheimer
10/11/2014

Rick Kelsheimer

Copyright © 2009 by Rick Kelsheimer

ISBN 1-4392-3711-5

Cover art by Ben Kelsheimer.

BookSurge
7290 B Investment Drive
North Charleston, SC 29418
1-866-308-6235 ext. 6
www.booksurge.com

Printed in the United States of America
Published April 2009

...for Ben, Anna, Meagen, Jim,
and especially Sofie and Luca Belle

Betsey Reed brewed some tea.
Leonard drank it happily.
When she saw that he was dead,
She clicked her heels,
And then she said
Arsenic...arsenic...
We all fall dead.

One

"Hurry, Betsey! You're going to miss the hanging." Isaac was already fifty yards ahead of his nine-year-old sister.

"Don't worry about me. I'll catch up." She wasn't about to miss the big event. It was the only thing that people could talk about. Will Davis had killed old Jeremiah Singer while stealing his fattened sow, and was about to receive frontier justice. Betsey didn't know what *justice* meant, but everyone sure seemed anxious for Will Davis to receive *his*.

A traveling judge found Davis guilty the day before, and sentenced him to be hung today at high noon. Word of the public hanging spread like wildfire as hundreds of people showed up to give Will a proper sendoff.

Betsey had never seen this many people in one place in her whole life. There were women singing hymns and men drinking whiskey. A preacher scolded Isaac for knocking his Bible out of his hand. There was an element of excitement in the air, but it was very unsettling for the girl. The crowd wanted blood.

"There he is!" shouted one of the whiskey drinkers. "It's Will Davis!" The mob focused on the tall, thin man who had a full black beard and was riding in the back of a flatbed wagon. The local sheriff, a barrel-chested man with a perfectly waxed mustache and a black overcoat, was driving the rig with a solemn look on his face. A loudmouthed deputy, wearing a buckskin jacket with matching moccasins, was shooing the crowd away so the wagon could be positioned directly beneath a low-hanging elm branch next to the gate at the entrance of the Hardshell Baptist Cemetery.

Jeremiah Singer's widow followed the wagon with the assistance of her sisters, seeking solace in the death of her husband's killer. The crowd encircled the wagon while several men shouted obscenities at the condemned man. Will

1

Davis remained silent, pretending not hear the insults. Betsey climbed a tree on the other side of the road in order to get a better look at the killer. She was surprised that Will Davis didn't look like a bad man. As a matter of fact, he looked a lot like the preacher who had just yelled at Isaac. He looked up and made eye contact with her. She couldn't help but feel sorry for him. He had very sad eyes. Not only was he going to die, but he also had to endure the wrath of an angry mob during his last few minutes. She began to sob.

The deputy fired his rifle into the noontime sky and the crowd became silent. He jumped onto the back of the wagon and pulled the prisoner to his feet. With wrists tied behind him, Betsey could see his knees tremble as the deputy placed the noose around his neck.

The sheriff pulled a sheet of paper from the inside pocket of his jacket. "Hear ye! Hear ye! And now, on this day, comes the prisoner in custody to receive the sentence of the court. By order of the Honorable Judge Joshua West, First District Court, Commonwealth of Kentucky, Will Davis, after being found guilty of the murder of Jeremiah Singer, you are hereby sentenced to be taken to a convenient place tomorrow at noon, and shall be hanged by the neck until you are dead, and the sheriff shall execute this sentence. And may the Lord have mercy on your soul. Seeing how it's noon and I'm the sheriff and this place is as convenient as any...we shall proceed with the hanging."

The deputy started to place a black hood over Davis' head, but he shook his head *no*. "Any last words?" asked the sheriff. Davis shook his head *no* again. He quietly looked into the sympathetic eyes of the little girl in the tree as the wagon lunged forward. The crowd gasped as Will Davis twirled helplessly. A woman screamed as he gasped for air and his face turned blue. Some decided to look away, while others watched with morbid curiosity. After a minute, he stopped struggling and went limp. Justice had been served.

Two

Say what you want about public hangings, one thing is for sure: the outcome is permanent for the one dangling at the wrong end of the rope. That was the unfortunate position in which Elizabeth "Betsey" Reed found herself on the morning of May 23, 1845, when she became the first and only woman ever to be hung in the great State of Illinois.

Over the years, many folks have given their version of Betsey's infamous demise, but as a first-hand eyewitness, I've found most of these accounts to be lacking and incorrect. Now that I've reached my golden years and seem to have an abundance of free time on my hands, I've decided to take pen in hand and write an accurate history of the incident. I personally witnessed most of the events firsthand, but I reconstructed some of the story from interviews of the principals involved, and also from their journals and letters, which I have in my possession. I suppose that I could cite a high moral purpose as the reason for recording these events, but I won't. It's because the true story of how Elizabeth "Betsey" Reed found her way to the gallows beside the Embarrass River is just a darn good, yet tragic, story.

My name is Nathan Crockett. With the exception of a brief stint in the U.S. Army and a two-year stint at Saint Gabriel College in Vincennes, I've spent most of my life wandering the rolling hills and hardwood forests along the Wabash River. I've seen the land go from a frontier wilderness, inhabited by hostile Indians, to a peaceful farming community where all the folks, for the most part, seem to get along just fine.

A wilderness doesn't tame itself. It takes a rugged individual with a pioneer spirit, a sturdy disposition, and an explorer's heart to bring civilization to the hinterland. Some folks look for fame and fortune. Some look for God in the new country. Others just want to see what's on the other side of the river. The one thing they all have in common is that they want a better life and are willing to fight to get it. They'll fight the land, disease, wild animals, and even sometimes each other, but rest assured that they aim to reach their goals. With all these kindred spirits moving into the new land, there were bound to be folks who crossed paths with people who had different agendas. Ruckuses were bound to break out.

And break out they did.

Just like in the Bible, people were all fighting for their piece of the New Jerusalem, except in this case the New Jerusalem was Crawford County, Illinois. In the last hundred years, Crawford County has been claimed by the Piankeshaw, Miami, Delaware, and Kickapoo Indian tribes. Throw in the French, the British, and finally the new Americans, and you have a recipe for bloodshed.

In the wilderness, only the strong are able to survive. In the long run, the American settlers were too numerous and claimed the new land for good. The Indians moved west, and pioneers came in droves. Hunters, farmers, and merchants all made their way to Crawford County to start a new life. You would think that there was plenty of room for everyone, but with human nature being what it is, there was bound to be trouble.

Sometimes you don't even have to go outside the family to find treachery. Cain didn't have far to go to find his victim. If I remember right, King Henry VIII removed the heads of several of his wives when the grass looked greener on the other side of the fence. So it was with Betsey and Leonard Reed.

"For richer or poorer...in sickness and in health...and till death do us part" are all vows that are part of the marriage covenant, but I don't think the Good Lord intended for us to speed up the process, especially the part about death parting us. A jury of her peers decided that Betsey Reed wanted to become a widow. They also decided that her husband Leonard wasn't ready to be dead.

Three

The first time I ever crossed paths with Leonard and Betsey Reed was in the summer of 1840, when I hitched a ride on their flatbed wagon on my way to the courthouse in Palestine. Normally, I wouldn't impose on anyone, but property tax was due and my horse, Newton, had gone lame. I've learned that you don't want to be in arrears where the government is concerned. The deed to your property has a tendency to end up in a politician's hand if the land tax is late getting into town.

I hiked up from my cabin on the west bank of the Wabash River that sits beneath five giant sycamore trees, which I call the Five Sisters, to Rennick Heath's tavern in Heathsville. The Heath Tavern was a large building of white oak logs, which were harvested from nearby virgin timber. There were two rooms in front, twenty feet square with a large stone fireplace in each, and a pair of small bedrooms in the back. The inn was used as a stagecoach stop on the Vincennes-Chicago State Road. Since it was the only route to Palestine, I figured it might not be too difficult to catch a ride from there. The Heath Tavern was also the same location where a young pioneer by the name of Abe Lincoln spent the night at the end of his first full day in Illinois, ten years earlier.

Just about everyone who entered Illinois by way of Vincennes had enjoyed some Heath hospitality on his way to the federal land office in Palestine. Rennick and his wife, Malinda, had made their way up from Virginia and North Carolina and founded Heathsville in the middle of the wilderness in 1826. Now that several years had passed, the village consisted of ten houses, a livery barn, a blacksmith shop, and the tavern. The tavern also served as the local trading post where you could buy whiskey, tobacco, and all the other necessities of life.

Rennick was a sturdy man who had served as a captain under Abe Lincoln during the Black Hawk War, but who now spent most of his days tending to his ever-growing orchard. He was constantly trying to develop a new variety of apple or peach that would carry his name.

Malinda Heath, a serious but caring woman, was the hub for all gossip throughout the neighborhood. She collected all the news from the outside world that was delivered with each visit of the stagecoach, and passed it on whenever she could. She wasn't concerned with the accuracy of the news as long as she was the first to know. She was also the first to arrive with food or supplies if anyone was in need.

I was a bit winded from the hike up from the river bottom, so I decided to partake in a little refreshment. I helped myself to a mug of apple cider and hoped to chase it with a snort from one of Rennick's jugs. Before we could pop the cork, I was startled by the unmistakable sound of a rifle shot just outside the door. After spending most of your life around hostile Indians, river pirates, and highwaymen, you learn to move quickly at the first sign of danger. Without thinking I ran out the door, only to find the front right hoof of Leonard Reed's bay gelding flailing toward my face. I tried to duck, but the back of the horse's shoe caught me square on the crown of my head. I was out cold before my body hit the ground.

After a period of about ten minutes, I woke up on the floor. Malinda was applying a wet cold compress to what felt like a mountain growing out of the top of my skull.

"Hold still, Nathan!" she demanded after I tried to stand too quickly. "You're lucky you didn't get killed. It's a good thing the horse kicked you in the head instead of someplace vital, although those blue eyes of yours seem to be knocked off center. "

"Glad to see you're still among the living." Rennick chuckled.

"I don't know how alive I am," I admitted. "There seem to be several cherubs with little harps flying around my head."

"Well, at least you haven't lost your sense of humor," he said.

"What happened?"

"As far as I can tell, just as Mr. Reed stopped his wagon out front, one of the Baker boys saw a timber wolf stalking one of my sows around back. With the bounty on wolves being so high, he decided to take his best shot. The wolf went down but the noise spooked Reed's horse. You ran out, and boom! Down you went."

"I guess I would have been better off if I had stayed put."

"Not at all," he said. "You seem to have fallen into a windfall due to your attempted heroics. The Baker boy felt so guilty that he gave you half of the reward for the wolf scalp. All you have to do is give him his half of the money when you cash it in at Palestine. And Mr. Reed felt awful bad, since it was his horse that nearly struck a fatal blow, so he agreed to give you a ride into town."

"I should try this more often," I said sarcastically.

"I wouldn't say that if I were you," whispered Malinda. "You still have to tolerate spending the day with that awful woman. She's from the Dark Bend."

"Mother!" scolded Rennick. "If you can't say anything nice, it's best to keep your mouth shut."

"It's the truth," she chided. "Nathan has a right to know that he's headed into harm's way. She's a witch, you know."

"Shhhh! They're right outside the door!" he whispered. "They might hear you."

"I don't care if they do. She is pure evil. Consider yourself warned, Nathan." Malinda pulled the compress from my head and stormed into the back bedroom.

"I've never seen her upset like that before," Rennick said.

"What have you gotten me into?" I asked.

"Oh, don't pay any attention to her," he assured me. "Betsey Reed isn't evil. A little odd, maybe, but not evil." Rennick helped me to my feet and walked me to the door. As he placed my coonskin cap on my head, he whispered, "On second thought, maybe you ought to be careful around that woman, just to be on the safe side. Have a good trip!"

Four

Leonard Reed was a thin, frail man with salt-and-pepper hair, an oversized nose, and a perpetual smile. He wore buckskin pants and moccasins and a gray wool shirt with several hand-sewn patches to cover the holes. His face was ruddy and hard-baked by countless hours of toiling in the hot sun. He offered his chafed right hand as I cautiously made my way past the horse that had knocked me for a loop. "Sorry about your head, young man, but Ole Hickory never did like the sound of a rifle shot, especially when he's not expecting it," he explained.

"Well, I don't seem to be any worse for wear," I replied. "Just as long as Ole Hickory doesn't make a habit out of it. I don't think I could handle any more of his *how-do-you-do*'s."

"He'll behave, I promise. And speaking of *how-do-you-do*'s, I'm Leonard Reed."

"Crockett, Nathan Crockett. Glad to make your acquaintance."

"Crockett! Any kin to Davy?"

"Shirttail cousin," I replied.

"You don't say? One of my cousins married one of his cousins, so that kinda makes us kin in a roundabout way."

"Sounds complicated, but if you say so, who am I to argue?"

"And this here is my wife Betsey," Leonard declared as he pointed to a woman hiding behind the far side of the wagon.

Betsey turned quickly and offered a poor excuse for a nod. She was wearing an extra long bonnet that covered both sides of her cinnamon-colored face. She seemed timid, and veiled her mouth and nose with a small, white handkerchief. From what I could see, she was much younger than Leonard, and much better looking, too. Her hair was silky brown and long, falling softly below her shoulders against a simple, gray, woolen dress. Her figure was sturdy, but still very feminine. But what really stood out were her eyes. They were emerald green, wide and wild, almost catlike. Not like your basic tabby or mouser, but more like a bobcat or panther: beautiful, but dangerous. Spellbinding! Within minutes, Malinda Heath's warning was completely forgotten.

In 1840, the Vincennes-Chicago State Road wasn't as formal as its name suggested. The folks around the area referred to it as the Vincennes Trace or Purgatory Road, since it crossed Purgatory Swamp just south of Heathsville. The road was actually an old buffalo trail that started on the west side of the Wabash River and headed directly for Chicago.

In 1831, the General Assembly of Illinois commissioned a team of surveyors to plot a new and proper road from Vincennes to Chicago using all of their fancy new scientific instruments. They planted their stakes, did whatever it is that surveyors do, and made a long-winded official report declaring their victory over the wilderness. But in all fairness to the old bull buffalo that first blazed the trail hundreds of years earlier, the surveyors never strayed more than a quarter mile from the original trace.

I perched myself on the back of the flatbed wagon next to two bundles of raccoon and beaver skins that Leonard had trapped last winter. There were also six barrels of winter wheat in the front of the wagon, which left little room for the six feet two inches of my frame. Leonard was an expert hunter, but he found that he could harvest twice as many pelts by setting traps along the Wabash. He grew enough wheat and corn to survive, but didn't care very much for farming.

As we left the tavern and headed north, the road was covered with dry, hard ruts made by wagons that had pulled through deep mud earlier in the spring. Leonard was trying to steer the wagon into the tracks already laid down, hoping that it would smooth the ride, but Ole Hickory wasn't cooperating. Kicking me in the head wasn't enough; he wanted to finish me off by hitting every bump in the road. I was beginning to think that maybe I should have walked to town.

By the time we reached Doe Run Creek, Leonard started to recite his life story, while Betsey, with her wild green eyes, looked in the other direction, careful not to give me a good look at her face. Leonard turned out to be very likable and a darn good storyteller, but Betsey remained standoffish and quiet. Within minutes, I was starting to wonder how this mismatched pair had gotten together in the first place.

Five

Leonard Reed was born in 1795 in Barren County, Kentucky, and was the oldest of ten children raised by Edward and Margaret Reed. Like most pioneer families that lived on the frontier, the Reeds struggled to scratch out a living in the poor mountain soil. The farming was tough, so you had to learn to hunt or starve. Being the eldest, Leonard learned to hunt before he learned how to use a knife and fork. Neighbors used to say that he could shoot the eyes out of a squirrel at fifty paces before he reached his fifth birthday. As long as Leonard could hunt, his family would eat.

When he was seventeen, Leonard answered the call when "Old Tippecanoe" William Henry Harrison asked Governor Shelby to form a Kentucky Militia of two thousand men to reinforce his regulars at Fort Meigs in Ohio. In typical Kentucky fashion, four thousand coonskin-capped men mustered at Newport.

Leonard's regiment hooked up with General Harrison and marched all the way to Lake Erie, where they participated in the Battle of Thames. It was at this battle that Leonard personally witnessed one of Colonel Richard Johnson's men kill the great chief, Tecumseh. According to Leonard, a private by the name of David King put two balls into Tecumseh's chest at point blank range. Johnson was wounded in the first shots of the battle, but took credit nonetheless, becoming an instant war hero. Leonard liked to tell that story, because at the time, Richard M. Johnson was Vice President of the United States under Martin Van Buren.

Leonard preferred storytelling to work any day. In fact, I would have to say that he could spin a yarn better than anyone else I have ever met. His favorite story was about a pig that marched all the way to Canada. I had known him for

11

less than an hour when I heard the story for the first time. In that same amount of time, Betsey had not uttered a single word.

"Back in 1813, we were getting ready to go fight Tecumseh and his red-coated friends when the regiment came upon a commotion at the edge of Newport, Kentucky. There were about two dozen drunken men circled around a pair of pigs that was engaged in a fight. The two boars seemed evenly matched, and for a while, neither one of them got the advantage. But one of the porkers seemed to gain strength whenever the men began to cheer. As the fight went on, more men arrived. When they started to hoop and holler, the pig got even stronger. Within minutes the crowd turned into a mob, and the cheers affected the pig like hair affected Samson."

Leonard looked back to see if I was paying attention.

I was.

Betsey wasn't. She acted like she had heard the story a hundred times before. (She probably had.)

"Well, with all that support, this pig bit the other pig's ear clean off, causing him to run away quicker than a rabbit with a wolf on his trail. The men gave a mighty roar in his honor and patted him on the snout, then started for the ferry on the Ohio River. Now, this pig liked being the life of the party, so he followed us all the way down to the river. As we boarded the rickety barge, the pig tried to climb on board with us. Needless to say, he was quite upset when we wouldn't let him. Normally, this is where the story should have ended— but then again, this wasn't a normal pig. As we started to pull away, Mr. Pig jumped in the river, and with some encouragement from the men, swam across and joined us on the other side in Cincinnati. When the march to Lake Erie began, the pig followed. He couldn't keep up as we marched, but he managed to find us each evening when we made camp. He would prance through the camp, proud as a peacock, squealing to high heaven as the men cheered. After he was properly welcomed, he would then run up to the front of the camp so he could get a head start in the morning. He became very popular with the men. It got to the point where they would save part of their rations and prepare a feast for his nightly appearance. When we got to Lake Erie, he must have realized that it was too big to swim, so he waited on the pier, broken-hearted, when he wasn't allowed to board the ship with the rest of us. Now, this is where the story should have ended again, but this wasn't a normal pig.

"After we landed on the other side of the lake in Canada, the militia was ready to take on General Proctor and Tecumseh when we heard that familiar squeal. Sure enough, it was our pig, big as life, standing on Canadian soil. He had somehow hitched a ride with the horses and mules and had followed them until he found our company. The men promoted him to the rank of captain and marched off to battle. He stayed with us as our good luck charm through some heavy Indian fighting. I am convinced that the battle wouldn't have been won without the good luck provided by our Captain Pig."

Leonard stopped to take a breath and wipe his brow as he got ready to finish his story. "Needless to say, our pig became famous, and he made the march all the way back to Kentucky. Just to make sure he didn't end up as Sunday dinner, he was promoted again to full Kentucky Colonel and was given to Governor Shelby at whose home he lived the rest of his days before going to hog heaven."

Betsey shook her head in disgust when he finished the story. "If I hear that damn story one more time, I'm surely going to kill you!" A sudden gust of wind silenced her tirade when her bonnet fell to the ground, exposing a deep scar on the left side of her face. The jagged cut was shaped like an upside-down letter J, starting high on her left cheekbone and ending at the center of her chin.

I tried my best to act like I didn't notice anything, but I guess I must not be a very good actor. She turned away, hiding her face in her hands. For an instant her wild green eyes showed a sadness that must have been all too familiar for her. *Who could have done such a thing? And why?*

Leonard hopped to the ground and had the bonnet back

on her head within five seconds. I would have never guessed that the little guy could have moved so quickly.

I sat in silence after her outburst. I was stunned that a woman so beautiful could be so difficult to look at. No wonder her disposition seemed so hard and distant. I guess what I felt was a combination of horror and pity. At the time, I didn't realize how ironic it was that the first sentence I heard Betsey Reed utter was a death threat toward her husband. I had heard men talk that way, but never a woman.

"Now, Betsey, don't get mad. I was just trying to be hospitable and entertain Nathan, seeing how Ole Hickory dang near killed him."

"I don't care," she bit back. "You're always trying to entertain somebody! If you spent as much time planting corn and shooting animals as you did storytelling, we wouldn't be living in that dirty one room cabin. I should never have left Indiana for this godforsaken place." She had replaced her pain with anger, and I could tell it was going to get rough for Leonard.

Leonard turned toward me to offer an explanation. "Sometimes the heat gets to her and she gets a bit cranky..."

"Cranky?" Betsey screamed. "I'll show you cranky! I'll show you more than cranky! I'll show you—"

"Hey folks!" I interrupted their argument before we found out what came after "more than cranky." "I've imposed too much already. My head's hurting pretty bad, so why don't I get off right here. I'll just lie down next to the creek bank up ahead, stay in the shade for an hour or two, and then walk into town. You two can go ahead, and I'll be fine."

They were silent. I had insulted them. Both looked like they had lost their best hound dog. I wanted to ease myself out of a sticky situation, but I never intended to bruise any feelings. I should have jumped off that wagon and stayed out of their path forever, but they managed to make me feel guilty. I don't know why I felt guilty; I just did.

I stood up quickly and faked a dizzy spell. "Whoa! Maybe it's not such a great idea for you to leave me alone right now. I guess I'll just tough it out and ride in with you. That is, if you don't mind."

"Why, no, it's no trouble at all. Is it, Betsey?" Leonard said, with a smile of relief.

"Of course not," she agreed. "Leonard, hand me the canteen."

Abruptly, she stepped off the bench seat and hopped into the back of the wagon next to me. Before I knew what was happening, she had my head on her lap and was rubbing cold water on my face with the edge of her apron. Leonard shooed Ole Hickory in the direction of Palestine with me sprawled out in the arms of his wife like a helpless baby. Part of me prayed that no one would see or hear about me ending up in such a compromising position. Another part of me enjoyed the surprisingly gentle caress of this woman, the same woman that Malinda Heath had just called pure evil. I had been warned, but didn't take heed.

This is wrong, I told myself as I halfheartedly tried to sit up. She pushed my head back into her lap. "Let me take care of you, Nathan Crockett," she whispered in my ear. "Just lay quiet, and everything will be just fine."

So, like a fly in a spider web, I laid there in silence.

Six

In Palestine, the Dubois Tavern was the center of activity after dark. The rooms were clean. The liquor was first rate. More importantly, the gossip was scandalous. A tuned fiddle was kept behind the bar and was used every night without exception. If none of the business travelers could play, there were at least ten regular patrons who could. It wasn't uncommon to have a dozen or more fiddlers in attendance at the same time. The fiddle would be passed around until every man got his turn. On these nights, there would be singing and dancing well past midnight. It was hard to get a good night's sleep, but without exception, I lodged at the tavern whenever I came to town.

Jesse Kilgore Dubois, the proprietor, was in the corner talking to three men who had the look of Eastern bankers. He gave me a wave as I made my way to the bar. Jesse was one of the richest men in the area. He served as a representative in the state legislature, and at that time was the receiver at the federal land office. He was later elected State Auditor, and was also one of Abe Lincoln's closest friends. Some of the local people were jealous of his wealth, but I knew him to be a generous man.

When my parents died of the milk sick, I was only twelve years old. Even though he barely knew me, Jesse Dubois arranged for me to stay with a local widow and paid my tuition at the local subscription school in Palestine. As soon as I turned sixteen, he paid for my tuition and board at Saint Gabriel College in Vincennes and never asked for anything in return. I did work for him occasionally, usually making deliveries of some sort. I never really needed the work, but I felt obligated to help him out whenever I could. I think he was disappointed that I never practiced law or went into business of some sort, but he never let it affect his kindness toward me. His wife, Adelia, had adopted me as one of her own and had become quite concerned that I had not yet found a wife. I could count on an introduction to one of her friends' nieces, daughters, or cousins on every trip into town.

I made my way to an empty table over by the fireplace. There was a cast-iron kettle filled with venison and potatoes hanging above a few hot coals. I ordered a bowl of the stew along with a mug of ale from a skinny, red-haired waitress by the name of Liddy Parker. She was a cute girl with a perpetual smile. She seemed eager to please and had a pleasant disposition. Unfortunately for her, I was not in the best of moods. My hunger had almost made me forget the knot on my head, but not completely. She seemed hurt that I didn't exchange pleasantries. I realized that I had offended her by the way she walked away. I would apologize later, but at that moment, all I wanted was to be left alone.

Fortunately, I had managed to make it into town without anyone catching a glimpse of me with my head on Betsey's lap. I know of at least twenty loafers and loudmouths who would have paid a day's wages to witness the event. I wouldn't have heard the end of it for years. At least for the time being, my secret seemed safe.

I finished the stew in minutes and ordered a second helping along with a second pint. I was starting to relax a bit when I heard a table of men roar with laughter. I was a bit surprised when I saw that the center of attention was none other than Leonard Reed. I looked around the room, but didn't see Betsey anywhere.

"Tell the pig story!" shouted a large, bearded man as he shoved a mug in front of Leonard. He didn't need much coaxing to start the story.

I hurried and finished my dinner, then slipped outside before Leonard noticed me. Not that I was trying to hide; I just didn't want the day's events to be the subject of one of Leonard's stories. I pulled up a chair and sat on the front porch. It was a very pleasant evening and the stars were extra bright that night. There were a few people moving about the street, but other than the laughter coming from inside the tavern, Palestine was quiet that evening. It felt good to sit and rest.

Just as I was ready to fall asleep, I was startled to feel a hand touch the sore spot on my head. I jumped up, ready for a fight.

"Oh! I'm sorry! I thought you were asleep." Even in the dark, I could see her green eyes. It was Betsey Reed.

"What are you doing? You nearly scared me to death."

"I just wanted to see if the bump had gone down on your head. I'm sorry, Nathan. I was worried about you. I just wanted to—" She never finished her sentence. She turned and ran toward the campground behind the tavern.

I sat in silence for a few seconds, and then I started to feel guilty. I knew that I shouldn't have been so cross with her. I probably should have left things as they were, but I didn't want her to feel bad on my account. Reluctantly, I made my way over to her campfire.

She was sitting on a blanket underneath their wagon with her face resting on her knees. She turned her head away from me as I approached. "Go away!" she calmly urged. "You don't need to worry about me. I'll be fine."

"I'm not worried. I'm sure you can take care of yourself. I just wanted to make sure that I didn't hurt your feelings. I didn't mean to snap at you. It's just that I was startled."

"Why should you care about my feelings? You don't even know me."

"What do you mean? I spent the better part of the day with my head on your lap. You single-handedly brought me back from the brink of death. I'd be pushing up daisies right now if you hadn't nursed me back to health." I was trying to be as overdramatic as possible as I sat down beside her.

"Now you're just teasing me." She made sure to keep her hand over the scar as she looked toward me. It was then that I realized the extent of her hurt. She had the same look that a dog has after it's been beaten all its life. She was cowering.

"Maybe I am teasing you a bit. I just wanted to see if you knew how to smile. It really doesn't hurt. You should try it

18

sometime." She hid her face even more. I couldn't tell if it was shyness or shame. I felt sorry for her. I gently touched the side of her cheek and turned her face so that she could see that I was being sincere. "I really am sorry. If I have offended you in any way, Mrs. Reed...I apologize."

The glow from the bonfire highlighted the part of her face that wasn't scarred. It proved that if you could look past her injury, she was really quite beautiful. Unfortunately, most people couldn't get that far.

She clutched my hand and held it tight against her face. "People aren't usually nice to me," she whispered. "All they see is the scar on my face and nothing else. I've heard people talk about me behind my back all of my life. I'm not who they say I am. I am not a devil or a witch or anything of the sort. I'm not a bad person!"

"I never thought you were a bad person. I don't even know you."

"I'm sure you've heard stories about me," she said.

"Not a one!" I replied. I never mentioned Malinda Heath's warning.

"Well, if you haven't...you will."

"Why do you say that?" I asked.

"Bad things always happen around me. Sometimes they happen to me. Sometimes they happen to someone else. But they happen! I'm one of those people who should have never been born." She then proceeded to tell me her life story.

She was squeezing my hand even tighter. I could sense that I was getting into a situation that I would regret later. "What about your husband? I'm sure he'd disagree with that statement."

"Not likely. He's just too lazy to divorce me." The subject of Leonard changed her mood as she looked down and let go of my hand. "He ain't much of a husband, anyway. After my first husband died, Leonard came and asked me to marry him and be a mother to his two boys who were still at home. His oldest son, Harrison, got married, and Leonard was left to tend for the younger ones all by himself. I told him no because we were first cousins."

"But you married him anyway."

"He had some land and promised to put half of it in my name. I figured that since he wasn't healthy, he wouldn't be around that long, and I would have a nice piece of acreage. People don't look down on you so much if you're a landowner."

"So it was a business arrangement?" I asked. I was starting to have second thoughts about chasing her over to her campfire, but to be honest, I found Betsey to be fascinating.

"You could say that," she said. "I took care of the boys and kept house for him. He was never around. He spent most of his time drinking whiskey at the tavern. He'd be gone for days at a time doing who knows what."

"That doesn't sound like much of a life," I said.

"It wasn't bad. I think the boys were starting to like me."

"What happened to the boys?" I asked.

"They got typhoid fever and died within a week."

"That's horrible."

"Yes, it was. He was gone at the time. I buried them myself in the back yard. The doctor said that the disease could spread if I didn't." She paused for a moment and took a deep breath. "It's an awful thing, to bury children. I don't wish it on anybody."

"What did Leonard say when he got back?"

"He blamed me at first, but I straightened him out real quick."

"What did you do?" I asked.

"I beat him within an inch of his life. I had done everything I could to save them. I wasn't about to stand for him blaming me for killing those boys. He should have been there anyway."

The tone of Betsey's voice never varied at all. She never showed any emotion as she recited the rest of her history with Leonard. As things turned out, Leonard had borrowed against the land. When he couldn't make good on the note, he lost the property to some Eastern speculators. Betsey was going to leave him, but had nowhere to go. When the land office in Palestine started selling land with a down payment of fifty cents an acre, they bought forty acres in southern Crawford County and tried to start a new life.

Apparently, Leonard had not been very ambitious, and they were having a hard time making ends meet. Leonard's son, Harrison, and his wife visited with them shortly after they arrived in Illinois. Harrison suggested that Leonard divorce Betsey before her name went on the deed in 1845. Needless to say, Betsey wasn't happy about that idea, and Harrison was forced to leave. She said that Leonard's health had been failing lately, and it would only be a matter of time until any one of the many contagious epidemics finished him off.

I was starting to realize that Betsey was unlike any woman I had ever met. I considered myself to be somewhat worldly and open-minded, but I couldn't imagine her socializing at the local church meeting or at the monthly quilting bee. In fact, I was having a hard time imagining her having any female friends at all.

"As far as I'm concerned," she said, "he can sit in that tavern and drink himself to death."

Even though I felt sorry for her, I was starting to feel uncomfortable being alone with her. "I really ought to be getting back inside," I said. "People might think that we ran off together."

"Don't go, Nathan!" She grabbed my arm as I started to walk away. "Please don't leave me alone."

"Really, it's not proper for me to be here." I tried to keep my voice down to a whisper. "You're a married woman. In this part of the country, a man could end up dead if he's found with another man's wife."

"Why did you follow me out here?" she asked. "It didn't seem to bother you before. Besides, Leonard doesn't care. He would probably pay you to take me off his hands. I'd take really good care of you, Nathan." She had gone from emotionless to out-of-control in a matter of seconds.

"I followed you to make sure you were all right. That's all! Nothing more!" I realized that I had made a mistake and needed to reverse course as quick as possible. "I want you to listen to me. I'd be worse than Leonard. I tend to drift like the wind. I couldn't stand to be tied down. It wouldn't be good for you. I'm not a good person. You'd only get hurt."

She stopped and became suddenly silent then pulled her hands away. "It's alright, Nathan. I understand. You don't have to lie."

"I'm not lying. You're a—"

"Go before you say another word," she interrupted.

"But—"

"Just go!" she screamed.

Seven

I turned and walked briskly back to the tavern. I knew that she was hurt and that I had done nothing to cause it, but I still felt bad. A little voice in my head was telling me to run and not look back, but I turned around anyway, just in time to see her kick an oaken bucket into the bonfire. She began to scream obscenities into the night, loud enough to wake up the dead. I decided to listen to the voice and ran inside as quick as I could. I was imagining myself turning into a pillar of salt. I made my way to the bar and downed a couple of pints of the Blue Ruin. The sound of fiddles playing and the laughter of drunken men filled the air, but I couldn't drown out the agonizing screams of Betsey Reed in my mind.

Leonard was in the corner, telling war stories to anyone who would listen, while his wife was outside howling at the moon. I finished another mug and decided that the night had become much too bizarre for my liking. I just wanted to bed early and hope for the best in the morning, but before I could move, the front door flew open with such force that it knocked an old man out of his chair.

"The stable's on fire!" shouted a voice from outside. The music stopped immediately and the room emptied. *So much for going to bed.*

By the time I made it out the door, half of Palestine seemed to be converging upon the pyre that used to be known as Taylor's Livery. It was obvious to anyone who had ever seen a building burn that this one was beyond saving. A few buckets of well water were not going to do any good against a fire in a hardwood barn full of hay. All you could do was try to keep the fire from spreading to surrounding buildings and hope that no one was hurt. While most of the tavern's patrons ran to join the bucket brigade, I noticed a man desperately trying to enter the burning stable. I saw him run into the smoky blackness only to reappear a moment later, crawling on his hands and knees. He was coughing violently and fell face-first to the ground. I realized that if he wasn't moved at once he was going to breathe in too much smoke and suffocate.

By the time I reached him, he was completely shrouded in smoke and had gone completely limp. I grabbed him by the collar of his shirt and dragged him to a nearby watering trough.

"Ole Hickory's still inside," he howled, choking on the smoke still lingering in his lungs. It was Leonard Reed.

"It's too late, Leonard! There's nothing you can do!" I moved him a little further back as the wind shifted, blowing the smoke our way.

"I saw him! He's still alive! I can get to him! The back of the barn is still in one piece!" He tried to stand up, but fell in a heap to the ground, coughing uncontrollably.

Whenever you face a life and death situation, it's usually a good habit to step back and think things through, to weigh the risks and rewards against each other and make a calculated decision. This was not one of those times. Leonard was not in any shape to go back, and I was feeling a little awkward for getting his wife riled up. Besides, saving a horse from a fiery death was as good a cause as any.

"I'll go," I said with a bit of reservation.

"I'll go—" (*cough, cough*) "with—" (*cough, cough*) "with you," Leonard stammered, as he tried to make it back to his feet.

At best, he would just get in the way. At worst, he'd end up getting himself, or me, killed. I didn't have time to argue with him, so I knocked him out with a quick punch to the jaw. "Sorry, Leonard," I mumbled to myself. "You can thank me later."

I peeled away my shirt and soaked it in the watering trough, then wrapped it around my head. I took a running start toward the entrance of the barn and jumped through the center of the fire. Luckily, I landed on the other side of the flames in the back of the barn. After getting my bearings, I unwrapped my shirt and used it to douse the fire, which had now started on my pant leg.

I figured that if I went fast enough I could get through the flames, but I hadn't counted on the extreme heat of the fire. I needed to get out, and I needed to do it quickly.

I saw Ole Hickory kicking at the door of his stall, desperately trying to free himself. His eyes were full of terror, and it looked like I was the last person on Earth he wanted to see. "Sorry, boy. It's me or nobody." When I pulled the pin out of the latch, he shot out of the stall just as a beam, engulfed in flames, cracked hard against the side of his neck. He ran through the fire and out the door without giving me a second thought.

I backed up against the wall in order to get as long of a run as I could. I knew there was another door in the barn, but I couldn't see three feet in any direction. I was going to have to go out the same way I came in. I had lost my shirt, and my eyes were stinging from the smoke so badly that I couldn't keep them open. I took two steps, tripped over something soft on the floor, and fell into a burning pile of hay. As I pushed myself back to my knees, I could feel the flesh of my palms sizzling like beefsteaks. I reached back to see what it was that had caused me to fall. It wasn't something; it was *someone!* As luck would have it, he was a very large someone.

I couldn't tell if he was dead or alive. He was probably dead, but I couldn't risk leaving him. I grabbed him underneath his arms and somehow propped him over the side of a stall. He was completely limp and felt like he weighed every bit of two hundred pounds, if not more. I backed up to the fence and pulled on his left arm, causing him to fall across my back. I hooked his legs with my right arm, and with a quick jerk, I managed to get him centered across my shoulders. My knees started to buckle, but after running into a wall I managed to stand up straight. Another beam fell beside me, and I realized I had to go *now*. I opened my eyes as much as I could to get my bearings, took a deep breath, and plodded slowly toward the fire and hopefully the door. I had been hoping to jump through the flames, but with the extra weight, that just wasn't possible. I thought the fire had been hot on the way into the stable, but it was nothing compared to the exit. It took me about five steps to get through. The force of the heat hit me like a hammer, and I knew immediately that I couldn't keep my balance. I also knew that if I fell backward, we were dead.

If we fell forward, we might have a chance. I felt myself falling toward the door. The momentum caused by the weight of my passenger started to push me forward to the point where I could throw him over my head and maybe into the clear. As soon as I let go of him I fell to the ground, and with a quick rolling motion I found myself outside and in the clear.

I tried to take a deep breath but could only cough. I struggled to get up but I was unable to move. There wasn't any air getting to my lungs. To make matters worse, my pants were on fire, and I could feel the fire eating at my skin. Mercifully, two men grabbed me and threw me into the horse trough.

I accidentally swallowed a large quantity of water and immediately vomited the liquid along with the smoke out of my lungs. The coolness of the water soothed my burns at first, but within seconds I realized that a good portion of my body had been roasted. It felt like thousands of bees were stinging me simultaneously. As they laid me on the ground, I felt myself growing cold and withdrawing into the back of my mind. I could see people running around trying to put out the fire while Adelia Dubois called for someone to carry me inside. Everyone seemed very distant as they lifted me onto a blanket. As we started toward the tavern, everything grew dim and silent. I was convinced I was dying. The last thing I remembered before things went black was Leonard Reed pouring a bucket of water over Ole Hickory's head.

How ironic, I thought.

Eight

"It's about time you stopped sleeping your life away," said Jesse Dubois. "We thought you were going to leave us."

"How long have I been out?" I asked. Everything looked foggy, and I could barely lift my head. I noticed that most of my upper body was wrapped up like a mummy from Egypt.

"It's been four days since the fire. Doc Logan's been feeding you Paregoric to kill the pain. You seared everything from your navel on up and from your thighs to your ankles, but Doc says it's not too deep. You should heal up just fine. He's got you covered in some sort of salve that is supposed to kill the infection. You had a high fever that finally broke last night. You're a lucky young man. What were you thinking? Running into that burning barn, trying to be a hero. I thought you had more sense than that!"

"I thought I did, too." I was trying to scratch an itch on my nose with my bandaged hand. Jesse pulled it away.

"Doc says you can't scratch anything. It'll make it worse," scolded the familiar voice of Adelia Dubois.

"Just a little scratch won't hurt," I pleaded

"If you do, I've got strict orders to tie you down. You don't want that, do you?" Adelia was laughing, but there was enough bite in her voice to let me know that she would follow through if needed.

"What happened to the man who was in the barn? Is he...?"

"Oh, he's fine." There was a hint of sarcasm in her voice. "Hardly a scratch on him. By the time he sobered up, he didn't have any problem walking over to the county jail."

"He's in jail? What for?" I asked.

"Arson. He was the one who burned down the stable."

"But why did he do that?" I asked. "He was still inside. It doesn't make sense."

"Who knows? His name is Doyle Popplewell, a river-rat from the Dark Bend. None of those boys has ever been known for his brains. Apparently, he made a pass at a married woman at the campground. She tried to shoo him away. He wouldn't leave, so she hit him on the head with a bucket and told him to sleep in the barn. He staggered to the stable. Two minutes later, it's on fire."

"Great. I saved a river pirate."

"That doesn't matter," she said. "It was a heroic deed. I suppose it would have made a better story if you had saved a fair damsel instead of a burly criminal, but it was impressive nevertheless. Besides, the horse you saved wasn't a criminal."

"I don't know about that," I moaned as I rolled on a tender spot. "He kicked me in the head earlier that day."

"Well, at least it adds color to the story. And don't be too hard on the beast. He *did* lose an ear in the fire."

"Did he? Serves him right." My skin was starting to sting. Whatever they had given me for the pain was wearing off.

"Looks like you need another dose of Paregoric," she said, as she poured the contents of a brown bottle into a small, pewter mug. "Drink it fast. That way it won't taste so bad."

I chugged the concoction in a single gulp. "That's horrible. What's in it?"

"Opium and alcohol, plus a little camphor thrown in for flavor."

"No axle grease?"

"That's the Nathan we've come to know and love," Jesse laughed. "I'd better be on my way. Doc says you should take it easy for a few days. I'll tell him you're awake; I'm sure he'll want to come by and see how you're doing. Maybe now you'll settle down and put that education to use."

"Maybe someday."

After drinking the horrible concoction I started to feel sleepy, but my mind was full of questions. "You said that Popplewell made a pass at a married woman. Do you know who it was?" I asked Adelia.

"I don't know her name," she replied as she was walking out the door. "All I know it that she has some kind of scar on her face. I think she's married to that little man who tells that story about the pig. She said that she has the gift of blowing fire away, so I let her say her chant over you on the night of the fire. I don't know if I believe in that white magic or not, but you seemed to take a turn for the better as soon as she left. Don't worry about that right now. Just get some rest. I'll be gone for a while, so Liddy Parker will be in to check on you later this afternoon. Nathan, I can't tell you how glad I am that you're going to recover fully. It truly is a miracle."

Coincidences. Without trying to sound too cynical, I just don't believe in them. Things happen for a reason. Two boys from the same family drown two years apart. People will say: What a coincidence! It's really not a coincidence. Maybe they went swimming at a dangerous swimming hole or never learned to swim in the first place. Who knows? Maybe Ma or Pa didn't want to have two hungry mouths to feed. Whatever the case may be, there is almost always a logical explanation for everything that happens. Many times, people don't look for the reasons. Looking can lead to answers. Sometimes the answers aren't so pretty. It was a coincidence that I was almost killed twice on the day I met Leonard and Betsey Reed. It was a coincidence that Malinda Heath had warned me about getting close to her. It was a coincidence that Betsey said bad things always happen when she was around. *Too many coincidences!*

The opium was starting to take effect, and I started to notice that everything was beginning to get a little cloudy. I tried to focus on all the coincidences that had occurred on the day of the fire. Betsey threw a bucket into the fire moments before a drifter made unwanted advances toward her. A few minutes later, the same man gets hit in the head with a bucket, then walks into a stable and burns it to the ground. Coincidence? Betsey had a man make unwanted advances toward her moments after she had made unwanted advances toward me. Another coincidence? Betsey Reed and Doyle

Popplewell were both from the Dark Bend. Too many coincidences! There had to be a reason for all these coincidences, but it would have to wait. I was drifting off to sleep with a vision of a one-eared Ole Hickory smiling at me.

Nine

"Green-Eyed Monster...Witch...Scar-face..." Betsey pretended not to hear the taunts and insults that people whispered as she passed them on the street. She made sure to never give anyone the satisfaction of knowing that the words had done damage. Women used to say she had the hardest disposition they had ever seen. Others used to say that she was quite homely, an absolutely false statement.

It was the scar on the left side of her face that made her so self-conscious. *"The mark of Cain...God's punishment... No God-fearing woman in her right mind would show her face at a social function with a scar like that!"* As a young woman, Betsey wanted to be accepted and liked by the people around her more than anything else, but it was never to be. She was a tainted woman.

To men, it was the scar that made her mysterious, a woman with a past, dangerous.

The fact that she refused to talk about its origin made her all the more intriguing.

Betsey was born the youngest of seven children to Abraham and Sarah Fail in the fall of 1807. It was a difficult delivery, causing Sarah to be bedridden for six months. She was never able to fully regain her strength and grew bitter as time passed by. She blamed Betsey, who essentially became a second-class citizen in her own family.

Betsey spent her early childhood in the forested hills of Barren County, Kentucky. But, like most early settlers in Kentucky, the Fails lost their land due to the fact that they had not filed a proper deed at the land office. They had settled and cleared the land before the arrival of surveyors, but the Commonwealth didn't recognize squatters' rights. Eastern speculators bought up the deeds to the newly plotted

31

frontier and promptly evicted the pioneers who had tamed the land. Abraham's only option was to move his family west and start over once again. He learned that the federal land office in Palestine was giving good paper on plots with favorable financing to pioneers that would settle the land. They headed to the open territory of Illinois and settled on the southern banks of the Embarrass River (pronounced *Ambraw*) about ten miles northwest of Lawrenceville in a region known as the Dark Bend. "Bend" refers to an area where the river comes south, then abruptly bends back to the north. "Dark" refers to the notorious deeds that were committed in that area. The Dark Bend was home to counterfeiters, moon shiners, horse thieves, and murderers. Lawmen had been known to enter the area in pursuit of a criminal and disappear without a trace. Any woman who grew up under such dubious circumstances was destined to have a reputation. Guilt by association was the rule of the day, especially in church-going circles.

When Betsey was eight years old, she dreamed about becoming a preacher's wife. In the wilderness, the local minister was often the glue that held the settlement together. The minister and his wife were held in high esteem, and were treated like local royalty. The wife of a preacher would wear the best store-bought dresses and only the finest hats. They sat in the front pew at church, and ate Sunday dinners that they didn't have to cook. Most of all, people respected a preacher's wife. It was definitely a life fit for a princess.

However, the reality of her life couldn't be further from her dreams. As an only daughter, Betsey was treated more like an indentured servant than a member of the family. She cooked, cleaned, and mended clothes. She chopped wood, made soap, and worked the fields like a man. She gathered roots and herbs for her father, who then sold them in town. Since there weren't any doctors around, neighbors would come to Abraham Fail for his herbal cures and remedies. He also claimed to have the gift of blowing fire, meaning that he could heal burn victims by blowing the fire awa, and the ability to stop bleeding, both internal and external. This practice was common among the mountain people back east. It was passed down from generation to generation, father to daughter and mother to son. Only one person could receive the gift, and it had to be a descendant of the opposite sex.

Since she was his only daughter, Abraham passed the healing secrets on to Betsey on her ninth birthday, but Abraham Fail was worn out by a hard life and soon became feeble and bedridden. Within a matter of months, he died of pneumonia. Sarah considered Betsey to be a threat to her position as family matriarch. She was consumed with jealousy whenever one of her sons paid any attention to Betsey. Soon after her father's death, neighbors started showing up with burns and cuts, knowing that Abraham had passed on his gift to his daughter. Sarah went into a rage when the people stated calling her a miracle worker. Betsey was beaten and belittled for every minor infraction. She was convinced that her mother would kill her and throw her body to the wolves if she could get away with it. It was a premonition that almost came to pass.

When she was thirteen, her mother traded her to a traveling wagon peddler by the name of Alfred Dean for a cast-iron skillet and five pounds of lard. She told Betsey that she was too much of a burden, and that she was lucky to have a man who wanted her. When she threw a fit and refused to go, her mother beat her until she lost consciousness. When she awakened, she was tied to the inside of the peddler's wagon under the influence of some type of opiate.

Dean raped her nightly and tied her to the wagon to keep her from running away. As the weeks passed, Betsey became numb and emotionless. She prayed every night for God to deliver her from this life. Death would be a much better option than the hell on Earth that she endured daily. But death didn't come. She felt totally abandoned and betrayed. What had she done to deserve this fate?

But when she thought things couldn't possibly get worse, they did. The peddler tried to draw into an inside straight and lost her in a poker game to a horse thief by the name of Eli Napier. At least Alfred Dean had kept her tied up in a covered wagon where she had shelter from the weather. Napier tied her to a tree for days at a time in the dense forest without feeding her. It was obvious that Napier never intended for her to leave the woods alive. After six weeks of being held prisoner, Betsey had wasted away to skin and bones. It was only a matter of time before she died of starvation or was killed by wild animals. After she had eaten all of the grass within her reach, Betsey reluctantly foraged for worms and insects as her only source of nourishment. It didn't matter; she already felt dead on the inside.

One evening, Napier came to the woods in a drunken stupor and was more agitated than usual. Betsey couldn't bear the thought of another assault by the dirty, long-bearded scoundrel. He smelled like a cross between a dead skunk and a horse stable. At first, she pretended to be asleep, hoping he would lose interest in her, but it didn't work. When he couldn't get a response, he cut the rope from her wrists and ankles and began slapping her across the face. After a sharp blow to the crown of her head, Betsey leaped from the ground and out of pure survival instinct somehow managed to throw a punch that hit him squarely in the throat. Napier immediately fell to the ground and began to make a gurgling sound. His eyes bulged, and his face started to turn blue. He was able to get back to his feet, and then he pulled out a large hunting knife and lunged toward Betsey's face. She tried to avoid his thrust, but tripped and stumbled against an oak tree. Her face stung as if it were on fire when the knife plunged into her left cheekbone. She was too tired to fight. Blood spewed out, covering her soiled wool dress. "Just kill me!" she screamed. Her voice was raspy from lack of water as she felt the blood pour down her throat. She poked her tongue through the opening in her cheek. She knew that she couldn't defend herself anymore; she was as good as dead. "Get it over with, you Pig!"

But instead of stabbing her again, Napier stumbled and fell to the ground. Within seconds, his gagging turned to silence. He was dead, done in by a one-in-a-million lucky punch. Betsey had been sold, raped, and almost killed, but she didn't die. She had killed her would-be murderer and felt no remorse. She made a vow over the bloating body of Eli Napier that she would never let anyone hurt her again. She made a poultice from some tobacco she found in Napier's saddlebag and a strip of wool from his horse-blanket, and held it against her swollen bloody face. Before leaving, Betsey doused Napier's body with oil from a lamp that was nailed to a nearby maple tree and managed to start a fire using his flint stone. As she left on the horse thief's coal-black mare, Betsey looked back to see the smoldering heap, who had only minutes before had tried to kill her, and felt empowered. She had a newfound desire to live and a newly acquired taste for vengeance.

Instead of riding to safety, Betsey rode at breakneck speed, looking for the wagon that had served as her prison before she was given to Napier. She would not rest until she found Alfred Dean.

Thirty days later, Betsey turned up at her brother Isaac's farm back in the Dark Bend, riding a stolen black horse. Isaac was the only member of the family who had ever shown her any compassion, and would have stopped Alfred Dean from taking her away if he had known about his mother's shenanigans. Isaac had actually gone after the peddler, but found out that he had been murdered ten days ago. "Seems like he was burned alive while he was asleep in his wagon," Isaac informed Betsey.

"He got what he deserved." Her teeth were clenched tight, and her eyes revealed an intense hatred above a fresh scar on the left side of her face. "He screamed like a baby when the flames reached him. I wanted him to suffer, just like he had made me suffer." She collapsed and fell to the ground, exhausted and near death.

Isaac knew that nothing good could come out of this situation. He hid Betsey in an abandoned cabin on the other side of the Embarrass River. He knew that their mother hated Betsey and would turn her into the law if she learned that she had returned home. After feeding her broth and stew for two weeks, he decided that Betsey had regained enough strength to travel. Isaac dressed her in buckskin hunting clothes so she would look like a boy, and under the cover of darkness, they rode east toward the Wabash River. When they crossed over to Vincennes, he bought passage on a riverboat named the *Juniata* to Logansport, Indiana in Cass County. He bought her a new dress and a bonnet. Her old clothes were nothing but rags, soiled beyond redemption. He gave her five dollars in silver, a box filled with biscuits and corndodgers, and a letter of introduction to their uncle, Jacob Fail. By five o'clock, she was steaming toward northern Indiana. She was thirteen years old and alone in the world.

Isaac told the Sheriff that Betsey had gone to live with her uncle in Indiana a full month before the untimely deaths of Alfred Dean and Eli Napier. No one in the Dark Bend would dare call Isaac Fail a liar, and after all, the men were considered scoundrels at best, so the murders went unsolved.

When Betsey arrived in Logansport, she found out that her Uncle Jacob had died during the past winter after a bout of dysentery. His widow, Abigail Fail, agreed to take her in as long as she agreed to work for her room and board. When Abigail, a practicing midwife, learned that Betsey possessed healing gifts and was experienced in harvesting roots and herbs, she decided it would be advantageous to keep her around.

Abigail Fail was a stern woman and had never been overly affectionate toward anyone, especially her own family. She pulled her hair into such a tight bun that people used to joke that it made it impossible for her to smile. Despite her hard disposition, she was not mean-spirited, and for the first time in her life, Betsey was living under the guardianship of a woman who didn't despise her. It wasn't a loving relationship, but at least it was safe and stable. Betsey assisted Abigail whenever she called on neighbors with her home remedies or delivered babies. By the time Betsey reached her sixteenth birthday, she had delivered over two dozen babies on her own and was given more and more responsibility by her aunt.

Betsey had never gone to school in Illinois, and Abigail

thought it was too late to start. However, she thought that every person should be literate and taught Betsey to read and write during nightly lessons. Betsey thrived under the attention she received, but only as long as she was protected under the covering of her aunt. Whenever she went in public alone, the other children teased her mercilessly about the scar on her face. They were relentless, but when she was in public with her aunt, the children wouldn't dare say anything. They all knew better than to trigger the wrath of Abigail Fail. This caused Betsey to withdraw even more, and eventually she refused to venture into social situations at all. She started to view herself as some sort of freak, a hideous monster, and believed that she was unlovable. Things only got worse when Abigail suffered a fatal heart attack while walking with Betsey to the mercantile. Abigail's brother from Ohio sold her house and took all of her belongings back east, leaving Betsey homeless and penniless once again.

Betsey found employment at a local boarding house that catered to river men and dockworkers. She cleaned and did laundry from dawn until dusk for the privilege of receiving one meal and a place to sleep on the back porch. Regina Hathaway was the pudgy, slovenly proprietor, who possessed a sour personality and was greedy to the core. She knew Betsey was in a desperate situation, and used her circumstances to take advantage of her any way she possibly could. Betsey had only lived with her for a few days when Regina noticed that her boarders were taking an interest in the new cleaning girl. She made it a condition of Betsey's employment to entertain the men in the evening after dinner. Her patrons weren't the type of men who would object about Betsey's scar, and they also weren't looking for committed relationships. At first, Betsey resisted their advances, but when Regina threatened her with eviction, she succumbed.

"A girl with a scar like yours is lucky to have any man look at her twice," she would tell Betsey when she started to complain. "Remember, if you don't earn your keep, you'll be walking the street, begging for a piece of bread, willing to do anything to get it." Betsey did whatever Regina asked her to do. It seemed like she was with a different man every night. Soon, their faces became a blur, and she looked for an opportunity to escape.

One day, a man named John Stone offered to take Betsey away from the boarding house. He wasn't very nice and wasn't much to look at, but anything was better than life with Regina, so without much thought she agreed to be his wife. They were married by a riverboat captain and lived in a rough cabin south of Logansport.

John Stone was fifteen years her elder and had a reputation as somewhat of a womanizer. He worked on the river, mostly loading cargo and taking keelboats down as far as Terre Haute or Vincennes. After ten years of abusive marriage, he left Logansport on a flatboat and was never seen or heard from again. Some said he ran off to New Orleans with a younger girl, while others said that he got drunk and fell in the Wabash just above the Darwin Ferry. There were even whispers around town that Betsey and her husband's business partner had conspired to kill him and disposed of the body in the river. No one knows for sure, and it still remains a mystery.

Betsey struggled to make ends meet as a midwife. She was scorned by most people due to the dubious reputation of her late husband, so when Leonard Reed appeared and asked her to marry him and raise his boys, she agreed. She was desperate and out of options.

Ten

It felt good to breathe fresh air again. Two weeks of the stale tavern variety had left me with the taste of mold and fireplace ash. My burns had healed up nicely. With the exception of a scab on my nose and several blotches of white on my arms, you couldn't tell I had been burned at all. Jesse Dubois purchased new clothes for me that were twice the quality of the ones lost in the fire. He acted insulted when I tried to reimburse him. I knew he would never accept the money, but I also knew he would be disappointed if I didn't offer. It was a matter of honor. It's a silly game that men play.

I needed to get back to my cabin. I was afraid of what I would find when I got back after being gone so long. For all I knew, bears and panthers might have moved in and decided to stay. I had thought that I would only be gone overnight, so I didn't secure the cabin for an extended absence. But as badly as I wanted to get home, I had to make one stop first.

Doyle Popplewell looked right at home behind bars in the Palestine Jail. For some people, incarceration is a fate worse than death. Lack of freedom has been the cause of hundreds of wars, rebellions, and skirmishes throughout the centuries. "Give me liberty or give me death" was the motto during our own local uprising. To most pioneers, freedom is the same as breathing air; it is needed to survive and flourish. But as is the case with any civilization, there are certain groups of people that survive by reaping what they haven't sown. One look at Mr. Popplewell confirmed that he belonged to one of those groups.

His clothes were torn and dirty, and his shirt was unbuttoned to the waist, exposing a swollen belly covered in fur. His beard was long and scraggly, and his snow-white hair looked as if it had been a year since it had touched a comb. River pirates, horse thieves, and slave traffickers all fell into that category. Time in a jail cell was just part of the routine for the path he had chosen. Three good meals, a nice warm bed, and not a bit of hard labor; all he had to do was give up a little freedom. A jail cell was definitely his natural habitat.

"Doyle Popplewell?" I asked.

"Who wants to know?" he asked as he looked out the window. He was careful not to look me in the eye.

"Crockett. Nathan Crockett."

He immediately turned and walked toward the front of the cell. "Why, you're the fellow who pulled me out of the fire. I guess I owe you my life. Much obliged, Nathan Crockett. Most people wouldn't risk their neck for another man."

"To be honest with you, Mr. Popplewell, I didn't even know you were in the barn. I went in to save a horse and happened to trip over you in one of the stalls."

"Well, however it happened, I'm thankful all the same. Now, what is it I can do for you, young man? Or is this a social call?"

"Just looking for some information," I said, trying not to place too much importance on his answer.

"Now, what kind of information are you looking for?" There was a guarded caution in his response. It was a natural response from a man who lives outside of the law to make his living.

"I just wanted to know how the fire started. I heard some different stories, and I was hoping that you could clear up some things for me."

"My mama didn't raise no fool, mister," he replied. "I ain't saying nothing!"

I was hoping that he would be willing to talk because I had saved his life, but it looked like he was a man who couldn't trust a stranger. Some animals were just meant to be wild, but wild animals could be trapped all the same. "I'm not a lawman of any kind. As a matter of fact, I try to avoid them as much as possible. They tend to give me a rash." I pulled out a full bottle of corn liquor that I had brought along from the tavern just in case Popplewell needed a little motivation. I pulled the cork out with my teeth and took a short nip. "Care for a snort?" I asked.

"Don't mind if I do, Mr. Crockett. It's been two weeks since I've had a taste of hooch." He took the bottle and downed half of it in a single gulp. "Ahhh! That hits the spot!" he roared, as tried to pass the bottle back between the iron bars.

"Go ahead and finish it off before the guard gets back. It looks like you need it more than me." An act of unexpected kindness goes a long way in building a new friendship, even if it's a friendship with an incarcerated river pirate.

He seemed more relaxed when I told him I knew the deputy was eating lunch and would be away for at least an hour. "I never seen a jail like this," Popplewell said after taking another drink. "They leave you all alone and keep the door unlocked during the day. The walls are three feet thick, so there's no way a man could get out of here without burning the place down, but it makes it too darn easy for someone to get in here and do a number on me."

"Who would want to harm you?" I asked with a hint of sarcasm. "The stable owner?"

"Probably that Fail woman, or whatever her name is now. I know for a fact she is capable of killin' a man, and I wouldn't put it past her to sneak in here some night and slit my throat. If not her, one of her kin." The whiskey was already starting to have an effect on his words. He was starting to slur his r's, and his voice was becoming more gravelly.

"Do you mean Betsey Reed?" I asked. "The woman with the scar on her face?"

"That's the green-eyed she-snake I'm talking about. Everybody down in the Bend knows that she killed a couple of varmints a few years back. Not that those two amounted to much, but killin' is still against the law, isn't it?"

"As far as I know, it still is."

"Well, anyway, her brother Isaac, who's the meanest man I ever met, sent her away and made it known that if anyone spoke of her to the authorities, it would be the last thing they ever said. Yesiree Bob! Fish food in the Embarrass River!"

"Would they have a reason to come after you?" I asked.

"They just might." He wiped his mouth on his sleeve after finishing the last of the bottle. "Say, you're askin' a whole peck of questions. Maybe they sent you here to finish me off." He displayed a comical scowl, and offered a bear-like growl that was interrupted by a hiccup.

"Think about it, Popplewell. Why would I pull you out of the fire if I wanted you dead? You were three-quarters dead when I found you. Besides, I was with Betsey Reed just before the fire started." I paused to see if he was paying attention. He was. "I don't think there was enough time for all the things that were supposed to have happened. There has got to be more to this story. As much as it pains me, I might be able to help you get out of this mess."

He sat silently for a moment, looking astonishingly sober for a man who has downed a quart of whiskey in less than ten minutes. "You were the one who got her all stirred up?"

"Yes," I answered.

"And you came here to help me?" he said in a reserved tone of voice.

"I did. That is, if you tell me what really happened and stop playing games with me."

"Well, I'll be damned. An honest-to-goodness Good Samaritan." Popplewell actually seemed to be touched. "Pull up a chair, Nathan Crockett, and I'll tell you the story. The good along with the bad." It was mostly bad.

I pulled a three-legged stool next to the door of the jail cell and plopped down with my arms crossed. "Now, give me the truth."

Popplewell cleared his throat before speaking. "Well, I got into town shortly before dark and decided to camp next to LaMotte Creek, then head up to Merom to see a man about a job. After getting settled in, I came up to town to see if I could find a jug of holy water to get me through the night. On the way back from the mercantile, I cut through the campground behind the stable and that's when I saw her, Isaac Fail's little sister, Betsey.

I remember her when she was younger. Before the scar, she was a beautiful young thing. It was the eyes that I recognized. Wild and green. Never seen another pair like those. She was setting up camp next to a wagon, but I didn't see a man around, so I decided to walk over and give my regards. She seemed upset when I told her I remembered her from her younger days down in the Dark Bend. I had already started on the jug, so I wasn't feeling any pain at the time. She told me I was wrong and must have mistaken her for someone else. She started acting all high and mighty, like she was better than me. I told her she was nothing but a murderin' whore from the river bottoms, and I was going to teach her a lesson." He paused to make sure I knew he was justified in doing what he was about to tell me.

"What did you do next?" I asked.

"I told her I would be back after dark to have my way with her. If she had a problem with that, I told her I'd talk to the law about those dead men she left behind."

"Didn't she tell you she was married?" I asked.

"She mentioned something about it," he admitted, "but I don't see how that has anything to do with me teaching her a lesson."

"Go on with the story." I tried not to display my disgust.

"I went down to the creek and finished off the jug. Then some trappers from Vincennes came by and invited me to drink with them. We polished off their supply, and I decided it was time to go up the hill and deal with little Miss Betsey. When I got to her campground, I saw her talkin' to a man. I thought it must have been her husband, but I guess it was you, instead. I was a bit drunk at the time, so I sat down next to a tree. I tried to listen to your conversation, but I was too far away. I must have dozed off for a spell, but I woke when she started to cause a commotion. I saw you go into the tavern, so I decided to make my move. I moved in quickly and snuck up on her from behind. I put my hand over her mouth and laid my hunting knife up against her throat. I was careful to make sure it was the dull side and not the sharp against her skin."

"You're quite the gentleman."

"I try," he said, proving that he could be just as sarcastic as me.

"This doesn't differ with the story the Reed woman told." I was almost ready to get up and leave. Curiosity satisfied. Case closed.

"This is the point where her story and the truth part company. After assuring me she wouldn't scream, I took my hand away from her mouth. She was completely calm and said that we should go over to the stable because her husband might come back at any moment. She took me by the hand and led me into the barn like a lamb to the slaughter. She walked back to a clean stall and laid right down on her back on a pile of hay. She told me to join her, but when I got to my knees, she reached into the hay and pulled out a small blacksmith's hammer. The last thing I remember was seeing it coming straight at my forehead. Everything went black. Then I find myself waking up in this jail cell. I didn't light any fire and didn't burn that stable down! If you hadn't pulled me out of the fire, I would have been dead. She had planted that hammer there all along and led me into that barn like a black widow spider." He was starting to sound a bit too self-righteous for my taste.

"What did you say to the sheriff?" I asked. "'I was going to rape her but she hit me with a hammer first?' That's not much of a defense, Popplewell."

"I can understand the whack on the head; it was an eye for an eye and a tooth for a tooth. But starting the fire with me in the barn...that would have been cold-blooded murder."

The sad thing was that he saw himself as some sort of victim in this dark, malevolent melodrama. I was starting to feel ill for allowing Doyle Popplewell to remain among the living. He might find the need to teach someone else a lesson.

"You didn't answer my question! What did you tell the sheriff about the fire?" I demanded.

"Not a damn thing!" he yelled back. One of Isaac Fail's men came by the day after the fire. He reminded me that the penalty for arson was a lot less severe than the penalty for rape. Not that it would matter."

"Why wouldn't it matter?"

"He made it clear that if I strayed one word away from Betsey's story, I wouldn't live to see the next sunrise. Dead men tell no tales."

"So you're going to go to the state prison for the arson?" I couldn't believe he would go so easily.

"Look at it this way," he said, "in five years I'll be a free man. Prison might not be much of a life, but it's a life. If Isaac Fail wants me dead, I'm a dead man, especially in this poor excuse of a jail."

"So there's nothing I can do for you?" I asked as I started for the door.

"Maybe sneak in another bottle of hooch," he said, as if we had sparked up some sort of lifelong friendship.

"I'll see what I can do," I told him from outside the door, knowing full well that I had performed my last favor for Doyle Popplewell.

I avoided all human contact for almost two weeks after leaving Palestine. I've never been a hermit, but my last encounter with civilization made me look for solace at my tiny oak cabin beneath the Five Sisters overlooking the Wabash River. It was so far off the beaten path, there was never any transient traffic. I spent hours talking to my horse, Newton, who was still slightly lame. He was named after Sir Isaac Newton due to the fact that he taught me the law of gravity on my first attempt to ride him. I moved him to a smaller pen, which made it easier for our one-sided conversations. I caught some bluegill from the river, shot a turkey out of an elm tree, and even planted some squash for a late autumn harvest. I decided I could be entirely self-sufficient on my insignificant twenty-acre Garden of Eden.

Life is complicated enough without river rats, scoundrels, stable fires, one-eared horses, and especially green-eyed scar-faced women, but for some reason, I couldn't get the tragedy of Betsey Reed's life out of my mind. She wanted desperately to be loved, but would never be able to accept love even if she found it. That part of her died somewhere in the Dark Bend, sometime around her thirteenth birthday. It was obvious that it would not be a happy ending for the Reed family. I vowed to stay as far away from that disaster as humanly possible.

I later found out that Doyle Popplewell had escaped from the county jail with help from unknown accomplices two days after our conversation. His body was found floating in the Embarrass River one week later. Dead men tell no tales.

Eleven

Everyone has a day of destiny. May 13, 1843 became that day for me. I had taken Jesse Dubois' prize draft horses and his heavy cargo wagon north on the Hutsonville Trail, and I crossed the Wabash to Merom, Indiana on a rickety flatboat ferry. Jesse wanted to serve the finest whiskey at his tavern, which meant buying corn liquor from James O'Boyle's distillery northeast of Merom. It was a bit of an honor to be entrusted with such a risky task. Eight hundred gallons of whiskey would be quite a haul for any road thief or river pirate. O'Boyle's stills produced twenty barrels of whiskey a day. That was much more than the local population could swallow, so most of the whiskey was shipped down to New Orleans by steamboat. Only the better public houses paid O'Boyle's premium of twenty-five cents a gallon when most local stills sold their hooch for a dime.

I paid a large, gray-bearded clerk with two hundred dollars in gold coins I had hidden in a pocket sewn inside my left boot. Jesse had those boots made especially for times when I carried large sums of money on his behalf.

"We don't have enough stock on hand to fill your order, but we'll have it ready to go by noon tomorrow if that is all right with you," he said in a heavy Irish brogue. "You can stable the horses at the white barn behind the Merom House. Then go into the tavern and see Mrs. Campbell. She'll set you up with a room. Tell her to put it on our account."

That was music to my ears. I knew from past experience that the fare at the Merom House was some of the best eating that could be found in the Wabash Valley.

I unhitched the horses and let them cool down during the half-mile walk back to the stable. After they were watered and fed, I handed them over to a half-pint stable boy by the name of Cletus and started toward the tavern.

Charlotte Campbell was a loud, cordial woman who was about as wide as she was tall. She claimed that there wasn't a man alive who she couldn't tame. Just fill them with cornbread, beef stew, and hot buttered rum, and you can march them down to the altar without a fight. She had tamed three different men in her life only to have them all die untimely deaths. I guess some men just weren't meant to sit on the nest. She came running to meet me as soon as I walked through the front door of the Merom House. "Nathan Crockett! You're a sight for sore eyes!" She gave me a hug that would have made a small bear proud. "What brings you over to the good side of the river?"

"Just picking up a load of corn liquor from O'Boyle's still. They can't fill the order until morning, so I have the privilege of enjoying your hospitality for the night."

"Throw your things in the room at the end of the hall, and I'll fetch some water so you can clean up before dinner. You smell like horse," she teased.

"You sure know how to charm a guy." I tried to act hurt, but Charlotte wasn't buying it.

Charlotte whisked past the open door and placed a pitcher of water and a block of lye soap on the table next to a small feather bed. "Make sure you wash behind your ears, Nathan. You might want to look your best tonight."

"Since when did my clean ears become a matter of concern to you, Miss Charlotte? It sounds like you're up to no good."

"Cleanliness is next to godliness," she said.

"You're up to something, aren't you?"

"Well, actually," Charlotte admitted, "There a nice young maiden who just came in on the boat from Terre Haute. She's got some kin living south of Palestine. Since she's going to need a ride down to your neck of the woods anyway, I thought that maybe…"

"You thought that you'd play matchmaker. You old busybody!"

"Nathan! It's time you settled down! It ain't natural that

48

a good-looking man your age is still single," Charlotte said.

"You know you're the only one for me, Charlotte."

"Don't think I couldn't have tamed you twenty years ago. I'd have you dead and buried by now." She stopped long enough to give me a sly wink. "Anyway, I was standing on the bluff and saw you coming with that wagon a couple of hours ago. I've made all of the arrangements. She'll be down for dinner in ten minutes. Her name is Eveline. Don't be late!"

Eveline Deal's smile hooked me like a night-crawler does a sunfish. It was her smile that made her beautiful. She wasn't made up with fancy store-bought clothes like some of the society wives in Palestine. She wore a simple, gray, wool dress and a white bonnet. She wiped her mouth after taking a bird-like bite of venison stew and set the napkin neatly folded on her lap. "Miss Charlotte tells me you went to college. I've never met anyone who went to school before."

"It's not much to brag about. It doesn't seem to help much when it comes to hunting for dinner or driving a team of horses. Maybe someday I'll grow up and put it to use."

"Well, you look plenty grown up to me," she teased. Her hazel eyes sparkled in the candlelight.

"I'm putting it off as long as possible," I said. "Too many responsibilities make me nervous." As a matter of fact, I was starting to get nervous at that very moment. I had avoided the bear trap called matrimony by fleeing at the first sign of a suitable candidate. Eveline was very suitable and certainly was a likely candidate. The little voice in the back of my mind was screaming his head off, but I wasn't in the mood to listen.

"Not me. I can't wait to get married and have lots of kids. Don't you want to have a house full of sons and daughters?" she asked sincerely.

"I never gave it much thought," I replied. "Maybe someday." It was at this time that I would normally be looking for a way to gracefully excuse myself and run for safety. I was definitely treading in dangerous water.

"Well, Nathan, you just haven't met the right girl yet."

"And I suppose that you could be the *right* kind of girl?" I couldn't believe how ridiculously giddy I sounded.

"Could be. You never know."

"Are you always this forward, Eveline?"

"I don't understand what you mean..." She started to twirl a single strand of her silky brown hair around her index finger. Eveline Deal was much more sophisticated than I had originally thought.

"I've known you for less than five minutes, and you've already let me know that you're available and the sooner we get things started, the better."

She sighed, then looked me directly in the eyes. "It's just that I know from experience that if a girl doesn't move quickly, she's likely to end up as a bitter old spinster."

"Somehow, I don't think you're going to end up as an old maid. By the way, how old are you, anyway?"

"Almost eighteen." She looked down at her plate like a child does when confronted by its parents.

"How old?"

"I'll be sixteen in three months. That's pretty close to eighteen," she admitted.

"I guess it's close enough." *Fifteen...sixteen... seventeen...*I stopped myself before I did the math. At this point, it didn't matter. It was close enough.

Watching a sunset from Merom Bluff was as close as you could get to an ocean sunset and still be in the middle of the country. The brown sandstone bluff stands over two hundred feet above the Wabash River on the Indiana side. As we looked to the west, toward Illinois, it seemed like you could see all the way to the end of the earth. Miles of green hardwood forest reached up to touch the multicolored sky on the horizon, while plumes of smoke rose beneath us from the cabins on LaMotte Prairie. You could hear men swearing while they loaded pork and whiskey on a new side-wheeler moored at the docks below us. To the south, there were two flatboats silently adrift, loaded with corn on their way to

New Orleans.

For the first time since we'd met that afternoon, Eveline was silent. She was deep in thought, almost spellbound by the view. She shuddered as a breeze started to blow from the north. I quickly took my buckskin jacket and wrapped it around her. As I pulled the front of the coat together, she grabbed my hand and held it tight against her. I didn't fight, as I felt myself falling for this girl who I had only known for a couple of hours. We stayed in that position until the sun disappeared completely. Neither one of us uttered a single word.

"My future's down there," she said, pointing to the west. "It's a whole new life, full of opportunity and adventure. Anything is possible."

"You're awfully optimistic, aren't you?" I teased.

"If optimistic means ready to kiss you...then yes. I am very optimistic." She turned and gazed into my eyes. I could feel my heart pound in my throat. I was trying to act calm and hide the fact that my knees were shaking uncontrollably. She wasn't about to wait for me to make the first move. With panther-like quickness, she grabbed the sides of my face and pressed her mouth passionately against mine. Her lips were soft and inviting, and I could feel myself giving up control. Maybe this *was* a whole new life. I pulled her tight against me. I wanted her to know that I wanted her just as badly. We maintained the embrace for several minutes until I spoiled the moment by pointing out the spot on the prairie where hostile Indians had massacred the Hutson Family several years earlier. Somehow, we overcame the awkward silence and kissed again.

As the night grew darker, we made our way over to a small bonfire behind the inn. Men were arguing about the unpopular southern policies of John Tyler, but it didn't matter. At that moment in time, Eveline Deal had become my whole world. As far as we were concerned, the outside world didn't exist.

Charlotte Campbell seemed happy with her matchmaking as she brought us pewter mugs filled with apple cider. "Not bad work for an old busybody, huh, Nathan?" she cackled, as she walked back toward the inn. I had to admit, I was happy with her handiwork. Eveline stayed in my arms for the rest of the evening. Finally, sometime after midnight, we made our way back into the foyer of the inn. Her face glowed from the reflection of the flickering embers in the fireplace. She had the most loving face I had ever seen. She was anxious, assertive, and a bit pushy at times, but somehow it was part of her charm.

"I keep wondering why you've never married, Nathan. Haven't you ever been in love?"

I shifted my weight from one foot to the other. "I loved my mother."

"That doesn't count! You're a good-looking man, you know. You have the bluest eyes I have ever seen. And with that silky brown hair of yours, there must have been other girls."

"Oh, there have been girls…from time to time."

"Aren't you quite the stallion?"

"It's not like that. It's just…"

"It's just that you're afraid to lose your freedom. You're afraid of becoming a caged animal." I could tell she enjoyed prodding me.

"I might like it. I've been alone most of my life. Since my parents died, I never knew a real home. I built a cabin and it's all mine, but it's not the same. It's not like the home I had when I was a child."

"I don't know," she sighed. "You've roamed wild so long; maybe you're untamable."

"I hope not. When I find the right woman, it won't be as hard to stay home. I may dream about adventures, but it will be her love that will keep me from straying."

"I have a feeling you'd be easy to love."

"No one has loved me yet."

"Goodnight, Nathan Crockett." She kissed me on the cheek one last time, then started up the stairway toward her room.

"Goodnight, Miss Deal." I probably should have gone

straight to bed just to make sure the night ended perfectly, but without thinking, I opened my mouth. "By the way, I didn't even ask... Who are the kinfolk you'll be living with?"

"It's my uncle and his wife, Leonard and Betsey Reed. Do you know them?"

I almost choked. "We crossed paths once. They gave me a ride into town."

"Great, that will make it easier." She seemed so happy as she disappeared into her room. I didn't have the heart to say anything. *So much for a perfect evening...*

I tossed and turned all night. Of all the people in the whole State of Illinois, why did she have to be related to Leonard and Betsey Reed? That little voice in the back of my mind was talking a mile a minute. I was trying my hardest not to listen, but it became more difficult as the hours passed. I tried to tell myself that things would work out fine, but the little voice wasn't buying it.

Twelve

Leonard was sitting on a hickory stump, puffing on a corncob pipe, as we approached, riding double on Newton. He seemed to have aged quite a bit since I had seen him last. He waved and motioned us over as soon as he saw us. "Nathan Crockett! Well, aren't you a sight for sore eyes."

"Good to see you again, Mr. Reed. It's been quite a while."

"What's this 'Mr. Reed' business? You call me Leonard. And who is this lass with you? Don't tell me you went off and got married."

"Oh no, no—Let me introduce—"

"Uncle Leonard, it's me, your niece Eveline." She smiled at me as she ran up and gave Leonard a hug.

"You can't be!" Leonard seemed genuinely happy to see her. "My niece is a skinny little girl with freckles and pigtails."

"I'm all grown up now and haven't had a freckle in years." She pointed at her face to offer proof.

"Well, I'll be darned," he cawed. "It *is* you. And look how you've turned out! Nathan, you better snap this one up before some of the local boys get a look at her."

"He already has, Uncle Leonard," she blurted. "You'll be seeing him on a regular basis." *So much for being subtle.*

"Nathan, is that true?" Leonard asked. "You haven't taken advantage of my niece have you?"

"Well, yes. I mean no." The whole situation was difficult and awkward. "I mean yes, it's true that I'll be calling on Eveline, and no, I haven't taken advantage of her. That is, if I have your permission to call on her."

"Why, of course you do. This calls for a celebration." Leonard slapped his knee with his hat, causing him to choke on the plume of dust it stirred up. "Betsey! Come out here!"

he shouted.

Betsey came out the front door, carrying a straw broom and wearing her long gray bonnet. "What's all the fuss?" she moaned.

"It's Becca's daughter, Eveline. And look who she brought with her—Nathan Crockett!"

"Well, isn't this a surprise." There was an awkward silence after Betsey displayed an obvious lack of enthusiasm.

"Oh, Aunt Betsey, it's so good to see you again!" Eveline rushed over and gave Betsey a hug. "Thank you so much for letting me stay here. I'm really a good house-keeper, and I'll do all the household chores. You'll be able to take it easy."

Betsey patted her on the back halfheartedly. She was not accustomed to being on the receiving end of an unsolicited show of affection. She looked at me with a bit of angst.

"It's good to see you again, Mrs. Reed," I said with a smile, hoping to ease some of the tension. "I want to thank you again for taking care of me. I really do appreciate everything you did."

"You're welcome, Nathan," she said apprehensively. "I was glad to hear you came out of the fire in one piece." She paid great attention to my response, looking for any indication in my face that I had knowledge of her role in the stable fire.

"I heard that crazy old drunk who started it got what he deserved when he tried to escape," I said. "I'm just glad that I was able to save your horse. How is Ole Hickory?"

"He's fine," Leonard said as he started to chuckle. "Best lookin' one-eared horse in the county, thanks to you."

At Leonard's request, Betsey went back into the cabin and brought four mugs of sassafras sweet tea on a pewter tray. She served Leonard first, because his had extra sugar in it, before serving Eveline and then me. Leonard said he had been having stomach problems, and the sassafras seemed to calm things down.

That night, there were pig stories, lies, promises, and Eveline's hope of a new start; there was talk of courtship and cabins, of crops and floods. Eveline and Leonard laughed and talked through an early supper of squirrel soup and cornbread, while Betsey tried to smile at all the appropriate times. I tried to convince myself that the Reed cabin would be a happy home, but the subtle voice inside me said otherwise. One look into Betsey's feline green eyes told me everything I needed to know. A jealous woman is a dangerous animal, sometimes even deadly.

The Reed marriage was a business arrangement, and bringing another woman into the nest was not good business for Betsey. Eveline was a threat and was in danger. I felt uneasy for allowing her to walk into this beehive.

A wild animal can smell fear, and Betsey sensed it in me. She never said anything, but her mood and mannerisms were more guarded than before. I possessed information that could do her harm, and she was going to be in possession of Eveline. I wanted to get Eveline out of there as quickly as possible, but it was too late.

Eveline helped Betsey clear the table while Leonard smoked some awful-smelling tobacco in his pipe. I walked outside and leaned against the fence rail next to a small, clapboard stable. Ole Hickory cowered as he approached me. The nub where his ear used to be had healed nicely. I patted and rubbed his nose and gave him a handful of corn from a nearby bucket. I don't know if he remembered me saving his life or not, but he acted as if he did. I told him he was a good horse in spite of our shaky start, and as far as I was concerned, he had a clean slate.

"How about me, Nathan? Can I have a clean slate, too?" Betsey had followed me outside.

I looked around and saw that we were alone. "I didn't know that you needed one, Betsey," I replied, not quite sure how to answer her question.

"You know what I mean," she replied. "I acted like a fool that day. I guess I was just feeling sorry for myself. Sometimes I get the idea that life is supposed to be fair, but then I get over it. Life is what it is. I just hope I can have a clean slate with you. I've felt so guilty about leaving town without seeing you, but I figured I had caused you enough trouble as it was."

She seemed sincere and contrite. She was more complicated than I had imagined. "None of that was your fault," I assured her. "Sometimes bad things just happen."

"They always seem to happen around me. Remember?"

"That's not what I meant. All of that is behind us. I just want to know if you're all right with Eveline moving in with you. If not, let me know, and I can make arrangements for her to go to Palestine or Heathsville."

"Why, of course she's welcome here," Betsey said, acting mildly offended. "Why wouldn't she be?"

"Let's talk straight, Betsey. You didn't look too happy when we showed up. I understand that. A lot of women wouldn't want another woman in the house. That's only natural, but I need you to be honest with me. If you don't want her here, let me know, and I'll take her away."

She looked down for a moment and then looked directly into my eyes. "Nathan, I give you my word. I'll take good care of her for you. You come see her as much as you want. She'll be a big help. Leonard's health has been declining, so I've been stretched pretty thin."

"So you're sure?" I asked.

"Don't worry about a thing. We'll get along fine, but now, be honest with me."

"About what?" I didn't know if I was going to like the question.

"I don't know much about a lot of things, but I think I am a bit of an expert when it comes to men. From what I can see, you're not the type to settle down."

"What does that mean?" I asked.

"I just figured it would take a lot more woman that that little girl to tie you down. I wouldn't dream of interfering, but when I was her age, older men made my life a living hell. I wouldn't want you to do that to Eveline. Please don't hurt her."

"You don't have to worry; I assure you my intentions are honorable." I was astonished how easily she had put me in a defensive posture. "Besides, she's not a little girl."

"Hey, what are you two talking about?" Eveline yelled from the cabin porch. "I hope you're not plotting against me."

"Oh no, dear," Betsey said, "I was telling Nathan about how it'll be such a blessing having you around."

"I'm the one who should be counting my blessings." Eveline said as she ran down and hugged me tightly. "Everything's going to be perfect. New life, new family, and best of all, a new husband."

"New husband?" Betsey howled, "I didn't realize you two were engaged already."

"Well, not officially engaged," Eveline explained, "but it's only a matter of time. Right, Nathan?"

"Uhhh, yeah...sure. Just a matter of time, Evie."

"Just think," Eveline said, "in ten years there are going to be five or six little Crockett children running around the cabin. I can hardly wait."

Betsey erupted in hearty laughter. "You're right, Nathan! She's not a little girl. It looks like maybe I should have been worried about you, instead, because it looks like you're going to have your hands full for the next several years."

"What is she talking about, Nathan?" Eveline asked.

""Don't worry, dear," Betsey said, as she grabbed her hand and walked her back towards the cabin. "I'll teach you everything you need to know. You'll make a fine wife for Nathan."

It was one thing to think about marriage and children, but it was entirely different to hear the words spoken during the course of a conversation with such certainty. I smiled and waved good-bye as they left. The little voice began to squawk again.

Thirteen

For the first couple of months, everything seemed to be going along just fine. I stopped by and visited Eveline several times without incident. She seemed to have grown quite fond of Leonard, and Betsey seemed to be on her best behavior. It was on the eve of a trip to Springfield when I realized there was a problem brewing. Jesse Dubois had contracted me to carry some land office documents to the land office in Springfield. The pay was good, and I was starting to think more about saving money as of late. I stopped by the Reed cabin to say goodbye and to let Eveline know I would be gone for two weeks. She met me at the road and asked if we could walk to some place where we would have some privacy. As soon as we were out of sight of the cabin, she grabbed me and kissed me passionately in a desperate manner.

"Let's get married now, Nathan!" she pleaded. "Please don't make me wait. Let's find a preacher and get married tonight. You know I love you, don't you?"

"Of course I do! But what has changed? What has got you so upset?"

"I don't know. Something is just wrong here; I can't really say." She started weeping uncontrollably. I held her head against my chest until she calmed down several minutes later.

"What is going on, Eveline?" I asked. "Tell me the truth."

"I think Aunt Betsey is going to kill Uncle Leonard." She hid her face as she buried it against my neck. "I can't believe that I actually said that. He seems to be getting worse and worse every day, and she keeps talking about the things she's going to do to the farm when he's dead."

"I don't think Leonard's health is all that good, Evie.

He's been sickly ever since I've known him. His health has been on the decline for some time. What makes you think that she's trying to kill him?"

"I don't know how I know," she cried. "She sits there in her rocking chair and stares at him by the hour. When he starts to cough and choke, she gets this funny smile on her face and starts mumbling things to herself like she's some kind of witch. She's an evil woman, Nathan! Please, can we get married now?"

"I thought you were getting along fine," I said, trying to sidestep the marriage issue. "When did all this happen?"

"It started as soon as I got here," she admitted. "Betsey told me that if I complained about it, you wouldn't want me anymore. She said you would think of me as a whiny little girl, and that it would take a real woman to keep you happy. She said if I told you anything about her, she would say awful things about me, and that you would believe her because she was a woman and I was only a snot-nosed little brat."

"I'm leaving for Springfield tomorrow, Evie. It's government business. I'm going to be gone for at least two weeks. I need you to be brave until I get back. I'll have something figured out by then."

"Two weeks? I don't know if I can last that long. Don't you want to marry me, Nathan?" She looked up at me, eyes moist with tears, and I remembered why I fell for her.

"Of course I want to marry you."

"Can we get married in two weeks as soon as you get back?"

"Yes, Evie, we can," I said. It was an act of submission. I knew that I loved her, and I guess I thought we were going to get married eventually, but I had intended to take things slowly. Maybe I had a fear of commitment, or maybe I was afraid that I would lose my independence. I had always tried to be a good person and take the feelings of others into consideration, but when it came down to it, I was basically a selfish person at heart. When it came to my life, I didn't like to compromise. I liked to do as I pleased and not have to ask permission to do it. I felt like a stallion that had just been broken.

I held her and kissed her and listened to her talk about our future children. I told her to be careful and say nothing to Leonard and Betsey about our engagement until I got back. She said it would be the longest two weeks of her life, but it would be worth the wait. I begged her to be careful, and I told her that if there was an emergency, she should go to the Heath Tavern and tell them that she is my fiancée. They would make sure she was safe. I waved goodbye as I left on Newton and rode for Palestine. I was consumed with the thought of losing my freedom and the changes that were about to take place in my life. If I were a better man, I would have been more concerned with the wellbeing of my young wife-to-be.

Fourteen

Pride is a terrible thing when it causes someone to come to harm, especially if the person is someone you love and care for. I delivered all the documents to the land office early in the afternoon and gave them to a bald, round clerk with bug eyes and a red nose spotted with giant pores. He told me to stop by in the morning, and he would have documents ready to go back to Palestine. I put Newton in a stable and found a room above a tavern across the street from the State Capitol Building. I decided to go downstairs and have a couple mugs of ale before dinner. I sat at a table next to the window overlooking the capitol courtyard and smiled at a lovely young lady who passed by on the sidewalk. She returned a half-hearted smile and went on her way. It was then that I realized there would be no more lovely ladies in taverns, church pews, or ice cream socials. In one week, I would be in front of a preacher, saying *I do*.

I wanted to be a good husband and take care of Eveline, but that selfish part of me worried about the loss of freedom that would accompany the bond of holy matrimony. I felt sorry for myself, asked for a bottle of whiskey, and started to get as pickled as a prize cucumber. As afternoon turned into evening, I joined some local patrons who were arguing politics and religion. The debate was bawdy, juvenile, and entirely a lost cause. Most of the men were uneducated, but they seemed to be good-natured. There was, however, a rather large, red-haired man with a long, unkempt beard who seemed to take an extreme disliking to me. He didn't say much, but kept a wary eye on me as if I were about to steal the family fortune. After an hour or two had passed, it came out in the course of conversation that I was a second cousin of Davy Crockett. For some reason, this fact seemed to antagonize this man.

"I don't believe you're any kin to Davy Crockett," he said in a deep, whiskey voice. "I bet you're nothing but a two-bit hustler with a big mouth."

"It would be a bet you'd lose, mister," I replied in what I hoped was a disarming manner. I reached into my pocket and pulled out a letter of introduction written on United States Land Office stationary, which confirmed that my name was Nathan Crockett and that I was in Springfield on government business. A man sitting next to me looked at the letter and confirmed its contents, which turned Long Beard's face a bright shade of red.

"Well, I guess it could be true," he said, "After all, Davy Crockett was nothing but a drunken bum who slept with bears and got what he deserved at the Alamo."

Immediately, everyone at the table stood up and took at least five steps backward, leaving Long Beard and I all alone. I had learned at an early age that there was no possible way to win an argument with an idiot or a drunk. Unfortunately for me, Long Beard was both; as a matter of fact, so was I. But I had been challenged. I had been called a liar, and the family name had been desecrated. Not to defend it would have been considered dishonorable and effeminate. I stood up abruptly, legs wobbly, the room a bit out of focus, and yelled with drunken elegance, "Mister, you had better take that back!"

Long Beard stood up slowly, exposing a height and girth that resembled the physique of an upright bear. He smiled widely, exposing a gap where his front teeth should have been, and slammed his mug down on the table, shooting shards of pottery twenty feet in every direction. He had baited the trap and I had walked into its jaws with all the finesse of a blind raccoon.

Whenever fighting a much larger opponent, it's important to have your first punch do as much damage as possible. If the first blow is well placed and hard enough, nine times out of ten it will end the fight before it gets started. Goliath went down in one blow, and I was hoping for the same result with Long Beard. I walked slowly toward him with my palms held out in a non-threatening manner.

"Mister, I'm sorry if I ruffled your feathers. I really didn't mean to. Why don't you let me buy you an ale, and we can—" Without warning, I coiled back and threw my right fist upward, using all of my leg strength, and delivered a direct blow to the bottom of his chin. Instead of falling to the floor as I had expected, he stood firm as an oak tree and gave me another toothless smile.

"Son, you're gonna wish you were at the Alamo with cousin Davy by the time I get through with you," he said, spit flying out of his mouth. He immediately put me in a bear hug and drove me to the floor with all of his weight pounding straight through my abdomen. The sheer force of his body knocked the wind out of my lungs, leaving me gasping for air. I was helpless and at his mercy. Unfortunately, he wasn't the merciful type.

He stood up and kicked me in the stomach five or six times. I could hear my own ribs breaking, and I was beginning to taste blood as it dripped into my mouth from somewhere inside my body. He pulled me to my feet without any help on my part and tossed me across a table into a solid wood wall. I opened my eyes momentarily only to see his black leather boot aiming for my forehead. His kick landed true, turning light and sound into fog and darkness. All pain left as I waited for the final blow that would surely do me in. My thoughts turned to Eveline and how I had let her down. I had broken my promise and left her in harm's way.

Somewhere in the distance, I heard Long Beard mumble something about catching his breath before finishing me off. I heard him take a couple of steps toward me. Then I heard the massive thud of him hitting the floor next to me. I somehow managed to open the eye that wasn't swollen shut. His face was drawn tight against the floor as he stared at me with the unfocused stare that can only occur once the soul leaves the body. *That's great,* I thought, as everything started to turn black. *Long Beard is waiting for me outside the Pearly Gates. I sure hope Saint Peter has a sense of humor about all this...*

...As black faded to gray, then gray to white, my mind became aware of my existence. If I was dead, then the great beyond looked remarkably like the inside of a jail cell, and my heavenly body had managed to retain all the damage incurred during my last earthly skirmish.

I started to roll over, but the pain in my ribcage immediately stopped me in mid-roll. I was alive, but not in very good shape. I managed to squirm up into a sitting position on the straw mattress, which covered a crude, rough, wooden bed frame. There was a dull, flickering light coming from a lamp on a tall, awkward table, which was on the other side of an intimidating set of iron bars. The wall was made from rough-cut limestone, and there was the unmistakable smell of raw sewage that is a common attribute in all jails. This was, however, the first time I had been on the wrong side of the bars.

I touched the right side of my face and found that it was swollen badly around the cheekbone and down to my lower jaw. I could feel that my upper lip was touching the tip of my nose. I tried to stand up but fell back to the cot as the room started to spin.

"Take it easy!" warned a white-haired old man with a weathered gray flannel shirt and dark wool pants. "You took one heck of a beating tonight, son. Doc said he'd be back in the morning and try to patch you up. He said he wouldn't know where to start until you told him where it hurt. I asked him if I could give you some whiskey for the pain, but he said it smelled like you had enough medicine in you as it was."

"Where am I?" I asked, while rubbing the collection of knots on the back of my head.

"You're in the Sangamon County Jail! Where did you think you were, the governor's mansion? The name's Charlie. I'll be your night host."

"Nathan Crockett's the name. I thought I might be dead," I said, half joking.

"The Grim Reaper may have come for you, but he took the other fellow instead."

"What happened?

"It appears that the fracas was more than the ole boy's heart could stand. It just plumb gave out. He fell deader than Brother Abel himself."

I took a deep sigh, which a person shouldn't do with broken ribs. I knew I was lucky to be alive. One more kick to the skull would have done it. "So why am I in the hooskow?"

"Son, you threw the first punch in a fight where a man ended up dead. They can't let you go until the case is disposed of officially. I wouldn't worry about it too much. Big Jesse Scott has been making more trouble than a fox in a hen house. Most folks around here will consider you aiding his demise as a public service. As soon as court convenes next month, they'll surely cut you loose."

"Next month!" I moaned. "I need to get out of here before then! I'm supposed to get married next week."

"Nothing you can do about it. The court comes to town every six weeks, so it won't be in session until a month from this upcoming Monday. I'd be glad to get some ink and paper if you want to write a letter to the bride-to-be. I can mail it for you first thing in the morning."

How could I get myself in such a mess? I had left Eveline in an impossible situation. She wouldn't even know that there was a problem for another week. Some provider and protector I turned out to be. I didn't see any way she could ever forgive me. I pounded my fist on my already knotted head. I knew better than to fight with a drunk who was obviously looking for a skirmish. I should have walked away at the first sign of trouble.

Still dazed from the effects of the fight and alcohol, I wrote an apologetic and very inadequate account of my predicament and addressed it to Eveline at general delivery Heathsville. Mail service in the southeastern corner of Crawford County was hit-or-miss at best and could take up to a month to reach her from here. I knew that service to Palestine was usually reliable, so I wrote a second letter to Jesse Dubois in the hope that he could use his political influence to secure an early release. Charlie took the letters and brought back a bowl of beans and biscuits left over from dinner. I tried to eat, but it hurt too much to chew. I set the bowl aside, lay on the mattress, and counted the number of flies caught in a spider web suspended from a ceiling beam. I was convinced they had also agonized over their plight and asked, *how did we get ourselves into such a mess?*

As I drifted off to sleep, my thoughts were of spider webs and spiders. Eveline was living much too close to Betsey, The Black Widow, while I was snared in a web of my own making. I said goodnight to my seven cellmates wrapped in their silky shrouds above me. *Don't worry, little bugs, the worst is over. You won't feel a thing. Don't worry Evie, I'll be back in two weeks. We'll get married and live happily ever after.* I hated myself and cursed the Grim Reaper for making such a horrendous mistake.

Fifteen

Every day spent behind bars seemed to consist of forty-eight hours. After the original anxiety from losing your freedom subsides, the progression of time seems to grind to a halt. Free will succumbs to the monotony and boredom of a caged existence. Once the cell door closes, you become less of a man, dependent on a jailer's generosity even for the slightest shred of dignity. Jail, however, is a great place to evaluate the path your life is taking. *How did I get here? What could I have done differently? Why did I go to the tavern in the first place? Why didn't I leave when I knew that I had more than enough to drink? Why did I antagonize a man twice my size? Why did I start a fight that I couldn't win?*

At first, I tried to rationalize my actions as being justified, but the little voice in the back of my mind kept insisting I was lying to myself. You hide from your conscience by self-involvement in the drudgery of the day-to-day business of your menial existence. You can work and fight and love and sin and die without ever being aware of being alive. The quiet solitude of the jail cell forced me to come clean and be honest with myself. When the questions were all answered, I didn't really like what I learned about Nathan Crockett. For the most part, I could go through life fooling myself that I was a good and moral citizen. Marry the girl and raise a family. I'm sure everyone would be happy. Except in the long run, it wouldn't be fair. It wouldn't be fair to Eveline, or to our children, and I am ashamed to say, it wouldn't be fair to the most selfish person on the face of the earth: me.

Deep down inside, I knew I had forced the issue with Big Jesse Scott. I had dismissed his type a hundred times before without incident, but this one had served a purpose. *Sorry, Evie, I couldn't make our wedding. I was busy defending the honor of a famous dead relative who I never actually met from a man of no significance who is, unfortunately, pushing up daisies. I didn't want to stay in that jail, Evie, but I didn't have a choice. I wanted to get married, but the sheriff wouldn't let me.*

The red-bearded man at rest in his grave had given me my alibi. I was tattered and bruised and beaten half to death, and I deserved every bit of it. It was the girl passing by outside the window of the tavern who had made me realize I wasn't ready for a life-altering commitment. It wasn't the fact that I considered pursuing the young lady that had bothered me, it was the fact that I couldn't. I knew I didn't want to be unfaithful, but I also knew I didn't want to be miserable. Maybe I couldn't hope for anyone as loving and wonderful as Eveline Deal, but she could do a lot better than me.

Sometime during my eighth night of incarceration, I made the decision to be honest and forthright with her. She may have been ready for marriage, but I wasn't. I loved her and would see her as much as she wanted, but it would be a few years before I was ready to tie the knot. The thought of hurting her, however, made my stomach wrench in knots. I might be throwing away the love of a lifetime because I wasn't ready to grow up and stop being selfish, so I decided to do whatever was necessary to keep her safe and help her find a new place to live, far away from the Reed household. Suddenly, the little voice finally went silent. I was able to get a good night's sleep for the first time since being locked up.

A tall, gangly, horse-faced lawyer with black hair named Lincoln (yes, *that* Lincoln) appeared at the jail with a court order for my release. After learning of my predicament, Jesse Dubois had sent a letter requesting assistance from his long-time friend. They had served several years together as district representatives in the state legislature. Lincoln convinced the state's attorney that I was being wrongfully incarcerated and should be released immediately. All accounts of the fight agreed that I was whipped soundly, and because I was unconscious at the time of Jesse Scott's death, I could hardly be held responsible. Lincoln shook my hand and said that Mr. Dubois had paid his fee. He told me to settle up with him upon my return to Palestine. I had been a resident of the Sangamon County Jail for thirty-six days. Lincoln's fee was ten dollars, and the wages for my trip as courier for the United States Land Office was eight. I shot a wolf on the way home and turned in his scalp to make up the difference.

Sixteen

It was a hard, cold rain for an August afternoon as I reached the side path that led to Leonard and Betsey's cabin. The dark gray sky seemed appropriate for my mood and the task at hand. Smoke from the fireplace was trapped by the rain and filled the small hollow that surrounded the dwelling. I tied Newton to a low branch of a sugar-maple tree to keep him as dry as possible, cleaned my boots off on a fence rail, took three deep breaths, and tapped gently on the door.

The door opened a few inches, just enough to reveal Betsey's wild green eyes. She seemed surprised to see me. "Who is out in weather like this?" shouted Leonard from somewhere behind the door.

"It must be a ghost!" Betsey said, as she opened the door the rest of the way.

Leonard was sitting at the table with a mug in front of him. His eyes widened as he took his pipe out of his mouth. "I'll be. Eveline! Look who's here!"

Eveline was bundled in a quilt with her back toward me in front of the fireplace. She remained silent as if she hadn't heard him at all. As soon as I saw her, my heart leaped.

"Eveline," he repeated. "It's Nathan!"

"Nathan?" She turned quickly, rolled her eyes, and fainted, causing a thud as she hit the floor. I ran over, scooped her up in a single motion, and laid her on a small bed in the corner of the cabin. I slapped her face gently and shook her shoulder. Her color was pale, and her eyes were puffy from crying. Her hair was matted and uncombed. She was wearing a frayed white sleeping gown and heavy woolen stockings. She opened her eyes slowly and started to cry again. "They told me you were dead!" She locked her arms around me and buried her face against my neck. "I thought you were dead," she kept repeating for the next few minutes.

I held her tightly against me until she fell sound asleep from exhaustion. Today would not be the day for truth-telling.

While Eveline slept, Betsey boiled some sassafras roots and poured three mugs of tea. "I can't tell you how glad we are to see you," Leonard said as he sipped his tea. "Green Baker came by here two weeks ago and told us you had been killed in a brawl up in Springfield. He said that a man on the stagecoach told everyone at the Heath Tavern that he had witnessed it personally. He said you started a fight with a man as big as a mountain and that he kicked you to death. He said the other man died, too. Must have been an awful mess. Everybody's been upset about the whole thing, especially little Evie." Leonard started to cough violently. He hacked and convulsed for the better part of a minute. Betsey brought him some more tea and he gulped it down with the vigor of a wolf. "I think it's a race between my stomach and my lungs to see which one kills me first. Betsey's sassafras tea is about the only thing I can keep down. So, Nathan, what did happen up there?"

"It was pretty much as the man said, except the part about me being killed—although he wasn't too far off. If the man hadn't dropped dead when he did, I'd have been a goner for sure. Didn't you get the letter I sent? I mailed it over six weeks ago."

"No, we haven't gotten anything in the mail," Leonard replied, "have we, Betsey?"

There was a slight hesitation before Betsey answered. "No, we haven't heard a thing. Not a single thing." Betsey was unable to look me in the eyes, which made me think she was not being totally honest with me.

"How did Eveline take the news?" I asked.

"How would you expect her to take it?" Leonard asked. "That girl's plumb crazy over you. She did nothing but cry for three straight days. Then, when she didn't have any tears left, she slept for another three. Since then, she's just sat in that chair and stared into the fireplace. Green Baker came over and visited her a couple of times, but she hasn't given him the time of day. I think he's sweet on her, but now that you're back, that won't matter. What did the letter say, anyway, Nathan?"

"It just said that I had gotten in some trouble and would be in jail for a few weeks until the court got back into town."

"We sure would have avoided some heartache if that letter would have gotten to us in time," Leonard said. "Betsey went by the post office in Palestine a couple of weeks ago and picked up a letter from my son, Harrison."

"If there ever was a letter," Betsey mumbled.

"What is that supposed to mean?" I asked.

"It wouldn't be the first time a man ran off and left a woman behind for weeks at a time."

I took a deep breath and didn't say a word. Betsey stared directly into my eyes with spite I had never seen before.

"Now, Betsey, if Nathan said he mailed a letter, he mailed the letter! He's as honest as the day is long. Don't forget what he did in that burning barn."

"There isn't a man on earth who isn't capable of telling a lie."

"What have I done to you to deserve this treatment?" I asked. "I don't have to put up with—"

"Nathan?" Eveline was awake and was starting to cry again.

I built a roaring fire of four hickory logs that were still somewhat dry, and joined Eveline on a bench in front of the fireplace. John Herriman, who lived in the first cabin east of the Reeds', was visiting family in Lawrenceville and would be gone for at least a week. Leonard was looking after the livestock and said it would be all right to use his place if we wanted some privacy. The ground was soft from the deluge, so I carried her the quarter mile on my back. She clung to my neck so tightly she nearly choked me on more than one occasion. She seemed thinner and frailer than when I had left her. Leonard said she hadn't eaten anything for days.

"I learned to hate you," she said. "It was the only way I could stand to take another breath. You were my whole life, and just like that, you were gone. You left me all alone with that witch."

"It's all right, I'm here now."

"It's not all right. I can't stand the thought of losing you again. How can I love you again when I've convinced myself that I hate you?"

"Shhhh…I'm here now. I won't be going anywhere."

"We both know better than that, Nathan. What Betsey said is true. You're not the type to settle down. You've gone to college. You know important people. You don't even know how to raise a crop. Why would you settle for a plain-looking, uneducated little girl like me? Betsey said you probably shacked up with one of the Springfield whores."

"Where is this coming from?" I was surprised that I was feeling a bit hurt by her rampage.

"Betsey said you had been with lots of different women. She said that you even tried to get her to run off with you. Even Malinda Heath said she couldn't believe that we were getting married. She said she didn't think you were the marrying type. It would be like turning a panther into a housecat."

"And you believe her?"

"Yes! No! Oh, Nathan, I don't know what I believe anymore. Just hold me tight."

I held her as tightly as I could. I wanted to say something to make her feel better, but it was best for me to say nothing. She was hurt and broken and Nathan Crockett was the breaker. Betsey had poured some oil on the fire, but this was still my fault. Maybe later I could fix things, but for now, all I could do was hold her.

After sundown, I pulled the feather bed close to the fireplace and she slept in my arms, waking periodically, making sure I was still with her. I knew we should be getting back to the Reed cabin, but she became upset every time I mentioned it, so I decided we would spend the night there. I had dosed off to sleep when I became aware of her hands roaming against my body.

"What are you doing?" I asked, half-startled.

"Isn't this what you like?" she whispered. "Show me how to be like those girls in Springfield."

"Stop it, Evie! There weren't any girls in Springfield. There was a fight and there was jail. That was it!"

"Am I so awful that you won't let me touch you?"

"No, of course not! It's just that…"

"It's just that you're trying to keep my reputation pure. We're already sleeping in the same bed, Nathan. With Betsey's big mouth, everyone will know that we spent the night together."

"But *we* would know that nothing had happened."

"What if I wanted something to happen?" she said, hiding her face against my chest.

"I wouldn't let you," I said. My head and my heart were engaged in a vicious tug-of-war.

"Why? Because I'm some sort of little girl, and my heart might break like a piece of porcelain? Why do you think I moved down here from Logansport, anyway? I was a girl with a reputation. Not that I did anything to deserve it. After my father deserted us, my mother took in boarders to make ends meet. One of them was a riverboat captain by the name of Quinn. Every time he stayed in town, he would visit my bedroom late at night. He held a knife to my throat and told me he'd kill me if I made a sound. This went on for almost two years. This spring when he showed up, I told my mother everything. Instead of protecting me, she was worried about losing the business. She called me a whore and kicked me out of the house with only the clothes on my back. That night I went back, stole ten dollars from her lockbox, and bought passage to Merom. Uncle Leonard was my only blood relative, so I knew he would have to take me in.

"I came here to get married and to have someone protect me and keep me safe. I met you and fell in love with you. I might not be very old, and I might not know much about the world, but I do know that you're the love of my life. I could never feel about anyone else the way I feel about you. I also know that you aren't the type to stay at home and raise kids and spend every minute paying attention to me. And *that* is what I require. I am so happy you're not dead, but I've spent the last two weeks mourning you. I've cried a river of tears and hurt so badly that I didn't want to live. I couldn't go through it again. Don't say anything. You know I'm right. I know I forced you into saying you would marry me. I saw it in your eyes that you really didn't want it. If you did, you would have married me before your trip to Springfield. I don't want to sit around for weeks at a time not knowing when, or if, you'll come home. I need more of a tame animal, and Nathan, you're anything but tame. Leonard's son, Harrison, just bought a farm down the road. I'll go live with him and his wife until I find a husband. I won't love him as much as I love you, but I'll be safe and raise lots of sturdy church-going kids. I can't change you, but I wouldn't want you any other way. We will be cordial friends, and you will kiss me on the cheek at my wedding and be present at all the baptisms. Someday, you might find a woman who tames you, but she'll never love you as much as I do. So tonight I'll love you as if we were just married. Tonight I'm Mrs. Nathan Crockett, but tomorrow I'll be Eveline Deal, and it will be over. I want you to remember this night for the rest of your life. I want you to lie awake at night and know exactly what you're missing. Love me as your wife tonight, Nathan. Cherish me with all of your heart. All you have to do is say 'I do.' Say it, Nathan! Say 'I do!'"

"I do," I whispered.

She was gone when I woke up in the morning. I should have been relieved that she had saved me the trouble of calling off the engagement, but all I felt was a hollow sensation of loss. Eveline was more mercenary than I ever could have fathomed, but she was definitely more woman than little girl. I knew that her brave speech was all an act for my benefit. All I had to do was say the word, and she would have been mine forever. I was too much of a selfish fool to realize how special she was. I should have dragged her to the nearest preacher and married her on the spot. Instead, I slipped out quietly, made a quick getaway on Newton, and slithered all the way to my cabin.

Seventeen

Over the next couple of weeks, I cut enough firewood to get me through two winters. The monotonous, mindless chopping made my muscles scream for mercy after the sedentary stint in jail. From dawn to dusk, I busied myself with all the manual labor I could find around my neglected cabin. Exhaustion and aches and pains couldn't mask what I was truly feeling. It was grief. The only other time in my life I felt this bad was when my parents died. I tried drinking the memory of her away, but that only made it worse. Eveline had managed to turn me into a blubbering idiot. It's a good thing I didn't have any neighbors living close to me. I would have never lived it down if anyone had seen me in that shape. Even Newton seemed to be ashamed of me.

But as the days passed by, the pain started to ease ever-so-slightly. I realized that I would survive. The sky didn't seem as blue as before, and the grass was a duller shade of green. I had been cut, bruised, and turned inside out, but I would live with the recurring thoughts of what could have been.

I decided to take my wrath out on a few of my fur-bearing neighbors, and within two weeks, I had enough furs to take to Palestine and stock up on winter supplies. I tied two bundles of beaver, rabbit, and raccoon pelts to Newton's saddle and headed west on the trail toward Heathsville. Sometimes, it is best to leave some things alone, but I seemed to be going through a phase where I was doing a lot of things that weren't good for me. Even though it really didn't matter, I decided to check on something that had been eating at me for the last month.

Neither Rennick nor Malinda had seen the letter I sent to Eveline from jail in Springfield. I knew that Charlie had mailed it, because Jessie Dubois had received his a week after it was sent. Since it was sent to Heathsville, the letter should have come to the tavern after arriving at the post office in Palestine. Malinda looked though all of the cubbyholes to make sure it hadn't been misplaced.

"Nathan, I sure am sorry that you and little Eveline split up," said Malinda. "I was starting to worry about you. We hadn't seen you in such a long time; I was afraid something had happened."

"It probably came as a shock to you when you found out I was still alive," I said, as I started to walk out the door.

"What do you mean by that?" I could tell by the look on her face that she didn't have any idea what I was talking about.

"You mean a man didn't stop by on the stagecoach and say that he saw me get killed in a fight in Springfield?"

"I never heard anything about your trip. Who would say such a terrible thing?" She seemed honestly upset.

"It's just a rumor that has been going around. I don't know who started it, but I have an idea I'm going to find out."

"One more thing, Nathan," Malinda added. "Eveline is seeing Green Baker now. I just thought you should know in case you see them together. She might be a little more than he can handle, but he sure seems smitten with her. I've never seen a girl in such a hurry to get married."

I didn't say a word. What could I say?

I stopped by the post office in Palestine after dropping my pelts off at Lagow Mercantile & Dry Goods. Uncle Tommy Boatright, a thin, white-haired man who looked as if he was a hundred years old, ran the post office out of his general store. He remembered receiving both of my letters at the same time. He had delivered one to Jesse Dubois at the land office, and a dark-haired woman with a scar on her face picked up the other one a few days later. He remembered her specifically, because she left with a red-haired boy who was half her age. At first he thought she was his mother, but they acted more like school kids with a crush. "It just didn't seem right," he said, "but to each his own."

I can accept fate. If things are meant to be, they're meant to be. If your number is up, it's up. But when someone deliberately causes pain to me or the people in my life, that's a whole different matter.

I stopped by the Dubois Tavern and paid the remainder of my debt for my legal fees in Springfield. After receiving a short lecture from Jesse, I ate an overcooked venison steak along with some sweet potato pie and chased it with a mug of cold buttermilk. I finished the meal off with a mug of brown ale, which had just arrived from Terre Haute. Instead of participating in the nightly debate, I went to sleep early in the same bed in which I had convalesced after the stable fire. I woke early in the morning and ate a breakfast of biscuits and gravy. I chased it with half a pot of coffee. I thanked Jesse again for his hospitality, and he refused to let me pay for the room. I told him I'd see him on the first of next month to make a whiskey run to Merom. I picked up Newton from the new stable and loaded him with supplies from Doc Lagow's store. I started south on the Vincennes Trail toward home, but decided to make a detour along the way.

Bristol Landing was a beehive of activity at this time of year. The landing was a big, flat knoll with dozens of loading docks at the base of a steep, wooded hill that towered over the Wabash River. It was two miles southeast of Palestine, the closest spot with access to the river. Flatboats were lined up for miles to the north, waiting to get their loads of grain and head south to the Ohio River and then on to New Orleans. It was also a place where a young man who wasn't afraid to work could find employment. Green Baker's flame-red hair made him easy to spot from a quarter of a mile away. He was loading corn onto a wagon in front of a warehouse, halfway up the hill. I waited until the wagon was loaded and the driver had pulled away to make my approach. Green had walked inside the dark, musty building and had no idea that I had followed him. I looked around and saw that we were alone. He headed over to a wooden keg that was labeled *Seven Jessie's Double-Distilled Whiskey*, popped off the lid, and dipped a ladle down into the barrel.

Even though I had decided to remain calm and not do anything I would regret later, I used the element of surprise to my advantage. I lunged at Green, grabbed a handful of hair in each hand, and pushed his face down into the barrel. He struggled wildly at first, arms flailing at the air, trying to free himself, but within seconds I felt him gag and go limp. I pulled his head out of the whiskey, waited for him to take a gulp of air, and then pushed his face back into the barrel for a second time. We repeated this process for the better part of five minutes until I finally picked him up and threw him onto a pile of feedbags. I remained on guard until I realized that he didn't have any fight left in him. He was drenched down to his thighs in whiskey, and coughed violently to rid his lungs of the poison. He struggled to catch his breath, and he finally started to breathe in a somewhat regular rhythm. "My eyes are burning," he yelled. "You've blinded me."

"It's just the alcohol burning; you'll be fine in a few minutes," I told him. "Quit acting like a baby. You're lucky I didn't drown you, Green."

"Nathan? Is that you?"

"Good guess," I answered.

"What do you want?" He kept scooting backward, away from me, until he fell off the pile and hit the back of his head on the ground. He shot up and threw a hay-bailer hook, which missed me by at least three feet. His momentum carried him past me, so I just kicked him on the backside as he went by and he fell on the ground in a heap. He was done.

"What I want is some information, Green. I already know *what* you did, but I just don't know *why* you did it. But you're going to tell me all the juicy details and not leave anything out."

"I don't know what you're talking about."

"Wrong answer, Green." I picked him up by the back of his collar and started dragging him toward the whiskey barrel for another session.

"Stop! I'll tell you everything. Please, I can't take any more."

"That's more like it. First of all, tell me why you and

80

Betsey intercepted my letter to Eveline and cooked up that story about me being killed in Springfield."

"You know about all that?" he said with a confused look on his face. "I thought you were mad because Eveline and I are seeing each other."

"What I'm mad about is you messing around in my business and causing a lot of pain and suffering for Eveline." After making that statement, I felt hypocritical because it was my actions in Springfield that really started all of the mess.

"It was all Betsey's idea, Nathan. She read your letter and said you were in jail and wouldn't be back for a while. She said you and Eveline weren't any good for each other, and we should do something about it. I know it wasn't right, but Betsey told me that if I didn't do as she said, she would..." He paused and seemed afraid to continue.

"She would what?" I stood over him and acted like I was going to grab him again for another whiskey bath.

"Or she would tell Mr. Reed and my folks that we had been meeting each other." He started sobbing. "I don't know how I got myself into this. She said that if I played my cards right, I would end up with Eveline. So I went along with her plan. I was supposed to tell Eveline that I met a man on the stagecoach who told me you were dead, except I said that he had told everyone at the tavern. I thought it made the story sound more believable, but Betsey almost killed me when I changed the facts. She said you would talk with the Heaths and find out that I had lied."

"She was right about that. But what did you think would happen when I got back? You had to know that I'd find out and would come looking for you."

"I didn't know what to do, Nathan. She said her husband would shoot me if he found out. And if he didn't, my Pa surely would."

Green Baker was no match for Betsey Reed. Once she had decided to seduce him, he didn't stand a chance. She had her claws in the boy and wasn't about to let go. She would keep him around as long as she needed, then throw him away when he was all used up.

"So she stirred up all this trouble because she thought Eveline and I weren't any good for each other? It just doesn't make sense."

"She's an awful jealous woman, but there's more to it than that," Green admitted. "She didn't want Eveline around when Leonard dies. She thinks he might leave the farm to Eveline or his son and leave her out in the cold. She thinks Mr. Reed's son is in on the plot too. She was awful jealous of you and Eveline. I don't think she wants anyone to be happy."

"She seems to want you and Eveline to be together." I realized that I was starting to sound like the spurned lover. "Forget I said that. Did she mention anything about wanting to kill Leonard?"

"No, but Eveline sure has a lot to say on the subject. She said she saw Betsey pour some poison into Mr. Reed's dinner. Betsey said it was just some sugar to sweeten up the stew, but Eveline said he got real sick as soon as he ate it. Betsey says that if Leonard doesn't kick the bucket pretty soon, the doctors are going to end up with the farm. I know for a fact that Mr. Reed had to borrow money just to pay for his last batch of medicine. He doesn't have much of a crop in the field, so I don't know how they're going to make it through the winter."

"But Leonard's health has been declining for some time; he's not going to be around that much longer. Why would she try to kill him?" I asked.

"Betsey thinks Leonard is going to sell the farm to his son, Harrison. She thinks that's why Eveline came to live with them, to make sure nothing happened to the old man. The doctor told her he is a tough old buzzard and could live for several years."

"You people are all crazy. What does Eveline have to say about the whole matter?" I asked.

"She hates Betsey as much as Betsey hates her. That's all she can talk about. Betsey this, Betsey that, Betsey! Betsey! Betsey!"

"I guess that leaves you stuck in the middle of the storm, doesn't it?"

"Like a sow in a mud hole."

"So what are you going to do about it?" I asked him.

"I don't know," he said hesitantly. "I've been thinking about hiring one of these flatboats and going downriver. Then you could have Eveline all to yourself."

"Don't do me any favors, Green. You've caused enough damage already. Running away from the problem seems a bit cowardly, though."

"What am I supposed to do, Nathan?"

"Tell the truth, maybe?"

"I wouldn't know where to start," he said, shaking his head, looking hopelessly at the dirt floor for some sort of answer.

"Do you know what happened to the letter?" I asked. I was beginning to regret not going straight home.

"Betsey told me to throw it away, but I hid it in the barn behind our cabin. I thought I might need it sometime."

"Well, you need it now, Green. After you get off work tonight, you're going to take that letter and make sure it gets delivered to Eveline. You're going to tell her the truth, and not leave a single word out. If I find out you didn't do as I've asked, I'm going to hunt you down and drag you back to her myself, and we can tell her together. I don't care if I have to go to New Orleans to find you. I'll do it. But if you set the record straight tonight, then as far as I'm concerned, the whole matter is over. If you can work it out with Eveline and she still wants you, more power to you both."

"It's not Eveline I'm worried about. Betsey is going to stir up a whole mess of trouble for me. She told me that if anyone found out, she'd make sure I wouldn't live to see my next birthday. She said she'd put a hex on me. She's a witch from hell, you know, and now I'm going to die."

"Don't be an idiot. Betsey's not a witch. She is crazy, but she's not a witch. Listen, Green, Leonard is too sick to care one way or the other, so why don't you just tell your father what happened before she gets the chance? He might belt you around a little bit, but he'll respect you for being honest. At least you'll be able to sleep soundly at night."

"Why do I have to tell Eveline the truth if you don't want her back?"

"She deserves to hear the truth."

"If you say so."

"I say so!" I could have talked to him for hours, but it wouldn't do any good. Green Baker was going to come clean with Eveline because I bullied him into doing it, not because it was the right thing to do. It disappointed me that Eveline would get involved with such a sniveling little boy, but then again, I didn't have any right to talk.

As I rode away from the warehouse, I saw Green pour buckets of water into the whiskey barrel to fill it back to the top and slap the lid shut. No one would ever know the difference. I laughed at the thought of an innocent tavern keeper swearing at a drunken customer for accusing him of serving watered-down whiskey. I decided not to make a second stop to confront Betsey. I had stirred things up enough. If Green had enough courage to go through with the confession, there was going to be a great deal of turmoil in the Reed cabin that evening. I had done enough damage for one day. Besides, I didn't want Betsey to put a hex on me.

Eighteen

The autumn of 1843 was quiet and uneventful beneath the Five Sisters. The trees turned shades of orange, red, and yellow; ducks and geese flew south, and the river started to rid itself of boat traffic. We had a short Indian summer interrupted by a week of cold, gray drizzle. I fixed the barn roof and doubled the size of Newton's corral. I made the promised trip to Merom for the whiskey, but avoided the Merom House. The last thing I wanted was to explain to Charlotte Campbell how I managed to foul things up with Eveline. I bought a book of short stories by Edgar Allen Poe and *Nicholas Nickleby* by Charles Dickens. I harvested some squash and corn and gathered hickory nuts, walnuts, persimmons, and sassafras roots for tea. I started clearing trees to give me a better view of the Wabash. A stray gray and white cat found my cabin and decided to stay. As a rule, I don't like cats, but this one was a good mouser and acted more like a dog than a cat. I named her Kate, after Kate Nickleby, a character from Dickens' book. She would follow me wherever I went, and even managed to win Newton's approval, which was no easy task.

As the days grew shorter and the wind started blowing in from the north, I knew that it would only be a matter of time before winter set in for good. After performing a quick inventory, I realized that I needed to get a few more supplies. I didn't need that much, so I decided to go to Heathsville instead of Palestine. Kate followed for half a mile before realizing that she wouldn't be able to keep up with Newton, and then turned back to the cabin. I wondered if she would be there when I got back. I hoped she would be.

Malinda Heath came up and gave me a big hug as soon as I walked through the door. "I've been worried about you, Nathan. You've been on my mind for the last few weeks. I

85

was just about to send Rennick over to your place and make sure you were all right."

"Why wouldn't I be?" I was a bit confused about all the concern. Malinda had always been nice to me, but she seemed to be sincerely concerned about my wellbeing.

"Oh, nothing, it's just...I really shouldn't..."

"Shouldn't what?" I asked.

"I promised that I wouldn't say anything."

"What did you promise, and what aren't you supposed to say?" I knew she was dying to blurt out whatever she had promised not to repeat.

"I can't stand it anymore. I know about you getting thrown in jail in Springfield. It must have been awful. Why didn't you say anything?"

"It's not something I'm proud of, Malinda. It wasn't all that bad. I survived."

"Don't lie to me, Nathan. I read the letter you wrote to Eveline. It's the saddest thing I ever read in my life. I could feel your broken heart with every word."

"How did you get the letter?"

"Eveline let me read it," she said. "She told me everything, Nathan. You two were doomed the minute you took her near that witch, Betsey."

I never imagined that anyone else would read the letter. I was thoroughly embarrassed. "Where is Eveline?"

"She left with her cousin and his wife a little over two weeks ago. She stayed with us for quite a while. I think she was hoping you would come and take her away."

"Why did she move in with you?" I was pretty sure I knew the answer to that question.

Malinda walked over to a pie safe, pulled out an envelope, and handed it to me. "This should answer all of your questions, Nathan."

The letter was already opened. "I suppose that you've read this also?" The look of guilt on her face answered the question.

My Dearest Nathan,

I've started this letter at least a dozen times only to have it end up as fuel in the fireplace. I half expected to see you after Green's confession, but realize that you probably wanted to stay as far away from me as possible. Nathan, I always believed that you had written that letter from jail. I never doubted you for a minute. You really didn't have to terrorize poor Green to prove your honesty, although I laugh out loud when I try to imagine you dunking him in that barrel of whiskey. It must have been quite a sight to behold.

You must have known that by making Green fess up about his affair with Betsey, you'd be stirring up a hornet's nest. As you probably expected, I was furious when he told me about their crazy plot. I stormed into the cabin and confronted her in front of Uncle Leonard. Uncle Leonard just shook his head and went out back. He didn't seem that upset or even all that interested in the matter. Betsey, though, was an entirely different story. She called Green a liar and accused me of getting him to stir up trouble. When I produced your letter, she flew into a tizzy.

She lunged at Green and started clawing at his face. Then she bit off a chunk of his left ear. He screamed, and then he punched her square in the nose. There was blood everywhere, and her eyes started to blacken immediately. It was awful, but I loved every minute of it. I hate to admit it, but I was hoping that they would kill each other. Finally, Green took off running with Betsey screaming that she would make sure he ended up dead. She demanded that I leave the cabin, but I had already started to pack.

I walked up to the tavern, and the Heaths let me stay with them. They've both been wonderful. Mrs. Heath hates Betsey as much as I do. I'm leaving today with my cousin, Harrison, and his wife, Mary. They bought a farm near Morea, about four miles west of here. They are a loving couple, and I feel safe with them. Harrison tried to get Uncle Leonard to move in with us, but he is too stubborn. He said that Betsey's bark is much worse than her bite. He would be fine and wasn't about to leave. He said that the new medicine was starting to help, and that Betsey was taking good care of him. Can you believe that? It would be like Eve going back to the snake for more advice in the Garden of Eden after the whole apple incident.

I also have some wonderful news to tell you. Remember when I told you that my father ran away when I was little? Well, the place he ran to was Vincennes. Harrison ran into him working on the ferry when he crossed the river. When he found out that I ran away from home, he came to see me right away. He said he thought about me every day, and had never forgiven himself for leaving me with my mother. I forgave him, of course, and we had a nice visit. He is going to try and find work in Palestine so that we can be close to each other. I can't even begin to describe what it means to me to have my daddy back.

Enough about me. It was very difficult for me to read your letter. I know you were battered and in a jail cell when you wrote, but you sounded so sincere. You apologized eight times, called yourself an idiot on four occasions, but you told me that you loved me twenty-three times. I counted every one of them over and over. I could feel your pain and I could feel your love with every word. Every night when I go to bed, I lie awake, remembering our night together. I have no regrets and hope that you don't either.

I heard someone talking about all the work you have been doing around your cabin. They said that you haven't been acting like yourself lately, and that you seem to be avoiding all of your friends. I can't tell how close I came to paying you a visit on more than one occasion, but I knew that if we spent a second night together, you'd be stuck with me for life. I know in my heart that you would be miserable being shackled to a demanding wife and a covey of hungry mouths to feed. I want you to know that I love you and always will.

Please go back to living your life as you did before you met me. I would sleep a lot better knowing that the Nathan Crockett I fell in love with is out there somewhere, living life to the fullest and without regrets. Thank you for being my guardian angel and not letting me make a mistake by marrying Green Baker. I'm sure I would have discovered their plot sooner or later, but thanks all the same. It's a shame, though. Green was easy to control. Believe it or not, Nathan, that's exactly what I'm looking for. I am free from Betsey Reed once and for all, and I'm on the prowl for the father of my children to be.

With all my love...

Your Eveline

I read the letter twice before tucking it into a pocket on the inside of my jacket. I didn't know what to feel. I was glad that Eveline got away from Betsey, but I still had that sick empty feeling inside. Maybe, I thought, she would come running to me, begging me to take her back. I don't think I would have turned her away if she did.

Malinda brought me a cup of hot apple cider and placed it on the table in front of me.

"If you had any sense, Nathan, you'd go after the girl and bring her back where she belongs. You're both acting like a couple of martyrs."

"I don't know if I'm ready to settle down yet."

"That's a load of horse manure. You're just afraid to grow up."

"You're probably right," I admitted.

"I know I'm right. If you're interested, she's at Elzey Higgins' old farm. If you hurry, you could have her back here by sundown."

I almost knocked Rennick over as I ran out the door. I jumped on Newton and headed west at a full gallop, dodging several low-hanging limbs along the way. The Morea Road was not much more than a deer path that followed a ridge through the dense hardwood forest. As I reached the top of the ridge, I could see the old Higgins farm, which Harrison Reed had just purchased. I paused for a minute to make sure that I had enough courage to go riding down the hill like a buck-skinned knight in shining armor. I decided to give it a try; I had absolutely nothing to lose.

There was smoke coming out of the fireplace and a pair of horses standing beneath a crude lean-to. I was trying to think of something clever to say when my heart suddenly sank into the pit of my stomach. I saw a young couple sitting on the front porch, holding hands. It didn't take a genius to see what was going on. I didn't recognize the young man, but the girl was definitely Eveline Deal. I had waited too long.

I immediately turned Newton around and headed back towards Heathsville. I packed up my supplies, which now included two jugs of the Blue Ruin, and started for home. I told Rennick and Malinda what had happened and asked them not to mention a word to anyone about me going after

Eveline. Even though I knew Malinda could never sit on a piece of juicy gossip of this magnitude, she agreed to keep it to her inner circle. She tried to console me, but realized that there was nothing she could have said that would have made me feel better. I reached my cabin at dusk, and found the new love of my life waiting for me on my front porch, Kate the cat.

Nineteen

That winter was colder than usual. The continuously bleak, gray sky seemed to match my mood. I spent most of my time inside my cabin in front of the fire, trying to convince myself that human contact wasn't at all necessary for my survival. Then I tried to pretend that the last year and a half was nothing but a bad dream. No Betsey. No Leonard. No Doyle Popplewell, Jesse Scott, Green Baker, no one-eared horses—and especially no Eveline Deal! Just wipe away the memory and move ahead with the adventure. I was happy before I met those people. I enjoyed barn raisings and turkey shoots. I occasionally even went to church on Sundays just to enjoy the company of other people. I was welcome at Little Church with the Hardshell Baptists and with the Methodists at John Fox's Meeting House. I wanted to go back and find the old Nathan, the one who didn't have a care in the world.

I had used the same strategy after the death of my parents. Just pretend it never happened. Just believe that they moved back to Tennessee and are living happily ever after. But as much as I tried, it didn't work then and it wasn't working now. We are the sum of our life experience. Denying the events of my past would be denying who I am. It wasn't until I saw my reflection in Newton's watering trough that I realized I needed to stop feeling sorry for myself. I saw an unshaven, shoddy-looking scoundrel who would have looked right at home with the horse thieves of the Dark Bend or a gang of river pirates on the Wabash. I was ashamed to have anyone see me in such a condition— not that they would have recognized me. I had fallen that far.

I boiled water in a large, black caldron, which hung above a roaring fire in my fireplace, and filled a large copper bathtub that used to belong to my mother. It was a silly thing for a single man to own, but I remembered how proud my mother was to have such a luxury in the hinterland. My father traded a swayback mare for the tub and gave it to my mother on their tenth anniversary. Even though I hated the thought of my weekly bath as a child, I couldn't imagine any reason on earth that would ever make me get rid of it.

After letting the water cool to an acceptable temperature, I went to work on myself with a cake of Malinda Baker's lye soap. As I scraped away the dirt and grime, I realized it was a good thing that no one had been downwind of me.

Without realizing it at the time, I was scrubbing so hard that my arm started to bleed. I had opened a scar that I had earned in the stable fire. I guess it was then that I accepted the fact that scars were nothing more than badges that proved I was a mere mortal. The burn marks on my arms, the knots on my skull, and my broken heart were going to be permanent reminders that life is a bumpy road, and if you want to make it to the end, you have to get past the storms to get to the rainbows.

I submerged myself completely and officially washed away the past. When I came up from my self-inflicted baptism, I realized that the old Nathan was back, ready to charge back into the world; he was a little bit tarnished but a little bit wiser. After shaving and cutting my hair with a sharpened Bowie knife, I wrapped myself in a wool blanket and sat in the rocking chair next to the fire. I felt fifty pounds lighter and ten years younger. The bathwater looked as if a shedding bear had gone swimming. Kate the Cat rubbed her arched back against my legs to remind me that I had neglected her during the bathing process. She must have thought it was a considerable waste of time as she demonstrated that all she needed was her tongue to do the same job.

It was a week before Christmas, and I was suddenly in the holiday spirit. I put a saddle on Newton for the first time in over a month and rode toward Palestine. I was only a mile from home when I came upon a flock of wild turkey foraging for food in the brush. I loaded my long rifle and took aim at a tom that had wandered out enough to give me a clear shot. He fell dead with a single shot to the head, but much to my surprise, the ball also hit a hen in the neck. Two kills with one shot. The world was beginning to look a great deal brighter.

I stopped by the Heaths' and gave Malinda the oversized tom. She declared that the bird would be the guest of honor at the Christmas feast, and my presence was required. I accepted, and promised to arrive shortly after the Christmas morning ceremonies in Palestine were finished. I left the hen with a frail widow by the name of Griggs. She had always provided cool water from her well on my numerous trips to town, so it felt good to pay her back. She invited me in for some persimmon pudding, which was absolutely delicious, and a mug of hot cider. She thanked me at least ten times before I could get out the door. Her son always brought a rabbit for Christmas dinner, so the turkey would be a wonderful substitution. She wanted to make sure I had someone to spend Christmas with, and admonished me for getting cold feet with Eveline. *So much for Malinda keeping it a secret.* When I assured her that I wouldn't be alone, she kissed me on the cheek and wished me a merry Christmas. It felt good to play Saint Nick and think about others for a change. I had been self-absorbed for much too long.

Palestine was busier than I could ever remember. Stores were all decorated in Christmas colors. Carolers, wearing matching red scarves, were singing hymns in the public square next to the land office. Children were lined up to get a free taste of the peppermint sticks that had just arrived at Uncle Tommy Boatright's grocery store. The Haskett Brothers' Dry Goods Store was the busiest store for thirty miles in any direction. Shelves were filled with dresses, hats, and shoes from back east, most of which were not at all practical for the wilderness of the Wabash Valley, but were coveted nevertheless by many of the society ladies in town for their numerous holiday engagements. There was a couple looking at rings in Peter Griggs' jewelry store. I debated about telling him not to bother buying a rabbit for Christmas dinner, but decided against the idea since he was so busy.

Augustus French waved from the window of a tailor's shop, where he was being fitted for a suit that would have put a proud peacock to shame. He had been appointed a receiver at the U.S. Land Office by President Van Buren and was also a successful lawyer in town. Like myself, his parents had died when he was young; however, since he was the oldest son, he had actually raised his younger siblings. I'd always admired him for his commitment to duty. I had also known his first wife, Clarissa Kitchell, a beautiful tall blonde, who was the daughter of the wealthiest man in Palestine. She died shortly after the birth of their first son, who passed away a month later. I have never seen a man grieve as much as he did at their funerals. I heard that he had just married a girl from a wealthy family in New York, so I stuck my head inside the store and offered my congratulations and wished him the best of luck. He thanked me and invited me to stop by his new country home, which he named Maplewood, so I could meet his new wife. I told him I would try to make it on the way home if at all possible. He seemed much happier now that he was married again.

I stopped by Gogin's General Store and bought some pipe tobacco from Virginia for Jessie Dubois, and some lace linen napkins and a tablecloth for his wife, Adelia. Auntie Gogin wrapped the gifts in red wrapping paper held together with yellow yarn, which was tied into an improbable yuletide knot. I also picked up several bags of sugar candy to pass around town on Christmas Eve.

When I arrived at the Dubois House, Adelia greeted me with a hug and asked me why my new bride wasn't with me. After explaining that I was still single, she scolded me for being such a fool and then ushered me to my regular room. "Jessie went to Vincennes to fetch a priest to deliver the Christmas Mass tomorrow morning. It would mean a lot to him if you attended the service, Nathan," she said, knowing that I would.

"That's why I'm here," I assured her. Jesse made a substantial contribution to the Vincennes Diocese each year, and in return they sent a junior priest to hold a service for Palestine's few remaining French Catholics. He had built a small chapel behind the inn, which served as the church whenever they were fortunate enough to have a priest or missionary pass through town.

Adelia had decorated the inn with red candles surrounded by conifer wreaths adorned with acorns, pinecones, and ribbons. The combined fragrance of cinnamon sticks, roasted chestnuts, and mulled apple cider left no doubt that Christmas was at hand. The Yule log, covered in flowers, silk, and ribbons, was displayed prominently by the hearth, where it would be offered to the fire at the height of the evening's festivities. Liddy Parker stood in the doorway between the dinning room and the kitchen with an expression that portrayed mischief and shyness at the same time. I couldn't help but notice that the skinny girl with freckles and flame-red hair had blossomed into a beautiful young lady. She cleared her throat as if she wanted to tell me something, but remained purposely silent.

"Got something caught in your throat?" I asked, puzzled by her peculiar behavior.

Exasperated with my response, she motioned for me to look up at the ceiling. I pretended not to see the ball of greenery hanging above her head. "It's mistletoe, Nathan! You have to kiss a girl when she's standing under the mistletoe, or you'll have seven years of bad luck."

"That's what you get for breaking a mirror." I hesitated for a moment, and then smiled to let her know that I was teasing. I leaned over and started to give her a peck on the cheek, but she grabbed my face with both hands and kissed me passionately on the lips. When I tried to pull away, she tightened her grip and kissed me harder. I finally submitted and reciprocated.

After twenty seconds she pulled away. She gathered her composure, took two steps backward, then looked directly into my eyes. "There's more where that came from if you're interested. And oh yes...Merry Christmas, Nathan." She scampered back to work in the kitchen and left me speechless beneath the mistletoe.

Liddy Parker had deep emerald eyes, perfectly round and as big as saucers. They sparkled with mischief in the candlelight. I was amazed that I had never noticed them before. Maybe it was going to be a good Christmas after all.

"Looks like someone's jumping straight from the frying pan into the fire," whispered Adelia as she walked past me with a handful of linen tablecloths and napkins. She had apparently witnessed the encounter.

"Just spreading a little Christmas cheer, Adelia," I said, trying not to let my embarrassment show.

"Just make sure you don't get too cheerful. Too much cheer has been known to result in autumn babies." She winked and went about setting the table.

Father Augustus Bessonies was almost as wide as he was tall. He was built like a tree stump with a head, no neck, and a pair of short arms and legs attached. His smile was infectious and his handshake was viselike. He was traveling with a French girl by the name of Josephine Pardeithou. She wore a simple, woolen, gray dress, and her dark brown hair was cropped short. I had once seen a painting of Joan of Arc in which her hair was cut in a similar fashion. Her skin was milky white and flawless. I noticed that she was standing directly beneath the same ball of mistletoe, but I didn't dare make a move under the watchful eye of Adelia and Liddy. I found out later that she was on her way to Terre Haute to join the convent of Saint Mary of the Woods. In two weeks, she would become Sister Mary Angelique. I assume that the penalty for kissing a Sister of Providence would be death by biblical plague, even if she was standing beneath the mistletoe, so in this case, discretion *was* the better part of valor.

Jesse hired Pryor Harvey and Bus Fuller, the two best fiddlers in town, for the night's entertainment. Father Bessonies apparently loved to dance, but didn't feel comfortable displaying his fondness for this leisure pursuit under the watchful eye of Bishop Brute in Vincennes. He jumped at the chance to participate in the various dances; the inn evolved into an impromptu ballroom for the night. He knew all the traditional line dances as well as some new choreography, which he had learned on a recent visit to France.

Some of the elderly women seemed shocked when he danced a waltz with Adelia. It was one thing to join in a line dance, where the dancers barely made any physical contact, but a waltz was an entirely different matter. What would the Bishop think about such a fleshly display in public? A man has to place his hands on his female partner and hold her in his arms as he whisks her around the dance floor. He soon quashed their opposition by dancing with every female in the room, with the exception of the future Sister Mary Angelique. I guess you have to draw the line somewhere. He was a most graceful dancer, much lighter on his feet than you might expect from a man of his size. He reminded me of a dancing bear that I had once seen at a traveling show in Vincennes.

The mulled wine and apple cider disappeared by the gallon. Even the dourest people in attendance were forced to join in the fun. I managed to find Liddy beneath the mistletoe on a few occasions, and I danced until my feet finally said 'no more.' I felt alive for the first time in weeks. When my thoughts started to drift toward Eveline, I simply grabbed Liddy and maneuvered her beneath the mistletoe once again. The more I kissed her, the further Eveline went away. At midnight, everyone walked to the public square and watched with trepidation as a few of the local war veterans attempted to fire a shot from the town cannon. The cannon, which had seen action with the Illinois Militia in both the War of 1812 and also in the Black Hawk War, was now relegated to a single burst annually to announce the arrival of the Christ Child. They front-packed the chamber with gunpowder, shreds of paper, wood, and pieces of brick. Two of the men started to argue about the proper amount of powder to use, which resulted in a fistfight. Some women became upset over the lack of decorum shown, while a few men placed wagers on the outcome. The argument was finally settled with a left hook. It was decided that *more* gunpowder would be used. This prompted any spectator with a lick of sense to take at least five steps backward, or to seek shelter behind a stout tree. The men drew straws to choose who would fire the cannon. A tall man with a Yankee Doodle hat was chosen, although it wasn't made clear if he was the winner or the loser of the selection process. He used a tallow candle to light the fuse, then quickly ran away.

Kaboom! The cannon flew up into the air and disappeared into a ball of white smoke. After the echo of the explosion subsided, you could hear the unmistakable sound of a falling tree somewhere in the distance, followed by the flapping wings of unhappy birds that were blasted awake from their winter slumber. After the smoke cleared, some men rushed over with buckets of water to douse a small fire that had started next to the cannon, which now rested upside-down and was missing a wheel. After making sure there were no casualties, the crowd cheered and broke into a Christmas hymn: "Joy to the World, the Lord Has Come…" Even the future Sister Mary Angelique joined in the celebration.

My headache was almost gone by the time I left for Heathsville. Too much wine and dancing, combined with very little sleep, had made for a very rough morning. As promised, I attended the Christmas Mass at Jesse's log chapel. I took two years of Latin in school, but had a hard time following Father Bessonies with his heavy French accent. The incense was extremely musty, and I almost became nauseous, but I somehow made it to the end of the service without incident. By mid-morning, the temperature dropped, and heavy, wet snow began to fall. I decided to leave early and get to Rennick's before it got dark. After gifts were exchanged, I spent a few minutes with Liddy and promised to call on her after the holidays. She kissed me goodbye and wrapped a red scarf around my neck as I left. She had knitted it for Jesse but thought that I needed it more.

I waved goodbye and headed south on the Vincennes

Trace. As soon as I passed LaMotte Creek, the wind picked up strength, blowing directly from the north. The snow became so heavy that visibility was limited to approximately fifty feet. I decided to bypass Augustus French's house and ride directly to the Heath Tavern. I was fortunate that Newton instinctively knew the way, because the road completely vanished somewhere around Fuller Chapel. Unable to distinguish any landmarks, I was beginning to wonder if we hadn't strayed off course. The snow was now blowing sideways, and visibility was down to five feet at best. I was considering finding shelter against a tree, but when we crossed the bridge at Doe Run Creek, I knew I was only a few minutes away. By the time I made it to the inn, the snow was already knee deep.

The aroma of pumpkin pie, sweet potatoes, and turkey overwhelmed my senses as soon as I opened the door. My fingers were numb, and my face felt brittle from the sting of the wind. I ran over to the fireplace and immediately began the process of thawing out. Rennick and Malinda were in the kitchen, arguing about something, while several of the neighborhood children sat around the Christmas tree eyeing their presents.

"You have no business going out in this storm, Rennick!" shouted Malinda, as the argument moved out into the front room. "Doc Logan says you need to take it easy on your heart! Wait till the storm is over and we will find some help."

"She could be dead by then. The baby was due over a week ago!" Rennick bellowed back. "I have to go!"

"What's going on?" I asked, realizing they didn't know I was in the room.

"Nathan! Oh, thank God you're here!" Malinda came over and clutched my arm. "Try to talk some sense into this stubborn goat. He's going to ride over to Will Fuller's cabin on the river and bring Hannah back."

"I have to agree with Malinda," I said to Rennick. "It's a blizzard out there; you'd get lost for sure."

"I'll have to take that chance," declared Rennick as he

wrapped a scarf around his neck. "John Herriman just dropped off this letter. It says that Will Fuller got his leg busted up in Pittsburgh, and he won't be home until spring. He says he wants me to get Hannah and bring her here to have the baby."

"Can't it wait until the weather clears?" I asked.

"Nathan, the letter is two months old. It says that the baby was due in the middle of December. Who knows what kind of shape she's in, or if she's alive at all? All I know is that if Malinda were down there, I'd do whatever it took to make sure she was safe."

It was an easy decision to make. Newton was still saddled up, and I knew the road by heart. I warmed my hands for a few minutes and went back into the blizzard, trudging through snowdrifts as I made my way across the river-bottoms, with the smell of my uneaten Christmas dinner still fresh in my mind.

Twenty

There were no signs of life as I approached the cabin. The barn was shut up tight, and there wasn't any smoke coming from the chimney. My stomach began to feel the clench of an invisible fist as I started to think about what I might find. Maybe Hannah had gone to stay with family or a neighbor. Maybe she was dead. The snow had drifted waist-deep in front of the cabin door, and there wasn't a footprint anywhere around. I was starting to pray that she wouldn't be inside. I kicked the snow aside, pushed the door open, and walked into the cold, dark cabin. I found an oil lamp hanging on a hook beside the door. At first I thought the cabin was empty, but as soon as I lit the lamp I could see the unmistakable silhouette of a human body lying beneath a heap of blankets in the corner of the room. It was Hannah Fuller.

She shuddered as soon as I peeled her blankets away. She was drenched and burning with fever. "Will, is that you?" she whispered.

"It's Nathan Crockett, Hannah. Will is stuck in Pittsburgh and sent word to take you to safety."

"Pittsburgh! What happened?"

"He broke his leg loading the boat. He's all right, but he won't be able to get back until the river rises in the spring. I'm supposed to take you to the tavern until the baby comes." It was obvious that she wasn't in any kind of shape to travel.

"It's too late for that. My water's already broke."

"What does that mean?" I was afraid to hear the answer.

"It means the baby is coming!"

"Oh no! You can't have the baby! Not now!"

"I don't think we're going to be able to do anything abowoh!" She dug her fingernails into my arm as she became rigid as a board.

"What is it? What's wrong?"

"It's the birth pangs. They're about twenty minutes apart." She relaxed and started to shiver uncontrollably.

"I need to go get help, Hannah!"

"No! You can't leave me, Nathan! I'm so afraid. I can't lose another baby."

"I don't know anything about birthing a baby. I really need to get help."

"No, you can't! Go fire three rifle shots in the air. All my neighbors know that I'm alone. Someone will come. I know someone will."

I ran outside, pulled the rifle out of my saddle holster, and fired three shots into the near-black sky. I cursed myself for getting into another impossible situation. I went back into the cabin and put three dry pieces of firewood on the few remaining coals in the fireplace. After a little coaxing, the wood ignited into a roaring blaze. I poured water into a cast-iron kettle to boil, wet a cotton napkin with warm water, and washed away the sweat beads on Hannah's face. Her face was pale white and sallow. I noticed some fresh blood on her lower lip where she had bitten down during one of the pangs. I felt entirely helpless. I didn't know exactly what the boiling water was used for, but I knew that it was a necessity at delivery time.

Hannah had two more birth pains accompanied by a blood-curdling cry for mercy. I ran outside and fired three more shots into the sky. The full moon, visible only a few minutes before, was now completely shrouded by heavy cloud cover as snow began falling heavily again. Even if someone had heard the shots and wanted to help, it would be foolish to venture out into the storm. The trail had completely disappeared, and the snow combined with the blackness of night would make it impossible to navigate by landmarks. I moved Newton into the barn, and much to his dismay, put him in a stall while he was still wet. I found some hay and a little bit of cracked corn and threw it in a trough, which seemed to improve his mood a little.

Hannah was having another pang when I returned to the cabin. This one, like the others, lasted for about thirty seconds before subsiding. She seemed to be withstanding them better than before. The cabin was much warmer now, causing her to shed some of her blankets. Hopefully, she would deliver the baby herself. After all, women have been having babies for thousands of years. It is a perfectly natural process. Even though I tried to convince myself that things would be fine, visions of young girls in premature graves kept popping into my mind.

Hannah's face, now an unnatural shade of red, couldn't hide the fact that she was terrified. There was nothing I could say to comfort her that wouldn't be a lie. She told me to get a clean sheet from the pie safe and cut it into small strips. The fact that I didn't know what to do with them reminded me of how helpless and useless I was going to be.

"Hannah, I need to be honest with you. I think it would be better if I went and got some help. The Higgins farm is only two miles away. I could be back with help in no time at all."

"You can't leave me, Nathan! I know I'll die if you leave."

"But I don't know what to do! How can I be any good to you?"

"I was about to give up before you got here. I prayed for the Lord to take the baby and me to heaven without suffering, and went to sleep not expecting to wake up. But an angel came to me in a dream and told me that help was on the way. I had nothing to fear. I would have a boy, and I would see him grow into a man. The Lord sent you, Nathan. That's why you have to stay."

"I'll stay, Hannah," I assured her. "Who am I to argue with an angel?" Of all the people the Creator had to choose from, I figured I would be the last person on earth he would send. At least, that was the case until I heard a knock on the cabin door.

A snow-covered woman carrying a cloth bag walked though the door. She was bundled up in a fur coat and wore a man's coonskin cap. Her face was covered with a scarf, leaving only her green eyes exposed. I knew who it was immediately.

"I heard you might need a midwife," she said as she peeled away her outer layers. Betsey Reed darted directly for Hannah. I guess God *does* work in mysterious ways.

"What are you doing here?" I asked rudely.

"From the looks of things, I'm going to help her bring a baby into the world. That is, if you want me to. If you've got everything under control, I can turn around and go back home." She backed away from Hannah's bedside and started warming her hands near the fire.

"No, don't leave!" Hannah cried. "Don't you dare leave me!"

Betsey looked at me, eyebrow arched slightly, waiting for a response. "Nathan?"

"Yes, Betsey, please, please, please stay! I'm glad you're here. I was afraid..." I decided not to finish the sentence. "She's in a lot of pain."

"Good. Now go outside and give us some privacy."

I walked outside and was surprised that I didn't find a horse. I could see the remnants of her footsteps leading back toward the road. It was at least three miles to her cabin. I couldn't imagine her walking that distance alone in the blizzard. I hated to admit it, but it was quite a heroic feat for her to venture out in such life-threatening conditions.

The door flew open suddenly. "Nathan, I'm going to need your help to turn the baby."

"Turn the baby? What does that mean?" I didn't like the sound of that.

"It's a breech baby; it's trying to come out feet first. It's going to tear her up if we don't turn it around." Betsey seemed completely calm in an obviously life and death situation. I, on the other hand, had no idea what she was talking about and was beginning to panic.

"See, Nathan?" Hannah screamed as another pang erupted, "I told you the Lord would send help. I knew my prayers would be answered."

"Yes. He did." I attempted to sound sincere. I was hoping it was the Lord who sent the help and not the other guy.

Betsey grabbed both sides of Hannah's face and positioned herself above her until their noses almost touched. "Hannah, I need you to pay close attention to me. Your baby is upside down and we need to turn it. I'm going to stick my hand inside of you and push the feet back up into your womb. While I'm doing that, Nathan is going to push the head down from the outside of your belly. It's going to hurt a little and you're going to feel some pressure, but whatever you do, don't push. You're going to feel like you have to push the baby out, but you can't. As soon as it's turned around you can push all you want. Do you understand me? Don't push until I tell you!"

Hannah nodded her head and whispered, "Don't push."

"What do you mean, Nathan's going to turn the head? How am I supposed to...?"

"Just shut up and pay attention!" Betsey peeled off the rest of Hannah's blankets, leaving her totally exposed. I pulled my hand back and turned my head. I was completely unprepared to see her lying naked.

"It's all right, Nathan," Hannah pleaded. "Please do as she says. I need you to be strong." She did her best to put me at ease with the situation, which in turn made me feel childish for acting so immature.

Betsey took my hand again. "The baby's head is right here. Can you feel it?"

I nodded my head yes.

"When I push from the bottom, I need you to gently move the baby's head down from her left side to the bottom of her womb. But don't push too hard, or you could break the baby's neck. Can you do that?" she asked in a soothing, confident tone.

"Down to the left and not too hard," I mumbled. My stomach was turning somersaults as I contemplated the odds of the baby surviving. Even though I was uneducated in the world of childbirth, it didn't take a genius to see that the situation was dire. Betsey remained soothing and in control as she calmed Hannah while instructing me at the same time. Amazingly, the baby turned exactly as Betsey said it would. I pushed its head from the top to the bottom in one continuous motion.

"We can take it from here, Nathan," Betsey declared. "I need you to pour some water in that basin on the table so that it will cool, then reach inside my bag and find my barber's razor. Wash it in the kettle and set it next to the basin."

I was happy to be assigned a menial task that sent me to the other side of the room. The cabin was much too small to provide any semblance of privacy. Even though I had just gone where no man, short of a doctor, is supposed to go, I felt like an intruder and tried to make myself invisible. As I washed the blade, Hannah yelled and cried, while Betsey commanded her to push, then stop, take deep breaths, and push again. It all sounded like a foreign language. I kept my eyes on my cleaning as I heard noises that didn't seem humanly possible. In the middle of a ghastly scream, a new sound joined the chorus. It was the unmistakable cry of a newborn. "It's a boy!" shouted Betsey gleefully. "And he's as big as a horse!" Betsey took the razor and cut the umbilical cord, then tied a small shred of cloth around the leftover part.

"Is he...?" Hannah whispered.

"He's perfect," assured Betsey. "Absolutely perfect. Ten fingers and ten toes."

Betsey carefully wrapped the baby in a tiny quilt, which had been saved for this occasion, and handed him to his mother. Hannah started crying as she held her son. Betsey's eyes began to well up when she saw them together. I knew I needed to leave the cabin before I joined them.

I excused myself, claiming that my horse was in desperate need of attention. After working out several tangles of matted, black hair in Newton's back and mane, I covered him with a saddle blanket and secured him for the night. I reached into my saddlebag and pulled out a frozen corn pone, and with a little effort, I managed to bite off a meager portion. Before I had a chance to wallow in self-pity for having an empty stomach on Christmas Day, fortune smiled on me. While opening the barn door, I spotted a fat cottontail nosing around a fence post only a few feet away. I grabbed my rifle, and with just enough moonlight to see clearly, bagged him with a clean shot. I was relieved to feel manly and useful again by providing food for the women. With some potatoes and carrots I found in the pantry, I made a nice rabbit stew in the fireplace.

Betsey forced Hannah to drink some broth to maintain her strength, but refused to eat anything herself. I wasn't bashful and ate two heaping bowls and considered a third, but figured I better save the rest for Hannah. I asked Betsey when she thought Hannah and the baby could be moved, and she thought they would be strong enough in a couple of weeks to make the trip to the tavern as long as both were kept warm. She told me that she would stay at the cabin until they were ready to travel. I said I would leave first thing in the morning, pick up enough supplies to get them through the week, and then check back next weekend to see if they were ready to go. I went back outside and brought in enough firewood for a couple of days, then split two large hickory logs and stacked the kindling next to the door. It would be more than enough to last them until I returned. I grabbed my trail blanket from the barn and went back inside to try to get some sleep. I flopped down next to the fireplace and within minutes was sound asleep.

It was a couple of hours before dawn when I opened my eyes, sensing some movement in the room. Amber coals cracked and popped in the fireplace, and a tranquil silence fell upon the cabin. Hannah was sound asleep as Betsey rocked William Nathan Fuller at the foot of her bed. She cooed a familiar lullaby as she held him tightly against her breast. Her voice was smooth and angelic, not her usual coarse, raspy tone. The glow from the fire softened her features, concealing her deformity as if it didn't exist. Without a doubt, she had saved the life of mother and child, an answer to Hannah's prayer. Hannah would have died without her intervention. I would be digging a hole in the frozen ground. Instead, I was witnessing a side of Betsey that I never would have believed existed. Betsey silently kissed the top of the baby's head as he clung to her pinky finger. She started to hum another tune, and seemed to drift far away in thought.

My mother used to tell me that there is *some* good in everyone, and Betsey had just proven her right. I couldn't help but think that if she could go far away to a place where no one had ever heard of her, she might be able to start a new life. It was a nice thought. It was probably too late for Betsey to change, but I realized that I no longer held a hatred for her. Regardless of her past transgressions, Betsey Reed had become a savior to this family. Will Fuller would return to the loving arms of his wife and hold his newborn son because Betsey Reed, the green-eyed monster, risked her life in a blizzard to save the life of a woman she didn't know. The least I could do was forgive her.

It was almost three weeks before Hannah and the baby were well enough to travel. Since a little over a foot of snow had accumulated on the trail, I borrowed a sleigh from Jed Higgins to make the four-mile trip back to the Heath Tavern. Even though four miles doesn't sound like a formidable expedition, the trail was rough and in some places impassable. It would require some tricky navigation through the woods and over three swollen creek beds, and at best would take the better part of three hours. Betsey helped me bundle mother and child in the back of the sleigh; then, she covered them with a fur blanket on top of three quilts and heavy woolen wraps. As I started to make room for Betsey next to me in the front of the sleigh, she grabbed my arm and told me that it wouldn't be necessary. She would walk home.

"Are you out of your mind? We're going to drive right past your cabin." I couldn't fathom any reasonable explanation for why she would be hesitant to accept a ride.

"Nathan, I thank you for your kind offer, but a midwife must walk to and from the house when delivering a baby. You go on without me. I'll be just fine."

"That's ridiculous, Betsey! Get in the sleigh."

"No!" she said forcefully. You don't want anything to happen to them after all they've been through, do you?"

"What could happen?" I asked, realizing that she was serious.

"Plenty of things. Look, Nathan, I don't want to argue with you. It's a rule! I didn't make the rule, but it's one I have to follow. So just go!"

"It's a stupid rule," I mumbled.

"Go!"

Newton navigated the trip like a seasoned arctic pack-horse and delivered us to Heathsville all in one piece. Half a dozen women were there to greet the Christmas Day miracle baby and the beautiful young mother upon our arrival. Amidst a chorus of cooing, they ushered Hannah into a back room that had been prepared especially for her. It had a small, single bed with a plush feather mattress, and a tiny rocking crib made out of tulipwood. There was a small corner table with an oil lamp, which was lit since there weren't any windows in the room. As the women argued like hens over who got to hold the baby, Malinda Heath helped Hannah out of her clothes and into bed.

Even though she was still weakened from loss of blood during the difficult delivery, Hannah went into great detail about her experience, telling how she prayed for help and how God answered her prayers. She fabricated the story when she told them how brave and noble I was before Betsey's arrival. "That's why I decided to change his name. I was going to name him William Wilson after my father, but when Nathan came out of the storm like a knight in shining armor, it just had to be William Nathan Fuller." Malinda helped Hannah sit up in the bed and offered her some freshly-brewed sassafras tea. "Oh, thank you so much. I've really acquired a taste for sassafras. Betsey said it was good for my stomach, so she made me drink three cups a day. Now, I don't feel normal if I don't have my sassafras tea."

"Nathan told us that Mrs. Reed was very helpful with the delivery," shared Sally Funk, a pudgy woman with doughy cheeks, who waddled like a duck when she walked.

"Helpful?" Hannah blurted with a hint of disdain. "I'll have you know that Betsey Reed walked three miles at night in a terrible blizzard on Christmas Day without any regard for her safety and delivered a breech baby for a woman who has suffered through two previous stillborn births. If you call doing all that helpful, then I suppose she was helpful. I tend to consider that she was God's gift to the Fuller family."

"I didn't mean anything by it, dear," Mrs. Funk stammered, "It's just that Nathan told us what had happened, and we thought that he might have exaggerated a little. You know how men are."

"Well, I can assure you that Betsey Reed performed a selfless act, was tender and caring, and refused to accept anything for three weeks of care, and—"

"Now, calm down, Hannah," Malinda interrupted. "You need to get your rest and let us play with that darling baby. And I guess we're going to reconsider our opinion of Betsey Reed."

Betsey was never going to win any popularity contests, but once word spread throughout the valley about her Christmas heroics, there was at least a new tolerance for her, and possibly a hint of respect. Her midwife services were called upon again; she delivered three more babies before the end of winter, and also dealt with numerous illnesses, including two serious burn victims. People didn't go out of their way to be sociable with her, but neither did they go out of their way to ostracize her. Most folks thought that her healing ways were a little too close to some sort of witchcraft, but they would seek her out without hesitation when they were in dire need of her services. I hoped that at last Betsey could find some peace and contentment. I was encouraged to find out that even Malinda Heath had softened her opinion toward Betsey and actually took her a rhubarb pie as a peace offering. I kept my fingers crossed.

Twenty-One

Heathsville had seen its share of quilting bees, threshing bees, spelling bees, harvest parties, cabin raisings, and barn raisings. Frontier families depended on each other as a necessity for survival. But in the spring of 1844, an event took place that gave communal cooperation a whole new meaning: a wedding bee. The unusually harsh winter had hindered travel throughout the valley, causing Justice of the Peace William Fox to fall behind schedule in his matrimonial duties. Much to his chagrin, he had received four requests to officiate weddings on the first weekend in April. Not wanting to disappoint anyone, he convinced all the parties concerned that the weddings should all be held at a central location. The Heath Tavern would host the area's first wedding bee.

Abner Lindsay would marry Soprina Ford on Saturday morning, followed by Asahal Styles and Lidia Ann Sackrider. On Sunday, after church services, Oliver Gogin would wed Eliza Jane Ewel. And then, for the finale, Thomas McKinney would marry Eveline Deal.

I always knew that Eveline would get married, but when I heard the news, I really had mixed emotions. At first I made the decision to be out of town at the time, but then I remembered my promise to Eveline to dance with her at her wedding and realized that I was just being childish. Despite my feelings for her, I knew that I wasn't ready to get married, and Eveline was way past being ready. Besides, this shindig was going to be the party of the year. I decided to put on a brave face and pretend that I was happy for her. I wanted her to be happy, but I had a case of having my cake and wanting to eat it too. I found out that Liddy Parker would be attending with some of her single friends, so I figured between her and a few snorts of the Seven Jessie's double-distilled hooch, I would somehow survive the weekend.

Wedding-goers started arriving as early as Thursday morning. Upon arrival, some made their encampments from clapboards, while others made tents from their bedding. Some made their beds in or under their wagons. Several log piles were turned into bonfires for cooking. The pleasant mixed aroma of corn pone, pumpkin pie, baked possum, fried venison, and rabbit covered the campground as dusk began to fall.

I had just tied Newton to a sapling behind the stable and started walking toward the tavern when I saw Eveline walking toward me from the other direction.

"I've been looking for you," she said, as she gave me a hug and a kiss on the cheek. "I was afraid that you wouldn't make it."

"I promised I'd be here."

"I know you did. Can we go for a walk?" she asked. "I'd like to talk with you, if you don't mind." We started walking east along a rail fence, away from the campground.

"I don't mind if your fiancée doesn't." I took a look around to see if Thom McKinney was anywhere in the vicinity. He wasn't.

"He's not going to be here until tomorrow. But he's not the jealous type. He knows that he's the second choice, and he doesn't have a problem with that."

"He's a better man than I am."

"No, he isn't. But he loves me and says he can't live without me."

"But do you love him?" I asked.

"He's a good man," she replied, stopping in mid-sentence.

"That's not what I asked."

"It's hard to put into words."

"What's so hard about it? Either you do or you don't."

"I suppose I do. It's not like the love I feel for you, though. I don't think I'll ever be able to feel that way with anyone else."

"Why are you marrying him, then?" I asked.

"What's wrong, Nathan? Are you starting to have some regrets?"

"Maybe a few," I admitted. Actually, it was more than a few, although I wasn't about to admit it to her.

"Good! It's a comfort to me to know that you still love me, too." She started laughing, then danced up ahead and hopped up on the fence rail now that we were out of sight of any potentially suspicious eyes.

"You're pretty sure of yourself, aren't you?" I said playfully after I caught up with her.

"About you? Yes, I am. You would never have gotten to taste the milk for free if I didn't know you loved me."

"Those words from such an innocent face. You're absolutely mercenary!"

She laughed out loud. "I'm only this way with you. With everyone else, I'm shy, sweet, and demure."

She jumped down from the fence and made her way through the woods on a deer path. I followed until she stopped at a tiny patch of thick bluegrass and lay down, motioning with her hand for me to join her. I hesitated, knowing she was to be married this weekend and no longer belonged to me. She pouted, and then smiled devilishly. "Come here, silly! I promise to be good and leave your virtue intact."

I reluctantly gave in and lay beside her. "What are you doing, Eveline? I don't know if this is wise."

"Oh, don't flatter yourself, Nathan. Nothing is going to happen. I just want to lie in your arms, one last time."

As I looked into those familiar hazel eyes, I couldn't help but recall the first time they had charmed me at Merom Bluff. She placed her head on my chest with the crown of her head tucked snuggly beneath my chin. I could feel the warm wetness of her tears against my throat. I wanted to say something, but realized that anything I said would be inadequate. So I held her, gently, as her quiet tears eventually evolved into uncontrollable sobbing. It was the death of us, as us. I realized that I would never hold her in my arms again, and felt the sting of grief that comes when you say goodbye for the last time. She looked up, saw the wetness in my eyes, and smiled without malice, pleased to see that I shared her pain.

"You asked me why I'm marrying him," she said, finally breaking the silence. "He's attached to the land. He bought forty acres over by New Hebron, and wants to spend his entire life with me in the cabin he's building at this very moment. He wants to have a dozen kids, raise crops, and go to church. He worships the ground I walk on and won't go over the hill looking for adventure. He's going to give me everything that I ever wanted. That's why I'm marrying Thom McKinney."

"Does he make you happy?

"Those things will make me happy."

"Then I'm happy for you," I lied. Down deep inside, I was jealous that it wasn't me making plans for the future.

"Thank you, Nathan. It means an awful lot to me to hear you say that, although I'd call the wedding off if I thought there was half a chance of you making the same commitment to me."

Eveline covered my mouth with her hand before I could say anything foolish in response. I realized that I loved her and hated myself for being such a coward about commitment, but there was a part of me that was wary of the cold-blooded way she made decisions. She was so calculating that I doubted if I could have ever truly trusted her.

"I want you to know that I'll dream of you every night, and that you are the one and only true love of my life."

"That's not very fair to your Thom." I was making a poor attempt at acting noble.

"Don't feel sorry for him. After all, it's his bed I'll be sleeping in."

"That's a horrible thing to say, Evie."

"Don't you go get uppity on me, Nathan Crockett. I know for a fact that you've been carrying on with that skinny redhead at the tavern. I always knew you had an appetite for the tavern wenches."

"Now wait just a minute—ahhh!" Eveline chomped down on my hand like a hungry wolf. I pinched her nose to make her release her grip, then placed her over my knee and spanked her soundly. We both fell over in a heap of laughter and kissed for a final time. It was over.

We engaged in small talk as we walked back to the tavern. Evie described the farm, and explained in great detail all the improvements Tom was going to make. I was a bit surprised, though, when she mentioned a visit to Leonard and Betsey.

"Harrison was worried about Leonard, decided to go for a visit, and insisted that I ride along to contradict anything Betsey might say that wasn't true. When we got there, Uncle Leonard came out to greet us looking ten years younger, and Betsey was as nice as a saint. He said that she had been mixing some herbs in his sassafras tea, and that it had made all the difference in the world. Maybe pigs do fly after all."

By Saturday afternoon, the party was well underway with the first two weddings going off without a hitch. Every musician in the county seemed to be in attendance, and everyone from children to the elderly joined in at least one dance. Leonard Reed held court around one of the bonfires, telling his famous pig story, while the men passed the jug. Betsey sat in the background and watched the celebration from afar. A few of the women went over to say hello, but Betsey seemed unable to be friendly long enough to make any female friends. It was frustrating to watch, and I truly felt sorry for her.

Liddy Parker, on the other hand, was very social. She loved to dance and sing, and enjoyed every minute of the festivities. She seemed happy when we were together without any strings attached. Even though she was a couple of years older than Eveline, she was much more innocent and not in any hurry to get married. She seemed to enjoy life as it came to her, without remorse. *Enjoy the day. Whatever happens, happens.* Later that evening, I realized that her outlook on life was much like my own. She had lost both of her parents at an early age, and found shelter in the care of Jesse and Adelia Dubois. She fended for herself and never looked for sympathy. I enjoyed watching how she interacted with other people; she never said a cross word or participated in insipid gossip.

After a few mugs of ale, Eveline Deal was the furthest thing from my mind. I was snared in a new web, entirely of my own free will. We sat in front of the fire until the wee hours of the morning. The fact that there was a chill in the air made it all the more prudent to keep her buried in my arms. She was comfortable, and she was there. When she finally fell asleep in my arms, I carried her to the wagon where her friends were waiting. I gently kissed her goodnight and let her go to sleep. It was a good night.

I was on the way back to my campsite as the last of the party started to dwindle. I took a deep breath and looked at the sky. The stars were exceptionally bright, and my mind was wandering back to Liddy's smile, when everything suddenly went white. I felt the crushing blow of a heavy stick across my skull. I fell to the ground hard and tried to gather my wits in order to defend myself. With my head still spinning, I was shocked to see Eveline standing there with a tree limb in her hand, her voice full of rage. "You could have waited!" she shouted. *So much for a cordial parting...*

"Waited for what?" I demanded, rubbing the knot on my head.

"Waited until my wedding was over before taking up with your wench." It was the stark, raw look of hatred in her eyes that took me by surprise. Her hands were trembling as she decided to take another swing at me. I rolled out of the way, and tripped her as she passed by. She landed with a sickening thud and went silent after hitting her head on a stump.

I was horrified when I saw a gaping gash in the middle of her forehead. Blood was spewing everywhere. At first I thought she was dead, but when she began to moan, I was grateful I hadn't killed her. I removed my shirt and wrapped it around her head to stop the bleeding. I slapped her face, but she failed to respond, and she slowly lost consciousness once again. I've always felt that I am calm under pressure, dependable in a crisis, but that night was an exception to the rule. After deciding that letting her lie on the ground until somebody found her wasn't an option, I carried her to the wagon of the only person I could think of who was an expert when it came to practicing the healing arts: Betsey Reed.

Betsey was sitting beside their campfire by the time I arrived, and seemed giddy at the opportunity to take care of the wounded bride-to-be. Leonard had long since passed out after a night of heavy drinking and was snoring loudly in the back of their wagon. Feeling the need to proclaim my innocence, I told her what had happened and begged for her help.

She immediately washed Eveline's wound with cold water, and much to my relief, Eveline gradually started to awaken. Her face had begun to swell, and her forehead obviously needed to be stitched up. "What did you do to me? I can't get married looking like this!" Eveline screamed, as she gingerly touched her forehead.

"I didn't do a thing, Evie! You were the one who sucker-clubbed me in the back of the head! You could have killed me." The last thing I wanted to do was alarm anybody, but I realized that it could look bad for me if I didn't set the record straight. Fortunately, Eveline admitted to the ambush, and even if she hadn't recanted, I would have had Betsey as a witness. Not exactly a reliable witness, but a witness nevertheless.

"Seeing you two together was more than I could bear. When I saw her kiss you, I wanted you dead. I hate you for doing this to me." Eveline buried her head on her arms and began to wail. People started to wake up and come over to investigate the commotion. The more I tried to get her calmed down, the louder she got. Finally, Betsey slapped her across the face and told her that she would wrap her head in an herb poultice that would take away the swelling by morning, but only if she quieted down. Eveline began to regain her composure, but then Thomas McKinney showed up and flew into a rage as soon as he saw me. I let him hit me twice, then dropped him with a blow to the stomach after he missed with a wild hook.

"You are all crazy! Every last one of you!" Realizing that there was no way of rationalizing with anyone involved, I stormed away in mock disgust and was relieved that McKinney didn't follow me. Not convinced that I wouldn't be ambushed in my sleep, I packed up my gear and headed for home while the going was still good.

Liddy's campsite was too close to the commotion for me to risk seeing her, so I walked to the tavern and told Rennick about everything that had transpired. He assured me that he would explain my sudden departure to Liddy and put out any fires that needed to be doused as far as my involvement was concerned. As I left, the little voice in my mind was saying *I told you so* all the way home. About an hour later, I was home in bed, thanking my lucky stars that it was Thomas McKinney who would be dealing with the temper of Eveline Deal instead of me.

I was still asleep that afternoon when I heard someone pounding on the door. With my head still throbbing, I grabbed my cast-iron skillet and stood next to the door. "Who is it?" I asked, as I readied myself for one of Thom McKinney's minions.

"It's Liddy. Nathan, are you all right?"

I breathed a sigh of relief, then wrapped a blanket around me as I opened the door. "Liddy, what are you doing here? Didn't Rennick tell you why I had to leave?"

"He told me, but…Oh, Nathan, it was horrible." She broke into tears and fell into my arms.

Still groggy and confused, I held her until she seemed to regain her composure. "What happened, Liddy? Did anyone hurt you?"

"It's Green Baker; he's dead. He fell off his horse during the race for the jug and hit a tree. It crushed his skull. He died instantly."

The race for the jug is a frontier tradition that takes place during a wedding party. All the young girls of courting age tie a yellow ribbon around a jug of whiskey, then place the jug at a well-known landmark, usually two miles away. All the available bachelors who have access to a horse ride at breakneck speed to be the first to recover the jug. The winner chooses a ribbon and the right to receive a kiss from the coinciding maiden. The second place finisher gets second choice, and so on for the rest.

"Did anyone see what happened?" I asked.

"Daniel Adams said that Green was in the lead and tried to go left, but the horse wanted to go right. Mrs. Baker fainted as soon as they brought his body back, and Mr. Baker went to dig his grave on a hill south of their farm. A few of the men tried to help, but he wouldn't let them. It didn't seem right to celebrate after that, so folks started to pack up and leave. The girls I came with went back to Palestine, but I needed to know that you were safe. I know that sounds foolish, and I hope you're not mad at me, but I needed you to hold me."

"Of course it's all right. You don't need a reason for that." I suddenly felt guilty for my harsh treatment of Green in the warehouse at Bristol Landing. Unfortunately, I'd never have a chance to ask for his forgiveness. "Did it happen before or after the weddings?" I asked out of morbid curiosity.

"Wedding," she corrected. "There was only one. Eveline and Thom called their wedding off."

"I was afraid of that. What happened?" I asked.

"From what I can tell, Thom McKinney called it off because he was convinced that something happened between Eveline and you. But Eveline brought him to my campsite, and I told him that we were together all evening. I went to look for you, and when you weren't there, I began to panic. Rennick finally found me and told me what had happened, so I relaxed a little bit, but I was still worried that McKinney was hotheaded enough to come looking for you. Then he calmed down, and the wedding was back on. But when Eveline woke up this morning, her eyes were swollen shut and her face was covered in sores. As it turns out, Betsey Reed mixed some poison oak into her poultice."

I started to laugh out loud. As inappropriate as my response was, I couldn't help but see the lunacy of the private war between Betsey and Eveline, two she-snakes simultaneously devouring each other. "I'm sorry, Liddy. It's just that those two deserve each other. What happened next?"

"Eveline looked so awful that McKinney postponed their wedding until after she healed. Eveline never stopped wailing. But it really got out of hand after Green was killed. She walked over to Green's mother and told her that Betsey had placed a curse on her son and was the cause of his death. To make matters worse, some women went to Betsey and confronted her about Eveline's accusations. Instead of denying the charge, Betsey started to cackle with a hideous laugh that made the hair stand up on the back of my neck. The more she laughed, the madder the women got. Things almost became violent, but Betsey finally decided to walk home. I've never witnessed such evil, Nathan. I never knew that people could be so cruel. I don't know why I feel so dirty, but just being around them makes me feel that I've been infected with some devilish malady." She held on to me as if she were drowning, and I completely understood the reason why. Betsey Reed and Eveline were a poisonous mix, and were quite possibly lethal on their own.

When someone young dies a senseless death, your first thought is of how precious life is, and that nothing is guaranteed. Your second thought is that you're glad it's someone else who's getting planted in the dirt instead of you. But then there's the part that reminds you of the loved ones you've lost, and reopens wounds that can never be completely healed.

Because Liddy and I lost our parents at an early age, we shared the need to feel alive. We also shared the need to not be alone. We held on to each other that night and for the next few days. Very few words were said, and there was no talk of the future. It was a time for healing and a time for burying the past. We lived in our own private world beneath the Five Sisters on the Wabash until the next weekend, when the real world beckoned and she went back to the Dubois House. I wanted her to stay, but knew that this wasn't the way to start the next chapter of our lives. "We'll know when the time is right," she said, as I left her in Palestine. As she waved goodbye, I realized an immediate awareness of being alone.

Twenty-Two

August of 1844 was the hottest month on record in the Wabash Valley. We had gone a month without any rain, and the crops were starting to wither under the droughty conditions. It looked like it might be a lean winter, and people were doing what they could to make sure that they would have enough to eat and survive it until spring. In situations like this, some people call in favors, and some borrow money while others lend it.

Sam McCarter was a lender. He was a successful farmer, and at times, a ruthless speculator. He had an uncanny knack of loaning money to people just before they were beset by some type of hardship, thus allowing him to foreclose and acquire their property for pennies on the dollar. Folks had begun to call him the Grim Reaper. Just like the angel of death, when you did business with the Grim Reaper, something bad was about to happen.

I was enjoying a mug of cool water beneath the shade of an ancient oak tree beside the Heath Tavern when Sam McCarter rode up on his prize dapple-gray stallion. He bounced off the animal with the gracefulness of a much younger man and led him to the watering trough. He was an imposing figure, second generation Irish, with a shock of wild black hair and a matching beard. He was six feet six inches in height and built like a bull with the fortitude to match.

"It's so hot that it's not fit for man or beast," he snarled, as he reached for a mug that was hanging on a post next to the well and dipped it into the bucket.

"You're a very observant man, Mr. McCarter," I replied. "Out collecting pennies from the widows?" I smiled to let him know that I was joking, although deep down, I wasn't. "What brings you out in this god-awful heat?"

"Out for a ride, looking at the crops. If we don't get a rain soon, there might not be any crops to look at. I've never seen it this bad." He guzzled a second mug of water like a bear.

"I don't suppose you'll be a little more forgiving with your debtors, will you?"

He turned red in the face. "Listen here, Nathan Crockett. When I lend my hard-earned money to a man, I have a right to expect prompt and full payment. If he can't meet his obligation, what recourse do I have? I have to take his collateral as payment."

"Whoa! Since when are you so touchy about me giving you a hard time?"

"Oh, I'm sorry, Nathan. I didn't mean to bite your head off. It must be the heat. I can't even think straight."

"Don't worry about it," I said, realizing that I had egged him on to begin with. I like to have fun with people, but at times, I push things a bit too far.

"Besides, it's something else that has me a bit upset."

"What is it?" I asked out of curiosity.

"You've had some dealings with Leonard and Betsey Reed, Nathan. What can you tell me about them?"

"What is it that you'd like to know?

"I don't exactly know how to put it…"

"Just say it," I told him. I had never seen Sam McCarter apprehensive about anything, but he was hesitating for some reason.

"It's a hard thing to say, and I wouldn't want to make a false accusation about anyone, but I think Betsey Reed is poisoning her husband."

"Whoa! That is some accusation. What makes you think that?" I was wondering if he had been having conversations with Eveline Deal.

He dipped his cup into the bucket, finished another gulp of water, then wiped his mouth with his sleeve and sat down on the log next to me. "You were right about the collecting debt part. Leonard borrowed a hundred dollars against his livestock in order to buy provisions to get through the winter.

He was supposed to pay me back with the furs that he trapped during winter, but he came down sick and never left the cabin. When spring came and he didn't have the furs, I foreclosed on his livestock. Not that I could get anywhere near a hundred dollars for those mangy animals, but I had to get what I could out of the deal. Yes, sir, I took a bath on that deal."

"McCarter! You're as bad as an old woman! What's that got to do with Betsey poisoning Leonard?" I knew that Leonard's herd of cattle was worth at least two hundred dollars, so I didn't know if I wanted to trust what he had to say.

"Hold your horses, Nathan. I'm a-gettin' to it. Leonard was feeling better last spring, and borrowed more money for seed and provisions. He put out twenty acres of corn, and until this drought hit, it looked as if he were going to harvest a bumper crop. There would be plenty to pay his debt to me, plus interest, and give them enough to get through the winter. But then it stopped raining, and it looks like his corn is all dying in the field."

"What's that got to do with poison?"

"I'm a-gettin' there! I stopped by their farm this morning to see if they had my money before I started foreclosure proceedings, but Leonard wasn't there. Betsey said he was feeling better and had gone out for a short walk. She was cooking some squirrel stew, and said that he would be back in a few minutes. I don't usually talk to women about business, but while we were waiting, I mentioned the loan to Betsey and inquired about receiving payment. She became irate and told me that the land was in her name, and if I thought I could throw her off her land, I had another thing coming. But what she said next really concerned me. She said that Leonard wouldn't live until the note was mature anyway, and I would have to take up the claim with his son, Harrison, who would serve as executor of the estate. She talked about him dying as if he were an animal. It sent chills up my spine."

"Betsey's been talking about Leonard dying ever since

I've known her. I wouldn't take what she said seriously. Besides, you came into her house like a buzzard circling a carcass, threatening to throw her off her farm. What type of response were you looking for?"

"I guess I shouldn't be surprised by what she said, but it's what she did that has me in a quandary."

"All right, McCarter, what is it?"

"Well, it was at about this time that Leonard walked in the door. He looked a bit pale and winded, but not all that bad considering all of his health problems. We exchanged pleasantries, and then he asked me to join them for a meal of stew. I almost accepted the offer, but decided to decline due to the hostility Betsey had shown. I also wanted to go to the land office and see if the property was indeed in her name."

"What about the poison?"

"I'm a-getting' to it! I had been watching Betsey as she was cooking the stew, and she tasted it every time she added an ingredient. But right before she served Leonard his meal, I saw her pour some white powder into his stew and stir it up real quick. Only this time she never tasted it, like she had done every time before. She placed the bowl in front of him, and after his second bite he became violently ill. He ran outside and vomited right outside the door. Then he fell to the ground all curled up like a baby. He convulsed, uncontrollably, for the better part of five minutes. I followed him outside to see if I could be any help, but all I could do was watch helplessly. Now, you'd figure that a wife would be out there doing whatever she could to help her husband, but not Betsey. She cleaned up the spilled stew and threw it out in the yard, then just went back inside and started cleaning, acting as if nothing had happened. He could have died right there on the spot, and she would have never known. She acted like she didn't care whether he lived or died. I tell you, Nathan, I've never seen a human being act so cold and unfeeling. It was the most shameful thing I've seen in my entire life."

"That's coming from a man who was there to foreclose on her farm. Leonard's had a bad stomach for some time, and I don't think he's going to last very long anyway. Why would she try to kill him now when he's going to die from natural causes on his own? If she was going to poison him, she would have done it by now. Leonard and Betsey have a loveless marriage, and I'm sure Betsey is waiting for Leonard to kick the bucket, but I really doubt that she is trying to kill him. I'm sure she was mad at Leonard for putting them in a vulnerable situation, giving you the mortgage to their farm, but I really doubt that she would poison him, especially with you there to witness everything."

"Maybe you're right. I'd hate to make a false accusation. Besides, I don't like to get involved in other folks' business. But if Leonard dies and I do nothing, I would feel responsible."

"Sounds like you have yourself a dilemma, McCarter," I chided sarcastically.

"Maybe you could say something?"

"Don't get me involved," I shot back, harshly. "If you feel that Leonard is in danger, his son, Harrison, lives two miles to the west. Go over there and tell him what you saw, minus the part about the poison. He'll go check things out, and you can sleep well tonight, knowing you performed your good deed for the day."

"Hey, that's a great idea! That's exactly what I'll do. Thanks for the help, Nathan."

McCarter took one last gulp of water, mounted his dapple-gray, and headed west toward Harrison Reed's farm.

I had serious doubts that McCarter was all that worried about Leonard Reed's well-being. On more than one occasion, he had sent families out into the cold of winter when they couldn't pay their loans, so his concern was hard to take as genuine. He was more than likely uneasy about Betsey claiming to be the deed-holder on the property. If Leonard died and Betsey owned the land, it would muddy the foreclosure, to say the least.

But what he said about Betsey *did* concern me. I wanted to believe that Betsey had changed and was on the road to leading a somewhat normal and socially acceptable life, but deep down, I knew she was capable of committing the act. Most human beings have dark sides, but those parts of us are usually kept far below the surface in the secret parts of our souls, and if we are lucky, they surface only in our thoughts. Betsey's dark side was much closer to the surface, where it could manifest with only the slightest prodding.

Was Betsey capable of poisoning Leonard? The answer was a definite yes! But the witness had an agenda, and that had to be taken into consideration. Besides, once McCarter told Harrison Reed about his suspicions, it would only be a matter of time before all hell broke loose at the Reed Cabin. I probably should have ridden over and investigated the situation myself, but I decided that it would be better to be as far away as possible from the upcoming episode.

An hour later, Harrison Reed came racing by on his workhorse, clutching his long rifle, with Eveline riding double and holding on for dear life. It was the first time I had seen Eveline since her ill-fated wedding day. I waved, but neither she nor Harrison acknowledged my presence. I don't know if they were consumed with concern for Leonard or hatred for Betsey, but they had fire in their eyes. It was the kind of expression you see just before a fight starts. If you know what to look for, the eyes let you know if someone is about to do you harm well in advance of the first punch. It was the same look Big Jesse Scott had in his eyes in the tavern in Springfield right before he beat me within an inch of my life. I was lucky that Big Jesse was the one pushing up daises instead of me.

Then it dawned on me that if I didn't intervene, someone might end up dead today. Against my better judgment, I jumped on Newton and chased after Harrison and Eveline. *So much for not getting involved...*

I didn't realize it at the time, but this was the beginning of a series of events that would change the lives of every person on the east side of Crawford County.

The door was open, and I approached the cabin apprehensively. I could hear someone shouting, but thankfully, I hadn't heard a gunshot. I started to run in, but was afraid that if I came in unannounced, someone could get jumpy and pull the trigger by mistake.

"Hello, Leonard? Harrison? It's Nathan Crockett. I'm coming in." I didn't hear a response, so with a bit of trepidation, I proceeded to walk to the threshold. Then I peeked around the corner. "Whoa! What's going on here?" Leonard was in bed with his head on Betsey's lap. Harrison was standing only a few feet away, rifle cocked and aimed directly at Betsey's face.

"This witch has been poisoning my father! That's what's going on! Now get on out of here, Nathan. This doesn't concern you. This is family business!" Harrison's high-pitched voice was jittery, and his trigger finger was twitching.

"Put the gun down, Harrison." I tried to keep my voice soft and soothing, even though my heart was pounding like a drum in a parade. "This isn't going to solve anything." Harrison was a soft, doughy man with a perpetual dull expression on his face. He seemed much more comfortable with taking orders than giving them.

"Don't listen to him, Harrison!" Eveline shouted as she poked him in the back, encouraging him to shoot.

"Evie! What are you doing?" Eveline was doing everything within her power to get Harrison to finish Betsey off.

"Don't you Evie me, you traitor! I always knew you would take her side."

"I'm not taking anyone's side," I pleaded. "I just don't want anyone to get hurt."

"Harrison! Put the damn gun down!" Leonard demanded. "Nobody's being poisoned. Where'd you get such a damn fool idea?" His voice was weak and pained, but he mustered enough authority to convince his son to put the rifle down.

"Mr. McCarter said he saw her put some white powder in your stew, and you got deathly sick right after you ate it," Harrison said.

"You'd believe that skinflint enough to shoot Betsey

without finding out the truth?" said Leonard. "The truth is that I'm dying. Doc Logan stopped by here and said I have a gangrened stomach. He said there isn't a thing he can do for me. He's been saying that for months, but Betsey has managed to keep me alive with her herbs and teas."

"But I didn't know—" stammered Harrison.

"How do you know that her herbs aren't the cause of your sickness?" Eveline interrupted harshly. "How do you know that she hasn't been poisoning you slowly for all these years? Maybe you're not sick at all."

"You caught me dead to rights, Eveline," Betsey declared dramatically. "I've been feeding him a recipe from my book of magic potions. Go ahead and burn me at the stake. That's the only thing that is going to make you happy."

"You no good witch!" Eveline shouted, her eyes red and piercing. Consumed with raw hatred for Betsey, she seized the rifle and fumbled to cock the hammer back. I lunged for the barrel, and with an uppercut I knocked it out of her hands.

Kabam! A sulfur plume filled the cabin as Eveline fell backward against the wall. A window in the roof, approximately the size of my fist, suddenly appeared.

For a short period of time, there was an eerie stillness in the room while everyone tried to digest what had just occurred. I knew that Eveline hated Betsey, but I couldn't believe that she had actually tried to shoot her. Jealousy and anger had replaced the warmth and tenderness. Betsey broke the silence with a low, soft laugh that sounded like the caw of a muzzled crow. Eveline sat down on a stool and started sobbing like a baby. Harrison stood in a silent stupor, and Leonard hacked and coughed uncontrollably, his lungs full of blue smoke caused by the spent gunpowder.

Prodded by Betsey's condescending laughter, Eveline started to regain her wits, and it looked like we were about to begin round two. With her eyes fire-red, fists and teeth clenched, knee-deep in humiliation, she lunged toward Betsey. Unlike her first attack, I could see this one coming. I stepped between them and caught Eveline with both arms.

She screamed and raked her fingernails across my face, frustrated again that she was not able to render harm to her target. I could feel the hot sting of my wounds as droplets of blood formed on both of my cheeks. She screamed again and started hitting the tops of my shoulders as I picked her up and carried her outside. Because I didn't see any signs of her calming down, I carried her to the horse trough, and much to Newton's disapproval, dropped her into the water. Enough was enough.

After a huge splash, she came up gasping for air. Her hair was pasted to her face, and she blew water out of her mouth and nose at the same time. "I hate you! I hate you! I hate you!"

"What is wrong with you?" I screamed. "What happened to the Evie I fell in love with?"

"She's dead! That witch killed her." She started to sob again, then went limp, and let herself drift back under water. I waited patiently for over a minute while she held her breath. Finally, she came back up, gasping for air once again. "Thanks for saving me—I could have drowned!"

"Stop playing games, Evie! You're out of control! What do you think they'd do to you if you had shot her?"

"Probably give me a medal."

"Or hang you!" I didn't want to banter with her, as she was still mad and showing no signs of remorse. I walked over to the trough, and without another word, grabbed a handful of hair from the back of her head and pushed her face back into the water. She began to fight back, but I held her firm. After a few seconds of fighting, I could feel her losing her strength. I brought her up long enough to take a deep breath, then dunked her down once again. This time she didn't fight back, so I let loose of her after counting to ten. She floated slowly back to the surface, with her nose stopping an inch above the waterline. I could see that she was breathing. She was panting at first, but soon her breaths became a bit more rhythmic. I backed away slowly and sat on a stump, folded my arms, and watched silently.

Eventually, she opened her eyes, but was careful not to

look in my direction. Her frown began to dissipate and she started to resemble herself again. The more I watched her, the more I wished that I could turn time back to that star-filled night at Merom Bluff. I knew, even then, that any contact with Leonard and Betsey was going to be bad news, but I didn't do anything about it. I was so busy protecting my freedom that I ignored the consequences. Maybe someday I would settle down and raise a family, but there would always be that voice in the back of my mind telling me I was settling for second best. But as much as I wanted her to be, the girl in the trough was not the same girl.

Everyone is responsible for his or her own actions, and Eveline had made her choices, but I had also made some choices that influenced her situation in a negative way. My insistence on maintaining my freedom, caused by an illusion of self-importance, drove a wedge between us. She had been a bit too anxious to make a deal, and I had possessed the same measure of reluctance. If I had worked a bit harder, she would be cooking dinner in my cabin instead of sitting, humiliated, in dirty horse-water.

I grabbed a clean blanket from my saddlebag and wrapped it around her as she stepped out of the trough. Even though it was the hottest part of the day, she was shivering when she fell into my arms. I sighed deeply, realizing that, once again, I had gotten a little too close to the spider web.

Eveline changed into an old sleeping gown of Betsey's and sat quietly on the front porch while her clothes dried on a low-hanging elm branch. I went inside and found that Harrison seemed convinced that nothing sinister was going on. "Pa says that Betsey's been taking good care of him, but she's awful tired and could use some help. We decided that Eveline should stay and help until I can find someone to take her place."

"Harrison, are you out of you mind? Betsey and Eveline will kill each other!"

"It'll be alright, Nathan. I don't hold any hard feelings towards her. We just need to sit down and have a talk and sort things out." Betsey spoke in a soft, calm voice, and sounded as if she was sincere. I didn't believe a word.

"I doubt that Eveline will agree. If you'll remember, she tried to kill you."

She's just upset about Leonard. Trust me. Things will be fine."

When Betsey and Harrison went to talk to Eveline, I pulled up a chair and sat next to Leonard's bed. His skin looked snow-white and paper-thin. His eyes were yellow around the pupils, and he looked as if he had lost twenty pounds that he couldn't afford to lose. "All this excitement can't be good for you, Leonard. Why don't you tell them all to leave you alone?

"Just tell them to let me die in peace, eh?"

"That's not what I meant to say," I protested, realizing I should have kept quiet.

"Don't fret, Nathan. I know what you meant. Let me put it this way. I've led a life that I'm not proud of. I've never tried to hurt anybody, but then, I never went far out of my way to help anybody, either. I've been a bad husband and father. I've done some good things, but have also done some hurtful things to the ones around me. I've let whiskey and womanizing ruin my life, and that is something I'll have to explain to Saint Peter before too long. But what's done is done. I can't change the past. The truth is, I'm scared. Scared of being alone. If Betsey weren't here to take care of me, who would be? I was never much of a father to Harrison. I was never around much, and he had to fend for himself most of the time. I think he stays around out of obligation."

"So you don't think that Betsey tried to kill you?"

"I didn't say that. She very well might be poisoning me, but if I accuse her, she'll either leave or kill me outright. Either way, I'm dead. All I can do is assume that she is trying to heal me, and hope for the best."

"That doesn't sound like much of a plan," I replied.

"What choice do I have?" I could see he was laboring to catch his breath. The ever-present twinkle in his eyes was nowhere to be found. He was now a frightened old man, full of regret, clinging on to life as his body betrayed him.

"Maybe it's best if Eveline did stay," I admitted, "but who's going to keep the peace between her and Betsey?"

"I was hoping you would, Nathan. You know what's going on. I couldn't count on Harrison; he hates Betsey, too. But they'll be on their best behavior if you're around. Grant a dying man this one last request, won't you?"

Twenty-Three

I relented, and promised Leonard that I would stop by daily to make sure everyone was on his, or her, best behavior. Eveline agreed to sleep in her old bed as long as Betsey didn't speak to her. It was an unusual setup, but as far as I could tell, things were functioning quite well. Eveline milked the cow and fed the animals while Betsey cooked and did the dishes. Eveline insisted on tasting Leonard's food as if he were the King of England, but despite all of the extra care, Leonard seemed to be getting worse. He was unable to eat anything solid, and was surviving on soup broth and sassafras tea.

Betsey spent much of her days gathering roots and herbs in the woods, returning at dusk with her harvest. Eveline kept close to Leonard and made sure that Betsey kept her distance. Eveline seemed formal toward me when we were together. She insisted that my supervision wasn't necessary, and that she was quite capable of caring for her uncle all by herself. I must admit that she had wedged herself firmly between husband and wife, and was, in fact, ruling the roost. I was a bit surprised that Betsey was acting so docile. It wasn't like her at all. It was apparent that she was on the outside looking in, and I could only assume that she was waiting patiently for Leonard to die. Like a buzzard circling the carrion, she was waiting around to claim the property.

On a day when I needed to go into Palestine for supplies, I stopped by their cabin early in the morning. The valley was filled with a low pocket of fog, which would disappear as soon as the sun rose above the trees. Leonard was sitting on the porch and seemed to have a little more color in his face. "Sit down and take a load off, Nathan. Beautiful day, isn't it?" His voice sounded stronger, and a bit of sparkle had returned to his eyes. He was clean-shaven and had recently been given a haircut. "You're just in time. Betsey's brewing up a fresh batch of sassafras tea."

"I wish I could stay, but I want to get to town before it gets too hot." I wasn't in a hurry to get there, but things seemed just fine, and I was starting to feel awkward about being around Eveline so much. She was cordial yet distant as she methodically went about her chores. "Yes, Nathan," and "No, Nathan," was the extent of her conversation with me. When I tried to pull her off to the side and talk, she would simply ignore me and walk away. Our relationship had become a lost cause, and there was no hope of revival, but I couldn't stand to see her living her life in such a state of despair. I wanted her to be happy and go on with the life she had planned. I wanted her to get married and have lots of kids. More selfishly, I didn't want to carry the guilt of breaking the little bird's wing.

Eveline burst through the cabin door, milk bucket in hand, and walked past me without turning her head. She marched to the barn like a soldier, with her nose pointing to the sky. Her apron was dirty and her hair was uncombed. Leonard looked at me and shrugged his shoulders. He had a lot more to worry about than his niece's tantrum. Even though I tried to avoid any confrontation with Eveline, I decided to put an end to this once and for all. I marched to the barn and found her sitting on a wooden crate beneath a scrawny brown milk cow.

"Eveline, we need to talk!"

"Can't you see I'm busy?"

"That can wait."

"Easy for you to say. You're not the one with an udder full of milk." The cow mooed right on cue, agreeing with Eveline.

"I said now, and I mean now." I grabbed her wrist and pulled her off the crate and into my arms. The bucket and a little bit of milk went flying, and the cow started bawling like a donkey.

"You bastard!" she yelled, as I pulled her tight against me. "Let me go!" She pounded her fists into my chest. I remained silent and still until she became placid from exhaustion, buried her face beneath my arm, and began to cry. After her breathing began to steady, I picked her up and set her on the top rail of the stall.

"Can we talk now?" I spoke in a tone slightly above a whisper. I firmly held her hand and could feel the first hint of acceptance.

She nodded yes, and, with a sudden sense of self-awareness, wiped the tears from her face and adjusted her hair, using her hand as a comb. "How can you stand the sight of me? I look so ugly."

"You look fine to me, Evie"

"No, I don't, but thanks for pretending."

"I'm sorry for not forcing the issue before now. I just need to know why you're treating me this way."

"I'm sorry. It's not your fault. It's just that my life is such a mess. Last year I was going to marry you, and that didn't happen. This year I was going to marry Thom McKinney, and you know what happened there. I should be on my farm and pregnant by now. I should be living my life, not this nightmare."

"Eveline, you're not even twenty years old. Your life is still ahead of you. You're a beautiful, loving girl, and you'll find someone who will make you happy."

"When I have my own home, then I'll be happy. Right now, I live with whoever will have me. Harrison's wife is going to have her baby, and I can tell she doesn't want me around. That's why he made me stay here. I'm living under the same roof as that witch, and there's nothing I can do about it."

"You don't have to stay here; I'm sure I can find some-place for you to go. What about Rennick and Malinda?"

"That's just it. I do have to stay here. Who will take care of Uncle Leonard if I don't?"

"What about Harrison?"

"He's too busy at his farm, and besides, once he found out that the farm was deeded in Betsey's name, he suddenly lost interest in his father's welfare."

"Are you sure it's deeded in Betsey's name?" I had my doubts that Leonard would intentionally defraud Sam McCarter.

"Harrison went into Palestine to the Land Office and verified it himself. It's in her name only. Uncle Leonard has some kind of lien on the property, so if she were to divorce him, the property would go back to him. That way, Betsey has to take care of him."

"But Leonard put up the property to get the loan from Sam McCarter; he can't do that if he doesn't own the farm."

"He didn't put up the farm," she explained. "He put up his interest in the farm. Uncle Leonard put up the mortgage that he's been holding over Betsey's head. When the note comes due this fall, McCarter will get the mortgage. Then he'll call in the note on Betsey, foreclose, and take the farm."

"So McCarter will get the farm either way. Seems like legal jargon to me."

"Nathan, you don't understand! If Uncle Leonard dies, the contract says that Betsey's mortgage can be paid in full for the sum of one dollar. Betsey pays the dollar, and she owns the land free and clear."

"And all McCarter gets is one dollar."

"Exactly." Eveline seemed relieved to bring me into her confidence, but I had the feeling there was something else she wasn't telling me.

"When is the money due to McCarter?" I asked

"October thirty-first, at midnight. But it doesn't matter. Leonard's crop is burned up. We could get a foot of rain and it wouldn't do any good."

"Midnight on Halloween. How appropriate."

"It is for that witch! She gets the farm if Uncle Leonard dies before Halloween. I know she is going to kill him! "

I sighed for a minute, not knowing what to say. A person knows that there is evil in the world, but you try not to go looking for it. When you come across evil, you do your best to convince yourself that it isn't what it is. I don't know if I believed that Betsey was evil or not, but I was convinced that she was dangerous. "This family is crazy, Evie, I'm getting you out of here now. Get your things. I'm taking you to the Heath Tavern, and we'll decide what to do when we get there."

She hesitated, pulled herself away from me, walked to the corner of the barn, and faced the wall with her back to me. "I can't go. There is something I haven't told you."

"Is it the reason you've been treating me as if I have the plague?"

"Yes, it...I'm so ashamed of myself. I don't want you thinking badly of me."

"That will never happen, Eveline. You can tell me."

"I can't keep it inside any longer. Sam McCarter offered Harrison half of the farm if he makes sure that Leonard survives through Halloween. Harrison is giving me half of his share for living here and making sure that Betsey doesn't finish him off. I'm supposed to keep him alive long enough so McCarter can take the farm. I'm an awful person, Nathan. I wouldn't blame you if you left and washed your hands of me completely."

I closed my eyes and drew a deep breath in an attempt to hide my reaction. I wanted to be true to my word and not condemn her for bad judgment, but I needed to digest her confession for a few minutes. Unfortunately, she took my silence as rejection and ran away toward the cabin. I decided to let her go. Words would have only made the situation worse.

Twenty-Four

I had been in Palestine for three hours, and I hadn't purchased any of my supplies. Even though I hadn't been drinking anything stronger than honey water, I felt like I'd done battle with a jug of the Seven Jessie's finest. My head was pounding, and my stomach was clenched tight. Even the most passionate of Liddy Parker's kisses couldn't ease my tension. *Stay completely away from that mess*, I kept telling myself. *Let them all kill each other. It's nothing to you.* It didn't matter how hard I tried to convince myself to stay away; I still felt somewhat responsible for Eveline's safety.

As soon as I made my decision, my headache immediately ceased. I kissed Liddy goodbye, and despite her objections went on my way south back to Heathsville. Newton must have sensed my anxiety; he opened up to a full run as soon as we reached The Purgatory Trace. He snorted with disgust as I tried to pull back on the reins. He sensed that I was in a hurry, and he wanted to run. He was a fast horse, sometimes too fast for his own good. I decided to give in and let him choose his pace. The sooner I arrived, the better. Something horrible was about to happen at the Reed homestead, and Eveline needed to be as far away as possible when it all went down.

If you live around treachery and evil long enough, after a while it doesn't repel you with its stench. It's like living next to a garbage dump. At first, the smell will overwhelm you. Within a few weeks, you won't notice the smell at all. You'll find yourself accepting the unacceptable as part of life. Eveline had lived with the stench of the Reed Family for far too long. I was determined to see that she never spent another night under their roof.

I was pulling back Newton's reins as we neared the last curve before the cabin when I got an eerie feeling that something had gone wrong. John Herriman, the Reed's next-door neighbor, was standing beside an unfamiliar black buggy hitched to a tall roan mare. His face was sullen and white. He looked like a messenger of bad news.

"What's going on, John?" I asked as I dismounted.

"It's Leonard. He's taken a turn for the worse. Doc Logan is inside with him now."

"He was fine this morning. What's wrong with him?"

"Doc says his stomach is in a state of gangrene. Incipient mortification, I think he called it."

"What the hell does that mean?" I asked. It didn't have a good sound to it.

"It means he's going to die, Nathan." The high-pitched, nasally voice came from the porch of the cabin. Doctor John Logan was a small, round, balding man, dressed in a ragged black suit, with a pair of golden round spectacles resting on the tip of his bulbous nose. He rushed past me and started fumbling through a black leather bag, babbling medical terms in Latin. "Here it is!" he exclaimed, as he rushed back to the cabin acting as though he didn't see us. He stopped abruptly at the doorway and looked back in our direction. "You two stay where you are! I'm going to need your help momentarily."

So we stayed and waited. Herriman told me that Eveline ran over to his cabin a couple of hours earlier, crying for help. After telling him what had happened, she rode off on Ole Hickory to find Doc Wynn. It was by chance that Doc Logan came driving by on the way back to his apothecary in Russellville. John waved him down, and the doctor had been with him ever since.

Logan appeared a few moments later with his coat off, wiping his shiny brow with a wet cloth. "John, have you told Nathan what the Deal girl said?"

Herriman hesitated, then looked down at the ground and kicked up a couple of wisps of dirt. "I didn't want to speak out of turn, seeing how he's so close to the Reeds and all..."

"What are you talking about? I know the Reeds, but I wouldn't actually say that I was close to them. What did she say that you can't tell me?" I demanded.

"Simmer down, you two!" Logan squawked. "John, there isn't any reason not to tell Nathan. I'd like to hear what he thinks about the accusation."

"What accusation?" I chirped mockingly. I knew it was not going to be anything good.

"If you'll give me a chance," Herriman spurted, "I'll tell you." He was struggling to find the words. "Eveline said that Betsey had poisoned Leonard, and that she had proof. That's all she said before she rode off."

"Do you think it could be true, Nathan?" Logan calmly asked. "Betsey seems genuinely distraught about Leonard's condition. It would be quite a performance if she were lying. Is she capable of such a heinous act?"

Now I was the one who was at a loss for words. I paused, took a deep breath, kicked at the dirt, and nodded. "Yes, she is."

"Oh my, oh my." Doc Logan started wiping his brow again. He was a staunch Hardshell Baptist and saw everything in black and white. Being an ardent advocate of law and order, he sent Herriman to find Eli Adams, the local justice of the peace. He paced back and forth on the porch, then darted into the cabin for a moment only to return and resume his pacing.

"Is it safe to leave Betsey alone with him in there, Doc?" I asked.

"It wouldn't matter if she did something," he blurted. "Leonard isn't long for the world either way."

"Isn't there anything you can do for him?"

He stopped pacing and looked at me with the solemn expression that is commonly possessed by doctors, preachers, and undertakers. "Short of administering a lethal overdose of opium and putting him out of his misery...no."

I sat quietly on the edge of the water trough and watched a water bug dance across the water with the grace of a dancing girl. I wondered if that water bug didn't have it better than us humans. As long as they stayed out of the hungry mouth of a fish or frog, they didn't have it all that bad. Since they only have a lifespan of six months, the odds were very much in their favor. Doc went inside every few minutes to check on Leonard and then quickly returned to the porch to resume his pacing, shaking his head in a negative manner. "Hope the law gets here first," he mumbled.

"So do I," I agreed. Neither one of us wanted to deal with Betsey alone, especially without any support. Doc was too honest to possess a good poker face, and I didn't want to lie to her. I had a feeling that things were going to get out of hand, and I really didn't want to be around when the trouble started. I was more involved than I wanted to be and angry with myself for not getting Eveline out of there earlier that morning. Now, she was in the middle of the whole stinking mess, and regardless of her innocence, she would be tainted permanently by the scandal.

Doc stopped his pacing when the sound of pounding hooves and a cloud of dust appeared beyond the bend of the Heathsville Road. "Finally!" he declared, as he walked toward the road to greet our reinforcements.

I gave a sigh of relief when I saw Doc Josiah Wynn's fancy black carriage pop into view. He was a reasonable man, and knew about Leonard's condition. He was a born politician and wouldn't let things get out of hand. My relief was short-lived as I saw Harrison Reed's horse following at a dead run, his long rifle strapped to his back again, only this time, there was fire in his eyes.

Doc Logan grabbed the bridle of his colleague's horse and they immediately went into a conference. Not only did they seem oblivious to Harrison's arrival, they seemed especially oblivious to the fact that he was heading into the cabin with his rifle. Part of me wanted to let him go into the cabin and keep my hands clean of the whole sordid affair. Unfortunately, the major part of me despised the hypocrisy of Harrison's actions. The thought of a man keeping his father alive long enough for the sole purpose of allowing Sam McCarter to foreclose on his property made my stomach turn. If he could fake outrage, I could fake sympathy.

As he neared, I hid the fact that I was coiled and ready to strike. Harrison Reed never knew what hit him. Both doctors scurried over and began to protest, but when they saw me commandeer the rifle from the unconscious man, they nodded in approval and went into the cabin to check on Leonard. I found a safe hiding spot for the gun beneath a haystack in the barn and returned just as Harrison began to awaken. He shook his head to knock loose the cobwebs, and then suddenly realized what had happened. I could tell by the look in his eyes that he wanted to give me a taste of my own medicine, but as soon as he got to his feet, he became dizzy and fell promptly down on his backside with a thud.

"What did you hit me with? A brick bat?" He rubbed his jaw as if he were checking that it was still attached to his face.

"Consider it a favor, Harrison. What were you planning to do with the rifle?"

"I was going to give that witch what she deserved—a quick trip to hell."

"Yeah, and you'd be sitting in jail waiting for the necktie party. Use your head! You can't kill her in cold blood. If she's guilty, let the law handle it. Herriman went to get the constable. He should be back any minute. Don't do anything until he gets here."

"You didn't have to hit me!"

"Just making sure you didn't shoot me by mistake."

Doc Wynn came out with Doc Logan right behind him, both men shaking their heads in unison, confirming the dire prognosis. They pulled Harrison aside and offered their condolences while he pretended to be the grieving son. But within seconds, he started pleading his case, claiming that Betsey put poison into Leonard's tea that morning. I was suddenly grateful that I hadn't accepted Leonard's invitation to join him for his morning tea party.

Harrison wanted to barge into the cabin and confront Betsey that instant, but Doc Logan stepped in his way and insisted that he not go. He said it could only upset his father, and that he was having a hard time buying into the poison theory. Betsey seemed genuinely distraught and was being quite tender with Leonard. "She's doing everything she can to keep him from suffering, and Leonard seems to be finding comfort in her care."

"I tend to agree with Doctor Logan," said Doc Wynn. "Your father has had stomach problems for years. She wouldn't have any reason to poison him. He probably wouldn't make it through the winter under the best case scenario. What would be her motivation? I don't buy it either."

"Oh, she had motivation, all right." Harrison told them about the loan with McCarter and the ramifications of his accelerated demise. He, however, forgot to mention the windfall that he would receive if Eveline managed to keep the old man alive until Halloween.

I could see some doubt appear in the doctors' demeanors, but they still insisted on Harrison not upsetting Leonard. If he wanted to see his father, he had to remain calm and not say anything that would make his last moments any worse. They were surprised when Harrison chose not to go into the cabin to say his goodbyes. "What a loving family," I mumbled.

Doc Logan deferred to Doc Wynn, since he had been treating Leonard on a regular basis for the last few months. "All we can do is wait and pray," Doc Logan said, as we stood quietly outside the cabin door. I don't know if doctors keep score or not, but I think that Doc Logan didn't want Leonard to show up on his ledger. From the scowl on Harrison's face, I could tell he was waiting, but he sure wasn't doing any praying. As the minutes went by, I inched my way away from the cabin door. I wanted to run away from this spider-web of a mess. I was too late to help Eveline, and all I could do now was stand back and look for a chance to escape without being noticed. Before I could get too far away, Doc Logan motioned for me to meet him by the barn.

"Nathan, how well do you know the Reeds?" he asked, making sure that Harrison was not listening.

"Better than I want to. Why do you ask?"

"Harrison is adamant about Betsey poisoning Leonard. He says that the Deal girl has undeniable evidence that will prove her guilt." He wiped his brow with the cloth again, pausing as if he wanted to find the right words to ask a difficult question.

"But you don't think that he's been poisoned. Do you?"

"To be honest, I don't know. His stomach has taken a sudden turn for the worse. It could be the result of a poisoning, but as Doctor Wynn stated, it was only a mater of time before his stomach killed him anyway."

"But like his boy said, she stands to gain financially if he dies before Halloween."

"I know what he said, and you seem to think that she is capable of murder, but damn it, Nathan, she doesn't act like a woman who's just poisoned her husband. She only sobs when he's not looking and is so tender and caring with him that if she did do the deed, she's the world's best liar."

"I don't know what to tell you, Doc. It's like she's two different people. If you're asking me if she did it, I don't know."

"What I'd like for you to do, Nathan, is to go in and see what you think. Is her grief sincere, or just a great acting job?"

"She'll get suspicious as soon as I walk in the door."

"I don't think she knows an accusation has been made. She hasn't left his bedside all day. Just go in and see what you think. I'd really like to get another opinion before the law gets here."

Reluctantly, I agreed. The cabin was dark and reeked with the smell of herbs, menthol, and death. Doc Wynn was hovering over Leonard's bed, checking his pulse, while Betsey sat on the side of the bed rubbing her husband's face with a cool cloth. "Mind if I come in?" I asked, meekly, as I poked my head in through the door. Doc motioned for me to come in while holding his index finger in front of his mouth, indicating that I needed to be quiet. I could tell by his mannerisms that he was expecting me as he politely made his way toward the door and whispered that he needed some fresh air. The room was hot and dark, the only light being supplied by a pair of tallow candles. I had to catch my breath when I got my first glimpse of Leonard. He looked about half the size of the man I had seen earlier that morning. He was lying flat on his back, stripped naked above the waist. His ribs, clearly visible through the thin veil of his pasty white skin, were heaving up and down as he labored to force every measure of air into his lungs. There were warm towels covered in pungent salve resting on his stomach. They were supposed to relax the intestines and ease the pain, but it was obvious that they were having little effect on him. In the stillness of the room, I could hear the beginning of the death rattle as each breath became more difficult.

Betsey, who at first seemed surprised by my arrival, seemed almost grateful to have me there, and she offered a gentle, welcoming smile. I noticed that her eyes were puffy, evidently from crying. Doc Logan was right. If she was lying, this was indeed quite a performance. This was the gentle, caring Betsey I had first witnessed on Christmas night in Hannah Fuller's cabin. Once again, her countenance was softer, and the hideous scar on her face seemed to disappear.

Leonard was suddenly awakened by a convulsion as he almost wrenched his body into a knot, and his face became disfigured with agony. Betsey forcefully held his upper body to keep him from banging into the wall, and as soon as the convulsion passed, she gently massaged his stomach muscles, allowing him to relax.

As she was rubbing his chest, he grabbed her wrist to make her stop. "Betsey, I can't tell you how sorry I am for being such a lousy husband. I know that you never loved me, and I never expected you to. Lord knows I never gave you any reason to do anything but despise me. I just want to thank you for putting up with me. You've taken real good care of me these last few months, and I wish I could leave you better off. At least ole' McCarter won't be getting the farm, although I'm sure he'll raise quite a fuss."

"Shhhh," she whispered. "Save your strength." As much as she tried, she couldn't fight back the tears. Finally, she put her head on his chest and started to sob.

"Now, don't go making a scene. I just wanted you to know that I love you." He feebly patted her on the back of her head. Her sobbing had now turned to wailing. Suddenly, his hand stopped as her sobbing died down.

"I love you, too," she whispered. But he never heard it. He was gone.

I was convinced that Betsey was innocent.

Twenty-Five

Eli Adams, the justice of the peace, arrived a few minutes later with John Herriman. Doc Logan took charge of the situation, since he was the one who had sent for him. Methodically, Logan presented the facts without prejudice, starting with Eveline's accusation and ending with my account of Leonard's final moments. Harrison, all the while, kept insisting that we should skip the trial and hang the murdering witch from the oak tree behind the barn.

Adams, a hard-working farmer who survived an Indian ambush as a young man and had just celebrated his seventieth birthday, listened intently without saying a word. After Doc Logan was finished with his report, the rail-thin justice walked over to the barn and began mumbling to himself. He seemed to be pondering his next move. He picked up a handful of rocks, and one by one he dropped them onto the ground. When his hand was empty, he walked directly to the cabin, leaving the door open so we could watch from the porch. Betsey was dressing Leonard in his best buckskins, her eyes still filled with tears. Adams removed his hat and offered his condolences. When he saw that he had an audience, he quickly kicked the door shut, making us feel guilty for being so nosey.

After a few minutes, he reappeared and declared that the widow needed time to grieve. Harrison started cursing and calling Betsey every vile name in his vocabulary. When asked if he wanted to view his father's corpse, he started calling the justice of the peace the same bad names, then pompously jumped on his horse and rode back in the direction of his farm near Morea.

Adams seemed to take everything calmly in stride, and started doling out orders. "Gentleman, there is not to be even a hint of accusation until Leonard is in the ground."

He immediately sent John Herriman to the general store in Richwoods to pick up a pine casket. Due to the high mortality rate on the frontier, they always had two or three in stock. Adams pulled me over to the side and had me describe Betsey's behavior. Finally, he asked me for my opinion, promising it would be kept in strict confidence.

"Betsey Reed is probably the most unlikable person I have ever met in my entire life. She is jealous, spiteful, and conniving. She is unstable, and might burst into flames if she ever entered a church. But do I think she killed Leonard? I think she was capable, but no, I don't think she is guilty. They had a strange, destructive relationship, but I think she honestly cared for him. All I can say is that anyone who saw her grieving and trying to ease his suffering would come to the same conclusion. I might be wrong, but I don't think so." I couldn't believe I was coming to Betsey's defense. Only minutes before, I would have bet money that she was the culprit.

"I agree. She seems to be sincerely upset about his passing, but Betsey Reed isn't the most popular woman in the valley. I've heard rumors that she has been involved in some sordid affairs." Adams rubbed his shock of long, white hair and loaded his corncob pipe with tobacco. "I need to talk to the Deal girl before I make up my mind. I owe it to the deceased."

"She'll see it differently; you can count on that," I said, a bit too sharply.

"If she does, we'll need to talk again. So don't be going too far away, Nathan."

I told Adams I would go to the Heath Tavern and remain there until twilight. After that, I could be found at my cabin if he needed me. I regretted leaving Palestine that afternoon and planting myself in the middle of the storm. I didn't care one way or the other for any of the Reeds and had only been around because I thought I could have given some help to Eveline. But instead of helping her, I ended up being a character witness to the person she despised. Now, Leonard was dead, and people were accusing Betsey of doing him in.

Why should I care? It wasn't my problem. *Let the law sort it out.* I didn't know if she did or didn't poison him. All I had was my opinion. *And everyone has one of those.*

As much as I tried to find a reason why I shouldn't get involved, my conscience kept reminding me of two reasons why I should. The first reason was because I could remember being held in the Springfield jail, accused of murdering long-bearded Jesse Scott. Even though I was innocent, there was still a remote chance that I could have ended up at the end of a rope. There wasn't a night in jail when I didn't lose sleep over that fact. I suppose that if I had been guilty, I could have accepted that I had it coming to me, but to be hanged as an innocent man...I couldn't imagine a more hideous fate.

The other one was the real reason why I couldn't shy away from this fight, and that reason was my mother. Though much of my memory of her had faded away into the fog of my mind, I clearly remembered that she made me promise every night, after saying my prayers, that I would always do the right thing. She was adamant about it. "A man must be true to himself, for only then can he be true before God," she always said before she kissed me goodnight. I don't know why she chose that as her only commandment, but those words were burned into my being. I would tell the truth because it was the right thing to do. And I also knew that my mother would haunt me for the rest of my life if I didn't. *To thine own self be true.*

Bad news travels quickly, and Leonard's death was no exception. I met Malinda Heath as she was leaving the tavern, driving Rennick's flatbed wagon with a basket full of food and a jug full of honey water. She was wearing her Sunday-go-to-meeting bonnet and had the determined look that women get when they're on a mission of duty or mercy, but in Malinda's case, I had the feeling it was a quest to be first with the gossip.

"Oh Nathan, isn't it awful about poor Mister Reed? I heard he suffered so much at the end."

"It was a rough way to go," I admitted. I knew she was fishing for information and that anything I told her would be repeated and twisted tenfold, so I decided not to expand on any of the particulars. She was a bit irked by my lack of candor, but left without too much fuss, figuring she would find out whatever she needed to know when she got to the Reed cabin. I assumed that either Harrison or John Herriman had stopped by the tavern with the news. Regardless of whoever told Malinda, the cat was out of the bag. Any hope Eli Adams had for muting the accusations was all but gone.

By the time I walked inside the tavern, Rennick had a mug of the Seven Jessie's sitting on the table. "Rough day?" he asked, as he poured my second mug full.

"I can't think of any worse ones," I replied with my throat on fire.

"Well, I have a sympathetic ear if you want to talk."

So I talked. The difference between Rennick and his wife is that Rennick could keep a secret. After I chronicled the sum of my day, he sighed. In a thoughtful manner, he poured me another mug and then one for himself. Even though Rennick was a staunch Baptist, he treated whiskey as a necessary commodity of the frontier; sometimes he found that a little snort helped him think a bit more clearly. This was one of those occasions. He took a healthy swig, then wiped his mouth with the arm of his shirt. "Well, Nathan, it looks like you stirred up a hornet's nest."

"That is the understatement of the year." I was hoping for something a little more profound.

"Remember when you met the Reeds for the first time and their horse tried to kick your head across the Wabash?"

"How could I forget? I've still got the knot on my head to remind me." I rubbed the back of my head to make sure it was still there. It was.

"Do you remember the warning Malinda gave you before you hitched the ride to Palestine with them?"

"I don't need an 'I told you so,' Rennick," I snapped at him.

"Don't get your feathers ruffled. Do you remember the warning?"

"I remember her saying that Betsey was a witch and to be careful."

"Exactly! Malinda didn't know her at all, but she knew her reputation. She's from the Dark Bend; that alone is enough for some to think that she killed him. She's a medicine woman, which to many is just another name for a witch. You know as well as anybody that there were all sorts of rumors that she tried to kill the man in the fire when you got burned. The fact that he was found dead a few weeks later didn't help her cause. She might have gained a little respect when she saved Hannah Fuller, but everybody is going to remember her laughing over the body of Green Baker. If Harrison and Eveline get things stirred up like you think they will, things might get hostile. It doesn't matter if she's guilty or not; people are going to believe that she poisoned him."

"I know that, Rennick! Hell, I believed she was guilty before I went into the cabin. I'm just saying that if anyone had been at his bedside and witnessed the way that she was grieving over him, they could only conclude that she was innocent."

"But you don't know that she didn't poison him for sure, do you?" He filled my mug again, but left his alone.

"No, I don't," I admitted reluctantly. "But Doc Logan and Doc Wynn don't think she did it either."

"You eat anything today?" Rennick changed the subject; he sensed that I was getting a bit agitated.

"Not a thing, now that you mention it."

He gave me a bowl of leftover possum stew with some biscuits and molasses. As a rule, I'm not very fond of possum, but it was sweetly seasoned and was tender like squirrel.

"Just as I thought!" he declared. "Your hunger was souring your disposition. You can't think clearly on an empty stomach."

"I'm sorry, Rennick, I've been acting like a jackass."

"It's all right. You've had a tough day, but I want you to listen to me and not say a word." After a nod from me, he continued. "As I said before, you don't know if she poisoned him or not. You have an opinion based on what you witnessed during Leonard's last few moments. You gave an accurate account to the local peace officer, who is a fair and honest man, and that is all you can do. Let the law handle it from here. There is no need to get worked up over this. There is likely to be a fuss, mostly name-calling, but the truth usually comes out in the end. The best thing for you to do is to get on your horse, go home, and stay there for a week until it all blows over."

"Why should I hide? I haven't done anything." I was a bit puzzled by Rennick's logic.

"That's just it, Nathan," he snapped back. "You won't back away from a fight. It must be that Crockett stubbornness. There's a storm brewing, and you're likely to get caught in the middle if you're not careful."

"What are you talking about?"

"Harrison Reed stopped by here a few minutes before you arrived. He was spouting off about Betsey killing his father and how you were covering for her so you two could run off together."

"Run off? Betsey and me? That's ridiculous!"

"I know it is, and I doubt that even he believes it, but he seems to be out of his mind, and I'm afraid of what he'll do."

"Don't worry, I hid his rifle," I answered, in a tone of voice that was supposed to let Rennick know I wasn't worried about Harrison Reed's intentions.

"Right after you knocked him out with a sucker punch."

"I stopped him from doing something he would regret later."

"Well, now he has another target in mind, and he's sitting across the table from me right now."

"He's harmless, Rennick. I've already disarmed him twice. He doesn't want any part of me. And if he does..."

"Trust me—he does! I realize that he's no match for you, but when a man's acting crazy, anything can happen."

"Do you really think he's that dangerous?" I asked.

"Let me put it this way. Suppose he comes after you, so

you have to defend yourself, and he ends up dead. People will say that you killed him because of his accusations, and you'll be the one they'll be looking to hang. If he kills you, he'll be the grieving son who killed the man who conspired to poison his father. Don't forget that you were held in Springfield last year as a murder suspect."

"No one would ever believe that," I claimed, a little less sure of my position.

"You won't be around to say otherwise, if you're dead. But if you're not here or at the Reed cabin when he comes back, he'll more than likely calm down and the truth will come out as it always does. You show up a week later, and your hands stay clean."

"I don't like running away, especially if I haven't done anything wrong."

"You are not running away, and you've done nothing wrong, but this isn't your fight!" He paused a moment, then took a deep breath. "Let me put it to you this way. If you're walking down the road and you accidentally step into a big heaping pile of horse crap, what do you do? You step right out of it. Well, Nathan, this Reed situation is nothing but a bushel full of road-apples, and you've planted your foot knee deep. All I'm asking you to do is to simply step out of it, at least for now."

With the image of a brown, stinking moccasin etched into my mind, I admitted to myself that he had a point. I didn't know why I had become so involved in the whole affair. I had returned to rescue Evie, but all I managed to do was stir up the coals. Leonard was dead, and I was alive. Harrison was upset because he wouldn't collect any of McCarter's money. Betsey was either grieving or laughing on the inside, and Eveline was out somewhere, trying to convince anyone who would listen that she had proof that Leonard was murdered. I had indeed stepped in it, and at that moment, I decided to step out. I thanked Rennick for sharing his wisdom, and with a jug of the Seven Jessie's nectar, I reluctantly headed for home.

That night, from a rocking chair in front of my fireplace,

I toasted Kate the Cat for her guile as a hunter as she dined on an uninvited mouse. Content with a good meal and a little attention from me, she purred a lullaby as sweet as my mother's. As I dozed off, my last thoughts were of Liddy Parker beneath the mistletoe.

Twenty-Six

When I was a small child, I believed that an ostrich was a giant, mythical bird that lived in the mythical land of Africa. Upon my birth, my father had purchased an ABC Picture Book to fulfill a promise to my mother that her children would be educated. It was the opinion of my mother that an educated man would never go hungry; therefore, my education started in the cradle. Each page of the picture book contained a letter of the alphabet and a corresponding drawing. "A is for apple" would be paired with an elaborate etching of an apple. "B is for boy" and "C is for cat" were paired with their appropriate illustrations, and so on. The letter "O," which was for ostrich, was my favorite. There was a drawing of a giant, awkward-looking bird with a long, pencil-like neck and a bald head that was buried in the sand. It was the funniest thing I had ever seen. My mother said that whenever an ostrich sensed danger, it would bury its head and hope that whatever was threatening it would go away. It made sense to a four-year old boy, but when I went to college, I found out that the ostrich's tactic rarely worked; an L for lion usually ate it.

For the past three days, I had felt like an ostrich with my head in the sand. It didn't seem right to hide and shy away from a potential fight, but a promise was a promise. I had made a pledge to Rennick that I would stay hunkered down in my cabin for a week, and even though I intended to keep my word, I was yearning to know what was going on at the Reed farmstead. I didn't know whether the fact that I had not received a visit from the justice of the peace was good news or not. I could see the wisdom of Rennick's counsel, and I knew he would defend my honor if needed, but to accept this plan of action was truly against my nature. I kept reminding myself that I was only upset because I wasn't in on the latest gossip.

I hoped that maybe a little fishing would ease some of the tension, so I dug up a few night-crawlers from a shady spot behind the barn and grabbed my fishing pole. After much consideration, I found a place on the riverbank just beyond the last of the Five Sisters and out of the late morning sun. The river was low as a result of the drought, causing a new sandbar to appear with a deep, calm pool behind it. Safely harbored from the subtle undercurrents of the main channel, it would be an ideal place for slaying numerous bluegills. Most folks in the valley preferred the meatier and bigger catfish or buffalo, but in my opinion, there is not a tastier treasure to be found in the Wabash River than the frisky little bluegill. However, because they are tiny, it takes several fish to make a good meal. It would take at least a dozen bluegill to equal the harvest of meat that could be found in a single, good-sized catfish, but the bluegill had a much sweeter taste, and since I seemed to have plenty of time on my hands, I chose taste over bulk.

The first two fish I caught were too small to eat, so I threw them back into the river. Unfortunately for the second fish, it landed in shallow water and flopped up onto the sandbar where Kate the Cat was patiently waiting. With all the skill of her cousin, the panther, she pinned it down with her front paw, grabbed hard with her mouth, and in a single bound disappeared into the cover of prairie grass. I had eleven fish on my stringer before Kate appeared again with a triumphant look on her face. She purred contently and gave herself a lengthy backrub against the side of my leg. She was uninterested as I pulled in my last fish and it landed on the ground beside her. She was more than satisfied by her earlier feast.

After beheading my catch and scraping the scales away, I dipped the fish in some raccoon oil and breaded them in corn meal. I poured a little more oil into my cast-iron skillet and then placed it into my homemade Dutch oven. An hour later, the fish were golden brown and fit for a king. Kate was upset when I booted her outside, but she changed her tune when I threw the heads and fish guts out behind the barn.

I warmed some corn pone and boiled a fresh batch of coffee, and for the first time since Leonard's death, I was starting to feel like myself again. The bluegill was tender, although I had prepared more than I could eat by myself. I poured a second cup of coffee and moved my rocking chair to the front porch, leaving the dishes for later. As the sun started to disappear behind some distant, pillow-like clouds, a bouquet of gold and red fingers filled the evening sky. I felt a cool, moist breeze blowing from the southwest, and my nose sensed that rain wasn't too far away. The sunset was beautiful, and I considered it a shame that I didn't have anyone to share the moment. Eveline had been willing, but I wasn't ready. I felt like Liddy was willing now, but she was careful not to mention marriage, being well aware of my fear of commitment. I was beginning to realize that my so-called fear of commitment was nothing more than my selfish nature and a refusal to become a full-fledged adult. I had always preferred the solitude of living by myself, but now I felt... alone.

The next morning found me with a more cheerful disposition. The much-needed rain had fallen throughout the night, providing the best sleeping weather in weeks. The parched, brown vegetation had miraculously turned green overnight. The world had a fresh new smell, and the sun glistened upon the ripples of the now-surging Wabash. I watched a doe on the Indiana side of the river carefully make her way to the water's edge to get a drink, much to the chagrin of a pair of squawking blue jays. I ate some wild blackberries straight from the bush and was starting to gather some kindling for a breakfast fire when I saw Rennick ridding his gray mare, leading an all-too-familiar one-eared horse. I suddenly got an uneasy feeling in the pit of my stomach. *So much for a perfect morning...*

"Congratulations, Nathan, you inherited a horse," Rennick shouted as soon as he got within earshot. Ole Hickory looked as horror-struck as I felt about the reunion. As much as I wanted to protest, I was more anxious to hear about the news from the Reed farm.

"Well, don't just sit there," I pleaded. "Tell me what happened." I could tell by the look on his face that it wasn't going to be good news. We tied the horses to the rail fence next to the barn as Newton came over to greet the visitors. He snorted in disapproval when he realized one of them was Ole Hickory.

"Got any breakfast? Malinda was in a foul mood this morning, so I rode off while the getting was good."

"Beans and bluegill."

"Sounds good," he howled. "You get the kindling started, and I'll grab some wood."

"What did they decide about Leonard's death?"

"Breakfast first, then gossip for dessert." I wanted to force the issue, but knew that Rennick would tell me when he was ready and not a minute before.

He finished the last of the fish and a heaping plate of beans. He declined seconds of the beans, but asked for another cup of coffee. He stared at the wall with a troubled look on his face between sips, but remained silent. "I forget how beautiful it is out here on the river," he said, finally breaking the silence.

That was enough. "Rennick! Tell me what happened!"

"It didn't go well for Betsey. They have her locked up in the jail in Palestine. She's charged with capital murder."

"Are you serious? I can't believe that Eli Adams would allow it. Both of the doctors believed that she was innocent, just like me. Why wasn't I called? I could have—"

"Hold your horses, Nathan. I can't tell you if you don't let me get a word in."

"All right, Rennick. Start at the beginning and don't leave anything out!" I decided to bite my tongue, or this would take all day.

"At first, it went just like I figured it would. Harrison Reed showed up with a musket that looked like it couldn't hit a barn at twenty paces. Anyway, he was hell-bent on putting some new holes in your hide, but ran out of steam when he found out you weren't around. Then he turned his attention toward Betsey, but Eli Adams put a stop to it before he could do any damage. Just when things started to calm down, Eveline showed up with Hiram Johnson, the justice of the peace from Morea, who claimed he had jurisdiction of the case because the Reed cabin was on the west side of the Vincennes Trace. Adams told him to shut up because *he* had jurisdiction north of Heathsville. Next thing you know, they got into a shouting match, and it would have come to blows if Doc Wynn hadn't stepped in between them.

"While all this was going on, Eveline stands on a wagon and starts screaming that she has proof that Betsey put poison in Leonard's tea. That's when everything went silent. She produced a small, tattered piece of paper, and handed it to Justice Adams. The paper had traces of a white powder, and Doc Logan said it looked like it came from his apothecary. He took a closer look, and said that it was arsenic. Eveline said she was outside the window and saw Betsey get the paper from between two plates in the cupboard. Then she took them inside and showed them the spot where Betsey had hidden the poison, and it was there that they found another identical piece of paper containing a quarter ounce of white arsenic. She said Betsey had thrown the paper outside the door in order to get rid of the evidence, but it had fallen through a gap in the threshold. While all of this was going on, Betsey was sitting next to Leonard's body, quietly combing his hair. She didn't utter a single word to defend herself. It was as if she hadn't heard anything that was said. In light of the new evidence, Doc Wynn and Doc Logan took another look at Leonard's body, and within minutes, they decided that he had died as a result of an arsenic dose. The two justices went out to the barn for a conference, and when they came back, Hiram Johnson announced that Betsey was under arrest for the murder of her husband."

"What did Betsey do when they arrested her?"

"It was strange, Nathan," he said, while pouring yet another cup of coffee. "She didn't react at all. It was as if she didn't care. All she asked was if they could bury Leonard before they took her away. So we loaded Leonard into a pine box, drove him up to Baker Cemetery, and planted him under a big maple tree. Betsey remained quiet until Doc Logan started to speak a few words over the body. That's when Betsey flung herself over the coffin and started bawling like a baby. I've never seen anything like it. It was just like you said, Nathan. If she did kill him, then she is the best liar in the county. This went on for at least twenty minutes, and Doc Logan finally gave up on the eulogy. I don't think he liked Leonard all that much anyway. Her act as the grieving widow must have had some effect on the two justices, because they wrote out an order for Major Gaines to summon a grand jury of twelve men to hear evidence."

"I don't understand. Why did they do that?"

"I think that Adams has some doubt about whether she is guilty or not. If twelve men think there is enough evidence for her to be tried, then they could indict her, and Eli wouldn't have any blood on his hands."

"So was she still under arrest?"

"I don't think so, but she wasn't free to go, either. Adams told her that she wasn't allowed to leave the cabin. Sam McCarter, who had come to foreclose on the mortgage, volunteered his two boys to stand guard to make sure she didn't run off in the middle of the night. Adams said that it wasn't necessary, but McCarter ordered his boys to stay anyway."

"Sounds like the fox guarding the hen house."

"Exactly. Adams told all the witnesses to appear at the Reed cabin at noon the next day for the beginning of the inquest."

"Why didn't you come and get me?"

"What could you say, Nathan? Betsey didn't act guilty while Leonard was on his deathbed? They already knew that! She didn't act guilty at the funeral, and she didn't act guilty when they accused her, either. I've never seen a more innocent-acting person than Betsey Reed. There no reason for you to get involved. Besides, I was convinced that Harrison was bound and determined to drag you into the mess. I was hoping it would be a case of out of sight, out of mind."

"Did it work?" I asked, a little miffed that I had missed all the excitement.

"Like a charm," he proudly declared. "Harrison tried to say that you and Betsey were in on it together, but Eveline set the record straight. She shamed Harrison by telling everyone that he was only saying that because you had punched him in the nose. Besides, everyone around here knows you, and for the most part everyone thinks well of you. After that, your name was never brought up."

"I suppose that I should thank you."

"No thanks needed. I'm just happy you didn't get involved in the ordeal."

"So what happened with the inquest?"

"Major Gaines rounded up the grand jury, and by noon, there were at least a hundred people gathered at the Reed place to watch the proceedings. Since the cabin wasn't big enough to accommodate everyone, they set up a makeshift courtroom in the barn. It wasn't much of an inquest, though. Since Gaines' term as constable expires at the end of the month, he didn't go out of his way to find an impartial jury. Most were farmers from around the area. Ben Painter, Carter Funk, Elias Brashear, Martin Fuller, and even McCarter's two boys were used, so you knew how they were going to vote before things even got started. Harrison had gone around the neighborhood telling everyone that Betsey had poisoned Leonard, so the jury members were already convinced that she was guilty before they heard the first shred of evidence."

"Who defended Betsey?"

"No one. The purpose of a grand jury is only to find whether a crime has been committed and whether Betsey should stand trial. They do that so a prosecutor can't put you on trial on his word alone."

"Sounds complicated."

"It's not, and it wasn't. Adams called Harrison first, who claimed that he suspected that Betsey had been feeding arsenic to his father all along and that she needed him dead before Halloween to keep McCarter from foreclosing on the property. He neglected to tell them about his agreement with McCarter to keep him alive. Not that it mattered. It was Eveline's testimony that gave them enough reason to indict her.

"She went into detail about how Betsey always talked openly about what she was going to do when Leonard died and who she was going to do it with. She told them about Betsey's affairs and how she promised to see Green Baker dead. She even said that she witnessed Betsey cooking up some kind of evil potion just so the Baker boy would come to a violent demise. She told them you were convinced that Betsey had started the stable fire in Palestine and was involved in the death of Doyle Popplewell. When she described how she watched Betsey stir the poison in the tea, the barn was so quiet you could hear a pin drop. They were hanging on her every word. Betsey was sitting by herself in the corner of the barn, looking away and acting as if she couldn't care less about what was being said. I've never seen anything like it.

"Both Doc Logan and Doc Wynn got up and testified that it was their opinion that Leonard died from a dose of arsenic. They also said that Betsey had probably been feeding him small doses for the last few months. Doc Logan went on to say that the poison was purchased at his store in Russellville, but he couldn't remember Betsey buying it. Finally, they asked Betsey if she had anything to say in her defense. She acted as if she didn't hear the question and never did say a word. They cleared the barn out so the men could discuss the matter in private. They made Betsey stand alone in the animal pen behind the barn, and that's when some of the people began to taunt her."

I couldn't think of anything that would be more humiliating. "Why not put her in stocks and throw tomatoes at her?"

"It was bad, Nathan." Rennick stared into his mug and shook his head. "I don't understand how self-professed God-fearing people can be so cruel. One woman called her a witch, loud enough for her to hear, while another called her *scar-face* and a *devil*. She pretended not to hear them, but her eyes started to moisten, and she hid her face in her hands. The jury was only out for a few minutes, but it seemed like she was standing in that animal slop for an eternity."

"I wish I could have been there."

"No, you don't, Nathan. You would have just gotten yourself into hot water. I'm embarrassed that I didn't do anything about it myself. Anyway, they called everyone back into the barn. Adams waited until everyone was situated and quiet. Betsey stood in the corner and stared at the ceiling, making sure she didn't make eye contact with anyone. He asked Ben Painter, who had been named jury foreman, to read the verdict. He said it was the opinion of the jury that Betsey was not a God-fearing woman, and, being inspired by the devil, gave Leonard a lethal dose of arsenic in his sassafras tea and should be indicted on the sole count of capital murder.

At first, nobody said a word, but then Harrison started shouting that she was a witch and should be lynched, right then and there. A couple of McCarter's cronies started doing the same, and before long, the mob was lusting for blood. Major Gaines took out his pistol and blew a hole in the roof, which immediately quieted the revolution. He calmly stated that if anyone made a move toward Betsey, he or she would shortly resemble the barn roof. He ordered everyone out of the barn, and when things settled down, he put Betsey in shackles and took her to the jail in Palestine. Even when they wanted to hang her, she didn't try to defend herself and never said a word. She just didn't seem to care."

"So what's going to happen to her now?"

"They'll try her in Palestine when the court comes to town, but that could be two or three months. They'll make sure she gets a lawyer, not that it will do her any good; everyone in the county is convinced that she killed him."

"Has everyone forgotten the fact that Leonard had been sickly for years?" I still didn't believe she was guilty.

"I don't think it matters," Rennick admitted. "People got it in their heads that she's as evil as the devil himself. Before things are all said and done, folks will be nominating

Leonard for sainthood. They'll demand an eye for an eye and a tooth for a tooth."

"Do you think they'll hang her?"

"If it's left up to the folks around here...they will."

Twenty-Seven

It was a humid, sunny day when General Looker came to town. Othneil Looker, a general in the continental army under George Washington and former governor of Ohio, moved to Palestine to be with his daughter, Rachel Kitchell. Even though he was in his ninetieth year, General Looker wanted to be with and care for his recently widowed daughter. Mrs. Kitchell might argue about who was performing the caretaking, but was glad to have her father with her nevertheless. Under normal circumstances, the arrival of such a prominent man and war hero would have been the main topic of conversation, but hardly a soul in town paid any attention.

Palestine was buzzing about the jail's new inmate. The fact that it was a female behind bars, and that she was to be tried for murder, made the affair all the more scandalous. Merchants seemed to be pleased with the prospect of new customers who would come to town to witness the trial, not to mention the hundreds of people who would show up for a public hanging. Everyone wanted a glimpse of the notorious Betsey Reed. Preachers were happy because there was new ammunition for Sunday sermons on the wages of sin. To those who hated Betsey, the news of her incarceration served as vindication for their beliefs. Children could be heard on the streets singing a song hastily composed to pay homage to the occasion:

Betsey Reed brewed some tea.
Leonard drank it happily.
When she saw that he was dead,
She clicked her heels,
And then she said
Arsenic...arsenic...
We all fall dead.

Earlier that year, an election was held, and it was decided to move the county seat seven miles west to Robinson. The problem was that the village of Robinson didn't yet exist at the time. Some politicians decided that the county seat should be in the center of the county. Since Palestine was on the Indiana border, Robinson was invented. As it turns out, the same politicians who orchestrated the move owned all the land where the new county seat was to be built. A new courthouse and jail would be constructed at that location, but for now, there wasn't any place to hold or try Betsey Reed, so Palestine would have one last hurrah as the legal center of the county.

It had been over twenty years since the last accused murderers were held in the Palestine jail. Back in 1819, three Delaware Indians, William Kilbuck, Captain Thomas, and Big Panther, were jailed and accused of murdering an Indian trader of dubious character because of a dispute over whiskey. The Indians traded some goods for what they thought was a voucher good for a barrel of whiskey. But when they presented the invoice to the still operator, it simply read: *Don't give these Indians any whiskey.* Fearing for his life, the whiskey-maker read the note to the three thirsty men and informed them that they had been hoodwinked. They went into a rage, and when the Indian trader was found dead, it was obvious who had done the deed. The three Indians were arrested and locked up before nightfall.

William Kilbuck was tried first. Proving that frontier justice is swift, the trial lasted only four hours. He was found guilty of murder and was sentenced to hang in five days. Captain Thomas and Big Panther were scheduled for trial on the very next day, and most certainly would join Mr. Kilbuck for a hempen demise.

That night, there were rumors of revenge from the prisoners' fellow tribesmen who were camped just outside the village, awaiting news of the trial. With the memory of the Hutson massacre still fresh in their minds, the people wanted to avoid an Indian uprising at all cost. Around midnight, the three Indians mysteriously escaped. It seemed that someone forgot to lock the door. Nobody raised a fuss, and the three men were never heard from again. The Indians, who had been perceived as a lethal threat, broke camp in the morning and the peace was preserved. Unfortunately for Betsey Reed, there were no hostile Indians lurking nearby on her behalf.

Crawford County's State Attorney, Alfred Kitchell, wasn't thrilled about the prospect of hanging a woman, regardless of the fact that most of the good townsfolk were demanding it. Rumors and insinuation had gotten so far out of hand that Betsey Reed Fever was spreading around town like malaria. Betsey was growing more sinister by the hour, and before long, she was not only guilty of murdering Leonard; it was said that she also killed Green Baker and Doyle Popplewell, along with several small animals, not to mention the widow Nash's milk cow. She was a sorceress whose rival hadn't been seen since the Salem witch-hunt back in Massachusetts. Kitchell couldn't fathom any way that Betsey would receive a fair trial in Crawford County, but that was for the judge to worry about. His job was to convict, and from the way things looked, even the most incompetent prosecutor could convince a jury of her guilt.

None of the local attorneys wanted to represent Betsey, but upon the insistence of his new bride, who was still considered an outsider from New York, Augustus French reluctantly took the case. It was rumored that he was considering running for governor at the time, so it came as quite a surprise that he would represent such an unpopular client. Potential voters could view the notoriety of being associated with the infamous Betsey Reed rather harshly. Nevertheless, French felt that Betsey deserved competent council and decided to do the honorable thing, and in doing so, appease his young wife.

Betsey, on the other hand, seemed uninterested in assisting with her own defense. She remained completely silent for the first few days she spent in the Palestine jail, refusing both food and water at every meal. Then, on the sixth day, she refused to get out of bed. Leonard Cullom, the newly elected sheriff of Crawford County, became alarmed at the prospect of losing his first inmate after only two weeks in office and entered Betsey's cell to check on her wellbeing. Not sure if she was breathing, he grabbed her shoulder and jostled her in an attempt to get a response. It was never determined whether Betsey baited the young sheriff into her cell or was simply was startled by the intrusion, but with her eyes still closed, she lunged at Cullom and locked on to his forearm with a vise-like bite.

According to the deputy on duty, the sheriff screamed like an injured raccoon and tried desperately to free his arm, but Betsey clenched her grip even tighter. Ready to faint from the pain, Cullom took his free arm and punched Betsey squarely in her nose, causing blood to splatter everywhere. She immediately released his arm and fell unconscious. Cullom locked the cell, not caring whether Betsey was alive or dead, and went home to tend to his wounds. He could be heard mumbling something about taking great pleasure in hanging her when the time came.

When Betsey came to, she vowed not to go down without a fight. From that moment on, Betsey was like a caged animal. She would cuss, spit, or throw her food at her caretakers whenever they came near her cell. Only a half-crippled custodian, who went by the name of Hopper, was able to bring her food and supplies. He was lame in his right leg and had a horrible scar on his face, which he had received when hot oil had been spilled on him as an infant. It was assumed that Betsey, knowing the hardships that went along with a disfigured face, felt sorry for the old man and let him do his job without being assaulted.

When Augustus French went to the jail to meet her for the first time, Betsey refused to tell him anything that would help her cause. When he inquired whether or not she was guilty, all she said was, "It doesn't matter. They're going to kill me anyway."

He met with her twice more, but the results remained the

same; she simply refused to say anything that would allow him to prepare an adequate defense. Out of desperation, he went to Eli Adams and inquired if Betsey had any female friends who could talk to her. Maybe they could persuade her to help him save her from the gallows. He became more frustrated when Adams told him that as far as he knew, there wasn't a female on the planet who would have anything to do with Betsey Reed. "If there isn't a woman, what about a man?" French asked. Adams told the lawyer that Betsey didn't have any friends at all, but that there was a young man present at Leonard's death who sincerely believed that Betsey was innocent, and he might be able to get Betsey to cooperate.

Guess who!

Twenty-Eight

I had just finished the last of the fried chicken, and Liddy was cutting into her delicious looking blackberry cobbler, when I saw the horse and rider galloping toward us across LaMotte Prairie. It had been a wonderful picnic up until that point. The day was sunny, but the temperature was comfortable, especially in the shade of a massive walnut tree. Liddy was in good spirits and had been receptive to my numerous advances. After several days of solitude and dwelling on Leonard's death and Betsey's predicament, I was soaking up every bit of Liddy's vivacious spirit. She was full of life, and I was hoping that she was contagious. As I watched her mannerisms and nuances, I could see that she was truly happy when we were together. I felt a tinge of guilt for taking her for granted. She had loved me unconditionally from the first time we kissed under the mistletoe, while I had used her as a bandage to ease the pain of losing Eveline. She never complained when I disappeared for weeks at a time and never mentioned marriage, even though I knew she had turned away three potential suitors. When I asked her why she tolerated my selfish nature, she replied, "I don't see you as selfish; I see you as you. You love your freedom, and you don't want to be fenced in like some kind of animal. I suppose that's why I feel the way I do about you."

"How do you feel about me?" I asked, as I tickled her nose with a long blade of grass.

"You don't know?"

"No, I don't. Tell me."

"I love you, Nathan. I have for years. I never said anything because I knew you didn't feel the same way about me. I was afraid that if I told you, you wouldn't see me again."

"But you're telling me now?"

"It's because you're acting different. I can see it in your eyes. You look like maybe you do care for me, and maybe…" She turned her head in embarrassment.

"And maybe I'll tell you that I love you, too?"

She nodded her head. "I'd just about given up hope, but…"

I reached over and turned her head so that she had to look at me. Her emerald eyes revealed that she was apprehensive about my response. "I do love you, Liddy. I've been too big of a fool to realize just how wonderful you are."

She kissed me gently and laid her head against my chest, pulling herself as close as possible. I decided not to spoil the moment by saying something stupid. Unfortunately, someone else did.

As the rider got closer, I recognized the stubby body and fancy eastern clothes of Augustus French. French, who was plain looking with a ruddy face and a bland disposition, made up for his conservative appearance by dressing like a peacock. He dismounted in a single bound and tipped his hat as he landed. Liddy jumped to her feet, brushed the grass away from her dress, and pulled her hair back into a ponytail. "Sorry to interrupt the picnic, Miss Parker, but I have some urgent business to discuss with Nathan. He can be a hard man to find, so when Mrs. Dubois told me I could find you here, I came at once. Please forgive me."

She told him it was quite all right, and offered him a slice of pie. He refused at first; then he saw that it was blackberry and changed his mind. He asked if I wanted to speak in private, but I said that it wasn't necessary. I told him there wasn't anything we couldn't discuss in front of Liddy, and judging from the look of approval on her face, that was the correct answer.

"I don't know if you've heard, but I've agreed to defend Mrs. Reed," he said disdainfully.

"It's hard to keep any secrets about anything where Betsey Reed is concerned," I replied. I had an uneasy feeling about the purpose of his visit, mainly because my contact with the Reed family was a direct result of my courtship of

Eveline Deal, a touchy subject to discuss in front of Liddy, to say the least.

"It's going to be an uphill battle as far as mounting a proper defense is concerned. Everyone in the area is convinced that she's guilty. I doubt we can find twelve men who will come into the trial with an open mind. On top of that, she refuses to speak to me at all. That's the reason for my intrusion today. I've come to solicit your help, Nathan."

"I don't know what good I could do for you, Mr. French. All I can do is testify that she didn't act guilty when Leonard died. From what I've heard, that's not going to carry much weight at a trial."

"You're right about that, although that wasn't what I was going to ask of you. In a conversation with Justice Adams, it was mentioned that you have some sort of familiarity with Mrs. Reed, which may be of some help. What I mean is that I was hoping you would accompany me to the jail and try to get her to talk."

"I'm not that close to her. I doubt I could get her to open up if you couldn't."

"I'm afraid I'm out of options. I can't defend her if she won't defend herself. They'll hang her for sure."

I could tell by the strained look on Liddy's face this was an uncomfortable conversation for her to hear. I decided to end it quickly. "I'm sorry, Mr. French. Betsey Reed has spread enough grief my way to last two lifetimes. I just don't see where I could do you any good."

French looked dismayed as he finished his pie. He licked his fingers, then carefully wiped them on a red silk handkerchief. "I knew it was a long shot, and I can't say as I blame you for your decision. Mrs. Reed isn't the most likable of clients. I was hoping—"

With a smooth and controlled tone of voice, Liddy interrupted the conversation. "Nathan, I think you should at least try to get her to talk to Mr. French. I know she doesn't have many redeeming qualities, but I remember when you told me how she risked her life in that snowstorm and saved Hannah and her baby, so there has to be a little bit of good in her. Besides, you told me yourself that you're not sure she's guilty."

"Thank you, Miss Parker. You are right. There is some good in every one of God's creatures, and Mrs. Reed is no exception. So, Nathan, if you would, please stop by my office first thing in the morning." French knew that only a cad could refuse after such a selfless statement. I nodded my head, since the decision had been already made for me. He thanked Liddy for the pie, and galloped back to Palestine.

I turned to complain to Liddy, but she cupped her hand over my mouth. "Don't say a word, Nathan. You just said that you love me for the first time, so if you weren't lying, just keep quiet and listen. I know the only reason you were down there at the Reed place was that you still had some feelings for Eveline. I always knew that you still loved her, and that as long as you felt that way, there was never going to be a future for us. But I can see in your eyes that you are finally over her, and maybe we can go forward from here. That being said, you need to close that part of your life completely. Help Betsey Reed with her defense; say your goodbyes to Eveline Deal if you must. But close their chapter in your life so that you can begin a new one with me."

Twenty-Nine

Much to everyone's surprise, Betsey allowed me into her cell. She had grown pale from lack of sunshine and was severely thin from refusing to eat. Dark circles had formed around her eyes from apparent lack of sleep, and her hair was matted and uncombed. She was very careful to hide her face when I entered, staring only at the puncheon floor. Augustus French and Hopper waited out of sight, but stayed within earshot in case she became violent. I had the feeling that I was approaching a wounded animal, so I proceeded with caution. I set a bag full of toiletries beside her on the unmade cot. Liddy thought it would be a good idea if I brought a peace offering as an icebreaker. She looked at the bag, then placed her hand over her face to hide the scar. "A lot of good that will do me in here," she growled. "The only person I see is Hopper, and he doesn't give a damn what I look like."

"I thought you might want to look good when they hang you." I ducked just in time as the bag came flying past my head.

"You Bastard!" she screamed. "Get the hell out of here!"

"I came to help," I said, trying to remain as calm as possible. "I thought you might want to save your life, but I can see that I was obviously mistaken. Hopper! Let me out. I can't do any good here."

"Wait! Please don't go, Nathan," she pleaded, as Hopper fumbled with his ring of keys. "I'm sorry. I don't know why I act like I do. Please…"

I nodded to Hopper, and he put his keys away while French pumped his fist to indicate his approval. Betsey ran to the far side of the cell, gathered the powder and soap, and hastily placed them back into the bag.

"Why don't we start over. I'm here to help. I need to

know why you won't help your lawyer defend you."

She solemnly looked at the floor. "There's no use. They're going to hang me regardless of what I say. I'm not going to give them the satisfaction of watching me beg for my life. I see the way people look at me. To them, I'm the green-eyed monster from the Dark Bend. They call me a *witch* and a *she-devil* just because I can heal people. They scorn me for my gift unless they need my help. Then they come running. Now they want to kill me, and they'll make a huge spectacle out of the trial and call it justice. But when it's all said and done, they're just going to kill me like an animal while all the God-fearing hypocrites watch with smiles on their faces. No sir, Nathan...They may kill me, but they won't watch me grovel. I won't ask for mercy. I won't ask them for anything. I won't give them the satisfaction." She turned away and began to sob, and then fell to her cot.

I let her cry for a few minutes without saying a word. French and Hopper peeked around the corner and then quickly went back into hiding. Finally, she regained her composure. "I really don't want to die, Nathan. I just assumed there wasn't any hope."

"There's always hope. And if it means anything, I don't believe that you poisoned him." I had been instructed by French not to inquire about her guilt or innocence. Many a neck had been permanently stretched as the result of a jailhouse confession that was overheard by eavesdropping lawmen. "Betsey, you need to talk to Mr. French. He's the only friend you've got right now. He's a straight shooter, for a lawyer, and wants to help. He's just outside, and if you'd like, I could get him right now."

"No! Not now! I don't want anyone to see me now. I must look awful."

I took her vanity as a sign that she might want to live after all. "How about tomorrow morning?"

"Will you come with him? I have an awful hard time trusting strangers."

"If you want me to."

"Please. It would mean a lot to me."

"Tomorrow morning it is." As I left her cell, I glanced back and saw her going through the bag of toiletries. I had an eerie feeling that I had only given her a measure of false hope.

Betsey seemed like a totally different person when we arrived the next morning. Her hair was washed and combed, and her clothes were crisp and ironed. She carried the scent of rosewater and jasmine and had a sparkle to her eyes that wasn't there before. She answered all of Mr. French's questions without hesitation. She said that Leonard had bought arsenic to kill rats and mice, but swore on the name of her departed father that she didn't poison him. She admitted she had never loved Leonard but had grown fond of him over the last few months. The main reason for her change of heart toward him was due to the fact that Leonard had signed over the deed, making her the sole owner of the farm.

French grimaced when he learned of Leonard's loan with McCarter, and he almost became ill when he learned that Betsey owned the land free and clear because Leonard died before McCarter's note came due on Halloween. He realized at once that it gave her a motive to kill her husband. Regardless of her guilt, the state's attorney would drive home the fact that she stood to gain a great deal monetarily, and with Eveline Deal's eyewitness account of Betsey slipping the poison into his tea, they were fighting an uphill battle.

French kept the meeting positive and told her that no woman had ever been executed in the State of Illinois, or even in the entire Northwest Territory, and he doubted she faced that fate. But he did admit that it might be hard to avoid a lengthy prison term. Betsey seemed to take his assessment in stride, which surprised me, but agreed to be cooperative with French in preparing her defense. French promised to return as soon as a date for the traveling circuit court was set. Betsey thanked me again for trying to help her with an awkward kiss on the cheek. She seemed sincerely grateful, but was very formal and aloof. After witnessing the way in which Betsey's disposition and moods could constantly change over the last few years, I didn't give her strange behavior a second thought.

Thirty

That night, an overly large, blood-red full moon appeared in the eastern sky. Liddy called it a witch's moon. She said that it looked like a witch had conjured it up to drop fire on some unsuspecting victim. I laughed and said it was a good thing that the area's only practicing witch was safely secured in the county jail. Liddy thumped my arm and scolded me for being mean. "You probably call me a witch when I'm not around, too!" she laughed, then hugged me to make up for the punch.

"I do, but I always make sure to say that you're a good witch," I teased, instigating another jab. We were sitting on the front porch swing of the Dubois House, which had been home for the last couple of weeks. Jesse was away on business in Springfield, and Adelia was entertaining guests who lingered in the dining room after supper. Someone had picked up the house fiddle and started playing a European sounding love song, and we watched the flickering dance performed by scores of lightning bugs. Liddy rested her head on my shoulder as we swung rhythmically with the music. Now that Betsey was cooperating with her lawyer, there wasn't any business keeping me in Palestine, but I found myself unable to leave Liddy.

After the death of my parents, I had guarded myself against loving anyone. Call it fear of commitment or immaturity, but I had kept myself in a position where marriage was not an option. In retrospect, when Eveline came along and wanted to get married, I wasn't ready. Because of her impatience with me, the relationship was doomed from the beginning. But Liddy was different. Her love wasn't suffocating or jealous in nature. She was patient enough to know that any talk of marriage would have to be initiated by me, and that was exactly the topic I had on my mind as we sat beneath the witch's moon.

I was ready to settle down, and had decided to ask her to marry me before the end of the evening. For now, though, I decided to enjoy the moment of having her on my arm, loving me unconditionally, while music played in the background. After all, the night was still young.

At the exact same moment, Betsey Reed was looking through the steel-barred windows at the blood-red moon. Over the last few days, her will to live had rekindled the fire that kept her life in constant turmoil. She was disappointed when she learned that there was little hope of acquittal. Augustus French was concentrating on keeping her from the gallows, and was trying to convince her that a lengthy prison sentence was an acceptable outcome. She knew that prison would be the same as death. She was hoping that her brother, Isaac, would use his influence with some of his cutthroat friends and attempt a jailbreak, but he hadn't even bothered to visit her. Betsey had learned that their ailing mother had moved in with him, and she envisioned her mother laughing and enjoying the fact that her only daughter was about to receive her great reward. She wiped a tear away from her cheek, angry that she allowed the mere thought of that evil woman to get the better of her. She waited until Hopper locked the outer jail door and went home for the night, then pulled out two small pieces of flint, which she had found in the corner of her cell.

Earlier that week, she had noticed that a large knot in the wall timber near her bed had broken loose. With a little prodding, she popped the knot out, exposing a hole six inches deep and six inches in diameter. Even though the walls were three feet thick and perceived to be escape proof, she suddenly realized she was one-sixth of the way through to her freedom. She grabbed her spoon and began digging and scratching into the hole, but soon realized she was barely making a dent. Sheriff Cullom had given strict instructions that she wasn't allowed to have anything that could be used as a weapon, so access to a knife or even a fork was out of the question. She honed the edge of the spoon handle against one of the cell bars until the edge became razor-sharp, but all she could manage to do was shave a few paper-thin strips away from the hardwood. After a half hour of hard work, she only had a handful of wood chips to show for her effort. She realized it would take years to cut her way out, and in a fit of rage she slapped her thigh, making the two small flint stones click together. The sound gave her an idea that was so obvious that she was dumbfounded she hadn't thought of it before. She could burn her way out!

So, over the last few evenings, Betsey systematically started, then extinguished, a number of small fires inside the knothole. She would let the fire go until the jail was filled with smoke and then suffocate it with a wet towel. Once the wood was charred, it would easily break away into brittle coals. She ground the coals into powder and tossed the remains around the cell and into her wastewater. She positioned her cot so that her blanket hid the ever-growing cavern in the wall, but since it was still summer and Hopper only lit a fire to make his coffee, it was becoming more difficult to hide the stale odor of smoke. She was using Liddy's oils and toiletries in an attempt to overpower the smell of burnt wood, but could see that Hopper was getting suspicious.

Betsey decided she was going to have to make her move that night. There would be no time to spare. She foraged the walls and floor for splinters that could be used for kindling, and after gleaning the proper amount, she built a small mound of fuel in the wall. With little effort, she flicked the flints until a spark caught. Within minutes, she had the fire crackling nicely. She knew she was going to have to let the fire go longer than usual, so she wet her towel in her drinking water and covered her face in order to breath when the cell became full of smoke. She could see that the fire was really burning fast, and was worried that it might get out of control, but decided to give it just a few more seconds. She knew time was of the essence and that the extra risk was necessary.

Liddy nuzzled even closer as the music continued to enchant the evening. With her head firmly planted against my chest, I inhaled the fragrance of her perfumed hair, thinking that I had never known a more alluring scent. She softly cooed in rhythm with the swing, rubbing the top of my thigh in a playfully seductive manner. She felt so familiar and comfortable that it was difficult to tell where I ended and she began. "I could stay like this forever," she whispered as she reached up to kiss me. "Nathan, I couldn't love you any more if I tried." As she looked up, I could see the reflection of the moon in her eyes as they sparkled like emeralds.

I would never find a more opportune time to propose to her. Instantly, my throat became dry and my tongue stuck to the roof of my mouth. My mind started racing with reasons not to go through with it, but I decided I had to do it now. It was time to silence my demons and ask her to marry me.

"Liddy, can you sit up for a minute? I want to ask you something." She held her breath, seeming to know what I had in mind. Even though I was somewhat confident, the fear of rejection unexpectedly tied my tongue. I started to stammer, my words sounding like some ancient middle-eastern dialect.

I stopped in mid-sentence, took a deep breath, cleared my throat, and got ready to start again. But before I could utter a single word, the mood of the perfect evening under the full moon suddenly took a turn for the worse.

"Fire!" somebody shouted in the distance. "The jailhouse is on fire!"

My heart seemed to jump into my throat. *How could this be happening?* I tried to ignore the commotion as people filed into the street and headed toward the town square. Betsey had caused enough grief in my life. Enough was enough! But as soon as I turned around, Liddy was out of her chair, racing for the fire.

"Hurry, Nathan, she could be burned alive!" she shouted, without missing a step.

"Liddy! Stop! I need to ask this now!" With my track record for commitment, I knew that I better get the job done while I still had the courage.

She stopped in her tracks and walked directly back to me until our faces were only inches apart. When I looked into her eyes my head started spinning. "Well, what is it?" She remained perfectly calm as she stared into my eyes.

"Liddy..." I stopped to take a deep breath. "I was wondering..."Another deep breath. "No, I was hoping..." Another breath.

"Oh, good grief! Of course I'll marry you, Nathan. I'll be a spinster by the time you spit it out."

"You will?" I was grateful she had taken control of the situation. I put her in a bear hug and twirled her around until we fell to the ground.

She grabbed me, then kissed me, then scolded me. "I've been waiting for months for this. I would have said yes if you had asked me under the mistletoe when you first kissed me. Yes! Yes! Yes! I will marry you. I love you with all of my heart. Now, let's get to the fire!"

Thirty-One

When we arrived at the jail, the entire building was engulfed in flames, and men were racing with buckets of water from the town well. Most of the blaze was concentrated in the area of Betsey's cell. After being all too familiar with what the inside of a burning building was like, I realized there was little reason to hope that Betsey could survive. When I saw Sheriff Cullom unable to enter the door due to the massive amount of black smoke billowing out, I feared that all hope was lost. A vision of Joan of Arc being burned at the stake came into my mind. Not to compare the two women in any way, but death by fire horrified me. Liddy turned her head at the same time, terrified by the thought of Betsey being trapped in the building. The joy of our engagement was suddenly gone.

To make matters worse, Squire Logan, a local shopkeeper and brother to Doc Logan, was running beside the jail when an exterior wall collapsed, trapping him in a pile of burning rubble. I ran over and helped move the timber that had him pinned down, but by the time we finally freed him from the fire, he was severely burned over most of his body.

It was at this time a voice yelled that there was someone moving inside the jail. After the collapse of the wall, the smoke was siphoned away from the front room toward the gaping hole. Much to everyone's amazement, there were two people, clearly visible, moving slowly in the front corner of the building.

Sheriff Cullom kicked the door open, disappeared into the veil of blackness inside the jail, and reappeared shortly through a shroud of smoke along with a staggering man who was dragging Betsey by her hair. As soon as they crossed the threshold, the roof collapsed with a thunderous boom. The building now became a giant bonfire, and without any hope to save the structure, the citizens of Palestine were forced to watch helplessly as their jail was reduced to ashes.

What started as a perfectly quiet August evening now threatened to become the most notorious night in the short history of the State of Illinois. Within thirty minutes of the fire alarm being sounded, nearly a thousand people had gathered at the public square to witness the commotion. It soon became evident that Betsey had somehow set fire to the jail in an attempt to escape and had lost control of the situation. It just so happened that a man by the name of Sam Garrard happened to be passing by and heard Betsey's cries for help. He grabbed an axe from a nearby barn, smashed the lock to the front door of the jail, and then ran into the fire. Even though the building was filled with smoke, he managed to find the ring of keys and open the door to Betsey's cell. By that time, though, the smoke was too thick, causing them to lose their bearings.

They crawled to the far corner of the jail and fell to the floor, where they found a small pocket of breathable air. Betsey broke away from Garrard by biting his hand, but was unable to find her way to the door and was forced back into the same corner with her lungs full of smoke. If the wall hadn't collapsed when it did, both Garrard and Betsey would have perished together. Sheriff Cullom found them immediately, but for some reason, Betsey refused to go. The sheriff was ready to leave her, but Garrard decided that he didn't risk his life only to watch her die in the flames. He reared back and hit her squarely on the jaw, causing her to collapse on the smoldering floor. While she was disabled, he grabbed her by the hair and dragged her out of the jail. He threw her next to the land office and revived her by pouring a bucket of water over her face.

Betsey erupted. Using language that would make a dockworker blush, she cursed the two men for pulling her out of the fire. She shot up like a wildcat and took a haymaker swing at Cullom, missing by an inch, and using so much force that she lost her balance and fell to the ground. Then she began cursing even louder, but as she tried to get up again, Cullom grabbed her by her arms and pinned her face against the building. "Grab a rope!" he demanded, as she struggled furiously to escape his grasp.

That's when things started to get out of hand.

"Lynch her!" shouted a voice out of the crowd.

"Hang the witch!" declared another.

As the crowd became more hostile, Betsey started berating people with curses, calling for a variety of maladies to befall their descendants. This caused even the most sympathetic of church-folk to side with the mob. Betsey became so incensed that she almost broke loose of Cullom's grasp on two different occasions, but when she savagely bit into the flesh of the sheriff's forearm, Cullom pummeled her with three open-handed blows, which landed squarely against her face. Battered and bruised, Betsey still refused to capitulate.

I could see that the sheriff had completely lost control of his temper, and if something wasn't done immediately, Betsey was going to end up dead tonight. I sent Liddy to get Newton, ride to Maplewood, and fetch Augustus French. It was going to take someone of his stature to restore order.

I breathed a sigh of relief when Cullom used the rope to tie Betsey securely to a nearby hitching post, but many were disappointed when he didn't make a noose. He ordered Hopper to guard her at gunpoint and keep the mob away while he went and dealt with the fire.

With Betsey bound to the post, she became an easier target for ridicule. "Throw her back into the fire! Burn her! Hang her! Shoot her!" She spat on a woman who strayed too close, inciting the crowd even more. Hopper was holding them away with his hideously long pistol, but he didn't stand a chance if the mob decided to act.

Through all the confusion, I realized the chief instigator of the riot was Thomas McKinney. Whenever things started to calm down, he would shout something with his booming voice and the mob would react. What shocked me even more was when I realized that Eveline Deal was lurking behind him like a puppet master, telling him what to say. Her face was so full of hatred that I had to look twice to make sure it was actually her. She barely resembled the girl I had fallen in love with. Eveline had seen a chance to get even with Betsey and was taking full advantage of it.

Doc Logan arrived on the scene and began tending to his brother's burns. Almost immediately, he began to shake his head, indicating that things didn't look good. Seeing this, Eveline quickly whispered something into McKinney's ear. "First Leonard and now Squire Logan!" he shouted. "How many men are we going to let the witch kill before we do something about it?" Eveline stood back with her arms crossed, satisfied that people wouldn't let her get away with a second murder.

Suddenly, the roof of the jail collapsed with a boom, and the timbers sent burning coals into the sky. The building became a blazing pyre, and the heat became so intense that people were forced to stand back away from Betsey. The few men who were still carrying buckets of water stopped to watch the blaze and realized it was hopeless; the jail was lost.

Sheriff Cullom, along with three other men, helped Doc Logan carry his brother back to his office, leaving Hopper to deal with the mob alone. With coaxing from Eveline, Thomas McKinney saw an opportunity; he began demanding that the citizens of Palestine take the law into their own hands, and like the regulators had done in other counties around the state, give Betsey Reed a full measure of frontier justice.

Hopper, aggravated that the inexperienced sheriff had left him in such a dire situation, took a position directly in front of Betsey and fired his pistol into the air. Since it was only a single-shot weapon, he now stood between Betsey and the mob without any form of deterrent. Meanwhile, Betsey started laughing uncontrollably, rotating her head wildly, as if she were worshiping the burning jail. As the fire became more intense, so did Betsey's frenzied behavior. That's when I realized she was simply mocking the mob. At that moment, she wanted to die and was doing whatever she could within her power to make it come about.

Sheriff Cullom, standing inside Doc Logan's apothecary, heard the shot and came running, but was unable to get anywhere near Betsey. Hopper had been disarmed and was thrown to the ground. I tried to fight my way to take his place but never got closer than ten feet. Thomas McKinney was the first to reach Betsey. Within seconds, Betsey was cut loose from the hitching post and was marched over to a large oak tree standing in the middle of the town square. Someone produced a rope and placed it around Betsey's neck as she continued to laugh and mock her accusers.

Realizing that Betsey was about to die, much of the crowd decided that they didn't want any part of a vigilante hanging, but the zealots had her surrounded and things were looking bleak. Augustus French hadn't arrived, and Sheriff Cullom was unable to get control of the riot.

McKinney and two of his partners pulled the back end of the hempen rope, hoisting Betsey into the air just high enough that her feet couldn't touch the ground. Half of the mob cheered wildly, while the other half protested in horror. Betsey kicked wildly, but she soon lost consciousness and fell completely limp.

Kaboom! Suddenly, the sound of an earth-shaking explosion silenced the mob. A ball of white, sulfuric smoke covered the crowd, forcing everyone to scatter. The hangmen dropped their rope, and Betsey fell to the ground like a rock with the noose still tight around her neck.

When the smoke cleared, ninety-year-old General Othneil Looker stood next to the town cannon in full military uniform, his bald head gleaming in the moonlight, and he brandished the sword that he received when the British surrendered at Yorktown. He waddled over to Betsey and ordered the sheriff to come to her aid as she struggled to remove the noose. "There will not be a lawless hanging tonight!" shouted General Looker with a tone of absolute authority. "I enjoy a legal hanging as much as the next fellow, but what you are doing here is against the law of this land, and more importantly, the law of God! I've spent my entire life fighting for freedom and protecting the rights of every American. This woman has the right to a fair trial, and she will receive one. A court of law may decide that she must meet her maker, but her fate will not be decided by a frenzied band of cutthroats. Not tonight. Not ever! As long as I can draw a breath, there will be law and order."

Thomas McKinney started to make a threatening move toward Betsey, but backed away quickly when General Looker pointed his sword in his direction. In the presence of the general, Sheriff Cullom handled Betsey with a bit more dignity and patience as he helped her to her feet. With many of the participants deeply ashamed, the crowd retreated to a safe distance behind the jail and watched what was left of the log structure burn to the ground.

Liddy and Augustus French arrived a few minutes later after the mob had started to dissipate. As soon as French noticed the rope burns on Betsey's neck, he realized she would never receive a fair trial in Palestine. After meeting with Cullom, it was decided that the sheriff would take Betsey to his cabin and shackle her to the bed in his upstairs loft until a suitable place of detention could be found. It was an act which, unfortunately, got the sheriff into hot water with his wife. Betsey was to be guarded at all times, and was not to be allowed to possess any material that could be used to start a fire.

Betsey was completely exhausted and accompanied Sheriff Cullom and Hopper to the cabin without incident. General Looker, with a hint of satisfaction on his face, limped back to his daughter's house, delighted to serve the public one last time.

I looked at Liddy, her hair windblown by the ride, her face covered in dust and soot, and realized that she was the most important thing in my life. Nothing else mattered. Just her. Forget the insanity of the night. Go marry the girl and take her far away, away from jails, fires, mobs, sheriffs, and crazy witches. I decided that I was going ride away with her that night and never come back. I was caught up in a treacherous windstorm that went by the name of Betsey

Reed, but I found my lighthouse and safe harbor before me.

Liddy smiled slightly, as if she had read my mind, and then beckoned with open arms. "Ask me again, Nathan," she cooed as we embraced.

"Liddy, will you marry me?"

"Yes, Nathan Crockett, I would be honored to become your wife." She reached up and kissed me passionately as the ambers and coals popped and crackled like fireworks in honor of the occasion.

As we stood silently, watching the crowd dwindle, I saw Eveline Deal standing on the other side of the public square, glaring intensely in our direction as she chastised Thom McKinney for letting Betsey continue to breathe. The fact that she had just witnessed Liddy accepting my proposal only added kerosene to her fire. When she realized I was watching her tirade, she began to march directly toward us. I started to usher Liddy in the opposite direction, but she stopped me. "We might as well face this now," she said firmly, "and we'll do it together."

As Eveline got nearer, I was shocked to see how much she had aged over the last year. Frown lines had appeared around her mouth, and her skin looked pale and dry. But it was her eyes that had changed the most. Warm, young, and inviting when we first met, they were now icy-cold and full of hate. "Why do you help her, Nathan?" screamed Eveline in a piercing tone. "After everything she's done to me...how could you? You said that you loved me, Nathan! That was a lie! If you loved me, you would have done away with the witch! But no! You protected her! You should have protected me!"

As I started to respond, Liddy gripped my hand forcefully to stop me. "I'm sorry, Miss Deal, we have never been formally introduced. I'm Liddy Parker, Nathan's fiancé."

Eveline took a deep breath, started to speak, but then stopped. She turned around, started to walk away, then tuned again. "You're going to settle for this redheaded tavern-whore when you could have had me?"

I didn't like where this was going. "Eveline! You need to

leave!" I said, and I stepped in front of Liddy, realizing I needed to end this situation. "I won't allow you to talk to Liddy that way."

"It's all right, darling, she's just hurt," Liddy said, pulling me back by the arm. "I don't know how I would react if I ever lost you." I could tell that her words cut through Eveline like a dagger.

"I wouldn't marry Nathan Crockett if he were the last man on earth! Besides, Thomas and I are getting married as soon as the circuit rider comes to town. The only reason we came to Palestine was to get our marriage license."

I started to speak, but Liddy quickly stepped in front of me. "We wish you nothing but happiness, Miss Deal," she said sternly.

"Well, Miss Parker, I wish you nothing but a trip to hell." With eyes full of tears, Eveline turned and stormed away with Thomas McKinney dutifully following behind.

"My, my, what a spiteful girl," Liddy said while patting my hand. "What did you ever see in her?"

"I don't know what's happened to her. It's like she's a totally different person." I paused for a moment to catch my breath. I had expected the confrontation to be worse than it had turned out to be. Because Liddy was polite and firm, Eveline didn't have an opportunity to make a scene. I had to admit that my future wife was much wiser than I realized.

"She's still in love with you," Liddy whispered playfully.

"That's ridiculous! You heard what she said."

"No, I saw it in her eyes when I introduced myself as your betrothed. Behind all of that hatred, I could see the pain my words had caused. It was as if I had stabbed her heart with a knife. I feel sorry for her."

"Don't feel sorry for her!" I said. "She's marrying Thom McKinney."

"She may be marrying Thomas McKinney, but unfortunately, he's not the one she's in love with."

"She's so consumed with hatred for Betsey that she doesn't have any room to love anyone." I felt sorry for her, too.

After the fire was completely extinguished, Liddy and I walked arm in arm east toward the Wabash River. Smoke from the fire lingered in the heavy night air, and the moon was now high in the sky. We were serenaded by thousands of crickets and a lonely bobwhite quail when we strayed close to her nest. I realized I was walking with the woman who was going to be my wife and the mother of my children. In the past, the thought of such an obligation had sent me running for cover, but at that moment I had never wanted anything more.

As we stood silently at the river, I spooned behind her with my arms wrapped tightly around her, her hands gently resting on mine. It made me remember the night when Eveline and I stood on the Indiana side of the river in Merom. It was ironic. That night, three years ago, we gazed at the river, dreaming of the future, falling in love. Now, I was contemplating my life with Liddy in our cabin beneath the Five Sisters.

I also remembered the voice in my head that told me to run away as fast as I could, especially when I learned that Eveline was going to live with Leonard and Betsey. I ignored that little voice, and our relationship ended in ashes, appropriately, at the fire tonight. Standing at the river seemed to be an appropriate place to wash away the memories of the past. I picked up a shiny black stone and tossed it into the Wabash, causing a splash and then a series of small, perfect rings. Within seconds, the rings disappeared forever, leaving only a fading memory of love gone bad...a Wabash tragedy. *Goodbye, Evie.*

On our way back to the Dubois Tavern, we stopped by Doc Logan's office to check on his brother. Augustus French was on the front porch, smoking his pipe. "I wondered where you two ran off to," said French. "From what I hear, congratulations are in order."

"Why, thank you, Mr. French," I said looking at Liddy. "I didn't realize anyone knew about our engagement."

"When Miss Parker arrived at Maplewood this evening, she introduced herself as your fiancé. All I can say is that it's about time you settled down, Nathan Crockett, although I shouldn't be surprised. I could tell you had him under your spell, Liddy, when I interrupted your picnic the other day. You should be proud of yourself; you've captured the most eligible bachelor in Crawford County."

Liddy smiled, and nodded politely as she rearranged a wisp of her hair. "Thank you very much, Mr. French. We're very happy, considering the circumstances. By the way, how is Squire Logan faring?"

"I'm afraid that things look very bleak. Doc Logan said he received severe burns to over half of his body, not to mention a broken arm and several broken ribs." French took another draw on his pipe and then sat down on a rocking chair. "Doc says he'll be lucky to make it through the night. Mrs. Reed was fortunate to survive the night also. But if Squire dies, a hundred crazy old generals couldn't stop the next mob. God help us all when that happens!"

Doc Logan joined us on the porch, his sleeves rolled up to his forearms, reeking of salve. He looked at French and shook his head, indicating that things weren't any better. "All I can do his give him opium for the pain and pray." He buried his face in his hands to hide his despair. "I don't know what else to do!"

Silence. I looked down at the ground, hurting for Doc, not knowing what to say.

Suddenly, Liddy jumped onto the porch and put her hands on Doc's shoulders. "Doc! You said the exact same thing about Nathan's burns. Don't you remember? You told Adelia Dubois that you had done all you could for Nathan, and the only thing left to do was pray."

"Yes, I remember, but Nathan is quite a bit younger than Squire. It's much easier for a healthy young man to heal. I'm afraid that Nathan's recovery was an exception to the rule."

"That's not what I'm talking about!" Liddy replied. "Adelia brought in a healer to blow the fire away. His burns started to heal almost instantly."

"Not that mountain magic again! It's utter nonsense!"

I saw where Liddy was headed with this. "No, Doc. It

does work," I said. "I was skeptical about the story too, but I witnessed a little boy's burns disappear almost immediately, right before my eyes. I know it sounds crazy, but what have you got to lose?"

Doc shook his head. "It goes against everything I've learned as a doctor. Even if I agree to this lunacy, where are you going to find a fire-blower in the middle of the night?"

I looked at Liddy and she nodded yes. "Mr. French, do you know the whereabouts of Betsey Reed?"

Thirty-Two

Doc Logan somehow persuaded Sheriff Cullom to escort Betsey to his office. More amazingly, she agreed to go. Without trepidation, Betsey entered the room and knelt beside the gravely burned body of Squire Logan. His face and chest were severely blistered, while the flesh on his arms and abdomen looked like a blend of charcoal and blood. Betsey smiled and lovingly ran her fingers through his hair, and to the dismay of Doc Logan, gently kissed Squire on the forehead. "I need everyone to leave the room," she suddenly demanded, oblivious to her circumstances.

"You've got to be kidding," declared Sheriff Cullom.

"I won't—no, I can't do this with everyone in here, especially at gunpoint," she responded.

"There's no way in hell I'm leaving you in here alone," said Cullom.

"Fine! Let Nathan stay!" She backed away, implying that she would only help under her terms.

"Oh, no! Keep me out of this," I pleaded. I could sense myself being led back to the quicksand.

"Quit playing games! My brother is dying, and it's your fault!" Doc Logan lunged at Betsey and slapped her sharply across the face. He immediately backed away, regretting his outburst, and ran out of the room.

Her demeanor never changed. "You're right. This is my fault and I'm trying to right my wrong. Nathan can stay; everyone else needs to leave."

Liddy nodded, indicating that I should do as I was told. "I'll make sure she doesn't go anywhere," I promised, as Liddy ushered the men out of the room.

"I'll be right outside the door, Nathan! I have no qualms about putting a lead ball into her if she tries anything," warned the sheriff as the door closed behind him.

As soon as we were alone, Betsey stood up and began to mumble something that sounded like a verse of scripture as she walked around the bed three times. I stood in the corner, trying to stay out of her way, as she focused all of her attention on Squire. She hovered over each part of his body and softly blew against his burns, rotating her hands, coaxing the fire away. Every time she repeated the ritual, Squire sighed deeply as if the burns were leaving his body. After what seemed to be an eternity, Betsey collapsed and fell to the floor. I ran to her side to check on her, but she was out cold. As I tried to revive her, I was shocked by a voice asking for a drink of water. Squire Logan was sitting upright with his feet on the floor, well on his road to recovery.

The news of Squire Logan's miracle recovery quickly spread through Palestine, but instead of swaying public opinion in favor of Betsey, it had the opposite effect. Many people were already convinced she was a witch, so her ability to blow fire away only confirmed their belief that she was a practitioner of the black arts. A substantial group of people, including prominent members of the religious community, wanted to rid the world of this green-eyed monster and daughter of the devil, with or without a fair trial. Fueled by the ranting of some who felt that they had been cheated out of a public hanging, it would only be a matter of time before vigilantes took the law into their own hands.

Augustus French, who was once, ironically, a member of a vigilante group in Edgar County, moved quickly to thwart the efforts of the lynching party. Without the jail, which also served as the county courthouse, all legal issues would be dealt with in a log cabin in Robinson. When French learned that Supreme Court Justice William Wilson was traveling to Carmi, he intercepted his stagecoach on the Hubbard Trail and convinced him to intervene on Betsey's behalf. Wilson ordered his coach to be diverted to Robinson, where he opened an emergency session of the Crawford County Circuit Court. After hearing French's plea and hearing the testimony of Sheriff Cullom, Wilson ruled that Betsey's life was in peril and ordered that she be transferred to the

Lawrence County Jail in Lawrenceville. Wilson stated that he would personally hear arguments when the circuit court resumed in September.

That night, under the cover of darkness, Sheriff Cullom, Hopper, and a posse of twelve men delivered Betsey Reed to the Lawrence County Jail. Cullom gladly presented the court order along with a copy of the indictment to Lawrence County Sheriff Sam Thorn. After informing Thorn about his ordeals and warning him of her treachery, Cullom wished him good luck, and with his thirteen deputies he rode back to Palestine, washing his hands of Betsey Reed forever.

After the deputies had removed her shackles, Sheriff Thorn went to her cell to introduce himself. He politely explained the rules of the jail and what was expected of all prisoners in his custody. Betsey remained silent and detached, so he asked her if she had heard him. She remained quiet, so he asked her again, only this time with a tone of authority in his voice. Betsey looked him directly in the eyes, smiled, and spat in his face. Sheriff Sam Thorn had been officially baptized.

Thirty-Three

After Betsey left town, things in Palestine started to get back to normal, proving the adage "out of sight, out of mind" to be true. While Betsey was incarcerated in town, she was blamed for every malady and infliction. From drought to constipation, if something bad happened, it was Betsey Reed's fault.

Now that she was in Lawrenceville, people had to look elsewhere for the cause of their tribulations. Wives blamed their husbands, husbands blamed the government, and preachers blamed the devil. There were more than a few who had a hard time looking into the mirror after their behavior on the night of the fire. If it wasn't for the fortitude of a ninety-year-old soldier, Palestine would have been scarred for many years because of the hysterical behavior of its citizens. It was decided that the jail would be rebuilt in Robinson, leaving only the charred foundation as a reminder of that infamous night.

Within a week, Squire Logan was back to work at his shop with only a few superficial burns left to heal. Within a month, the fall harvest started, and folks were too busy to worry about Betsey Reed. In September, when Judge Wilson changed the venue of the trial to Lawrenceville, it caused very little commotion. By Christmas, with the harshness of an early winter to endure, the Betsey Reed incident was a fading memory.

Sam McCarter convinced a justice of the peace to rule that Leonard and Betsey had defrauded him, and immediately took possession of the farm. He sent Betsey's personal effects to Sheriff Cullom for safekeeping and moved his oldest son into the cabin. Since Leonard hadn't survived until Halloween, Harrison Reed and Eveline Deal received nothing.

Eveline Deal and Thomas McKinney were married that winter and lived in a small cabin near New Hebron. They were planning on moving west, but they were forced to stay in the area because Eveline was the star witness for the prosecution at the upcoming trial. Without her testimony, Betsey would surely be acquitted.

Liddy had been planning to visit her Aunt Matilda in Cincinnati, so we decided that she should make the trip before the wedding. Since Matilda Parker and her two daughters were Liddy's only living relatives, she hoped they would accompany her back and attend the wedding. It would also give me a chance to get the cabin under the Five Sisters a bit more female friendly.

Upon her arrival, Liddy found her aunt to be gravely ill with malaria, and she was needed to help with her care. After two months she recovered fully, but wouldn't be able to travel until spring. We made the decision to postpone our wedding until Liddy's aunt could accompany her back to Illinois after the threat of bad weather had passed.

While she was away, some of the leaders of the Illinois State Democratic Party approached Augustus French about running for Governor. At first he denounced the idea as folly, but after persistent coercion, he decided to throw his hat into the ring. That's when he approached me about studying for the bar exam.

"Me, a lawyer? You've got to be joking!" I laughed out loud. "I'd be the butt of every joke in town. I'm usually the one telling the jokes. Where can you find a good lawyer? The graveyard."

"Very funny, Nathan," French laughed sarcastically. "But isn't it time you grew up? Now that you're getting married, you have to think of more than just yourself. It's one thing to get by on odd jobs when you're single, but you're going to have children to think about. I know Jesse Dubois paid for a fine college education, which you've failed to put to use. He agrees with me. He believes that you would make an outstanding lawyer."

"You've discussed this with Jesse?" I was feeling guilty

for my arrogance. Jesse Dubois had done so much for me and never asked for a thing in return. The fact that Augustus French, the leading Democrat in town, would meet with Jesse Dubois, the most influential Whig in this part of the state, to debate about my future both honored and humbled me.

"I wanted his input on a proposal I was thinking about making to you. I know he's like a father to you, and I wanted his blessing before proceeding. He made some suggestions, but overall he thought it would be an outstanding opportunity."

"What is it that you had in mind?" I asked cautiously.

"Work for me as my legal assistant while reading law every afternoon. I've decided, foolish as it may be, to make a run for the governorship. I've built what I feel is a successful law practice here in town, and I don't want to lose it if my campaign doesn't come to a triumphant ending. I would need you to handle the day-to-day operations of my office in my absence."

"But I don't know anything about the law," I protested.

"I didn't, either, before I studied under a crotchety old judge back in New Hampshire. Besides, I'll be handling all the legal matters. What I'll need from you is filing motions, meeting with clients in my absence, managing paperwork, gathering facts, and soliciting depositions."

"It all sounds like Greek to me," I said as my head spun wildly. "I don't know if you have the right man for the job."

"Nonsense! I know I have the right man! I watched how you handled Betsey Reed. You're a born barrister if there ever was one. Not to mention the Crockett name. Your Uncle Davy was a hero. That would certainly work to your advantage. But what it comes down to is whether you are willing to work hard and take advantage of a once-in-a-lifetime opportunity. Nathan, if you put your nose to the grindstone and study like I think you can, you'll be able to take the bar exam in a year. When you pass, I'll make you my partner. If things work out as I hope, being the law partner of the Governor of Illinois would be quite an opportunity for an ambitious young man, not to mention something to make a young wife proud."

By the time our conversation was finished, I realized he had presented his case in a manner that made it impossible to say anything but yes. He used guilt, obligation, duty, and family, all sugar-coated in a syrupy molasses pill, to get what he wanted. If he talked to the voters the same way he talked to me, I was convinced he would be elected governor. But Nathan Crockett Esquire...

Sheriff Sam Thorn realized that he didn't have the patience to deal with Betsey on an everyday basis, so he gave the job to the deputy county clerk, John Seed. Reverend John Seed, an Irish immigrant who had been successful in every venture he attempted, served as pastor for the local Methodist Church. Reverend Seed was the most saintly and non-judgmental soul in the county, and if he couldn't get along with Betsey, then it just couldn't be done. At forty years old, he had the demeanor of a man in his sixties, charming and grandfatherly. He saw only the good in people and prayed that the bad was only a temporary manifestation of the devil's influence. He saw Betsey Reed as a prime candidate to receive the Lord's salvation, and he went to work immediately.

When he first attempted to talk to Betsey, she ignored him, which only encouraged him to try harder. When he saw that Betsey had not touched her stew for dinner, he told her he didn't blame her for not wanting such poor fare, and he immediately marched home and brought her a basket containing fried catfish, cornbread, yams with butter, and a huge slice of peach cobbler. At first, Betsey was afraid to accept the food; she was sure there were probably strings attached, but she reluctantly gave in when her hunger triumphed, and she devoured the food like a ravenous wolf.

They repeated this ritual three times a day for the first week until Betsey finally gave in and spoke to Reverend Seed. She asked him why he was being so kind. If it was her soul he was trying to save, she told him not to bother; she was way past saving. "That's nonsense!" he told her, trying to be as sincere as he could. "I see you as God sees you. You're beautiful in his eyes."

"Then God must be blind," she replied, not exactly sure how to answer such a preposterous statement. She felt as if she were the most unlovable person in the world. It was a nice thought, but she believed she was beyond redemption.

Betsey eventually began to converse with Reverend Seed when he delivered her meals, and soon it became the highlight of her day. The talk was light and cordial, and there was never a word about the trial. At night, he would read stories from the Old Testament, followed by a short prayer. Betsey listened quietly with her eyes closed as Reverend Seed, with his heavy Irish brogue, made the characters come to life. She identified with the mark of Cain and the shame he must have felt. She gently ran her fingers over the scar on her face, all too aware of the insults that the mark must have incited. She also identified with the rejection Jacob's first wife must have felt when she realized that her husband wanted Rachel instead of her. After he left for the night, Betsey would close her eyes and envision herself in the deserts of the holy lands, being saved by a biblical hero. It helped to pass the time, but as soon as she opened her eyes, the reality of the iron bars of prison was there to greet her.

Every day was the same as the day before, and with the trial still several months away, she felt trapped and caged, despondent without hope. With a long prison sentence or even public execution in her future, Betsey started to contemplate committing suicide as a viable option to incarceration.

Sensing he might not be able to breach Betsey's granite-like disposition, Reverend Seed enlisted the help of his wife, Emily, and of Julia Ann Hennissee, the wife of the county clerk and a member of his congregation. He prayed that one of them would be able to kindle a friendship and hopefully help her let go of the inner turmoil that held her captive.

With Liddy in Ohio, I took up residence at the Dubois Tavern during the week and went home on the weekends to prepare the cabin for her return. Each afternoon, after completing my work at the law office, I spent two hours reading court records and decisions before dinner at the tavern. In the evening, I read ancient texts on the theory and history of the law by candlelight. If at all possible, I wanted to finish my studies and take the bar exam before Liddy's return.

The physical labor I performed on the weekend became a joy, as my muscles were begging to be used after a week of inactivity. I shingled the roof, added two windows to the south side of the cabin, and built a new outhouse that would be more suitable for my bride. I added a new stall to keep Newton and Ole Hickory separated and built a pen that would hold a new milk cow. To make the house more hospitable, I bought a new cast-iron skillet and an oversized kettle along with a new walnut table and matching chairs. I also purchased a cherry double bed and a new feather mattress along with new linen, which Adelia Dubois had chosen. It was a difficult period of separation, but it gave me comfort to turn the cabin into home for Liddy.

In the meantime, Augustus French was spending much of his time in Springfield, positioning himself for political advancement. French had become close friends with Stephen Douglas, Illinois' most prominent politician, whom many prognosticators thought would one day become president. Douglas was responsible for French seeking higher office at the next election. It was believed that the next governor would certainly be a Democrat, as the Whig party had become so unpopular on the frontier. Lyman Trumbull, who was serving as Illinois Secretary of State, was considered a front-runner for the 1846 election, but as a staunch abolitionist, he was considered too divisive. If nominated, he could tear the party apart, allowing the Whigs to win by default.

Douglas thought that French would make an ideal compromise candidate, as he had no political enemies, and with his steady, methodical approach to solving problems, he should be agreeable to all. However, some of the powers that be were concerned about him representing the notorious

Betsey Reed in her murder trial. News of her arrest and jail-burning had spread throughout the state like a prairie fire. Almost everyone had an opinion about the situation, so regardless of the outcome, half of the potential voters would be at odds with her lawyer. French refused to renege on his promise to defend Betsey, but did agree to find co-council and allow the other attorney to act as lead. French approached the flamboyant Usher Linder, from Charleston, who never missed an opportunity to get his name in the newspapers. Linder jumped at the chance to represent Betsey in the highly volatile case.

Governor Thomas Ford once made the statement that Usher Linder would be the greatest statesman the State of Illinois ever produced if it wasn't for his foul language and excessive drinking. No politician has ever spoken truer words. At 27 years of age, Usher F. Linder was elected Attorney General of Illinois and appeared to have an unlimited political future in the state. But Linder became an ardent states' rights and proslavery advocate, and in 1837, he incited the mob that murdered Elijah Lovejoy, the leader of the abolitionists, at an antislavery congress in Alton. Lovejoy became a martyr, and Linder was vilified. He moved to Charleston, where he was elected to the state legislature and started a law office, but because of the Lovejoy incident, his political career was doomed. He was appointed as a traveling circuit lawyer along with Abraham Lincoln, and they traveled from town to town whenever the courts were in session. It was during these court sessions that Linder earned his reputation for getting his clients acquitted, regardless of guilt or innocence. If anyone could keep Betsey Reed from the gallows, it was Usher Linder.

In early December, I was sent to Lawrenceville to inform Betsey that Mr. Linder would be arguing her case at the trial. Another reason for my visit was to see if two months in jail had softened her disposition to the point where she would assist in her own defense. Up to this point, she had refused to give her account of what happened during Leonard's final days, allowing Eveline's testimony to go unchallenged. It was imperative that she testify at the trial or at least cooperate enough that Linder could fight the allegations. Regardless, I was apprehensive about the visit.

The new Lawrence County jail and courthouse were two substantial, red brick buildings that sat in the middle of the public square on a hilltop above the Embarrass River. The jail was a much more secure facility than the former log structure in Palestine. The new jail was completed in the fall of 1844, and ironically replaced the old log jail that had been built by Isaac Fail, Betsey's brother.

Reverend Seed and a stubby jailer with tobacco stains on his shirt escorted me up a steep stairway to Betsey's cell. Seed was a tall, slender man with brownish-red hair and a long, well-groomed beard. Seed had an air of authority about him, yet seemed very humble in his mannerisms. "Ladies, may we enter?" he asked. Her cell was covered with a large patchwork quilt, which was used for privacy when needed.

Julia Ann Hennissee, a matronly woman in her thirties, pulled the quilt away and motioned for us to enter the cell. I could tell by the expression on Betsey's face that she wasn't expecting me. "What are you doing here?" she asked, as she suddenly sat upright and adjusted her hair nervously.

"Mr. Crockett is here on behalf of your attorney," interceded Reverend Seed. "He told me that you were acquainted, and there wouldn't be a problem if you met privately."

"I'll stay if you want me to," Mrs. Hennissee offered, as she looked at me skeptically.

"No, you can go," Betsey assured her. "I trust him."

Reluctantly, Mrs. Hennissee agreed, and she hastily closed her enormous Bible and strutted out of the cell. "I'll be down the hall if you need me," she declaied as she left, obviously not feeling comfortable about leaving us alone.

"And I'll be down the hall as well, if it's *you* that needs the help," Reverend Seed whispered into my ear as he closed the cell door behind me.

There was a small beam of light shining through a small, rectangular window in the middle of her cell. "How are they treating you here?" I was trying to act as professional as I could, but I had a hard time not feeling hypocritical due to my involvement with her over the past few years. I moved a wooden stool so I could sit directly across from her.

"Like the Queen of England," she blurted with a tone of cynicism. "It's jail. How do you think they're treating me?"

"They're not mistreating you, are they?" I asked.

"Why? What does it matter to you? And as a matter of fact, why are you here, anyway?" She sprang up from her bed and walked over to the window. She seemed uncomfortable when we made eye contact.

"I'm handling Mr. French's legal affairs while he's in Springfield. He wanted me to make sure that you are being treated well, and wanted us to do some groundwork for your defense."

"Are you some kind of lawyer now?"

"Actually, I'm studying to pass the bar exam." I moved my stool back against the wall to give her more breathing room, and she took her seat back on the cot.

She laughed brazenly. "Do you know how silly you seem in a suit? You look more like an undertaker or a snake-oil peddler if you ask me."

Biting my tongue, I agreed with her. I did feel like a fish out of water in the suit. "Please, Betsey, the reason I'm here is to try to help get you out of this mess. Your life is on the line; if you don't help your lawyers, they won't be able to help you."

"Lawyers?" She seemed surprised. "I have more than one?"

"That's one of the things I needed to talk to you about. Mr. French brought in the best defense attorney in the state to plead your case. His name is Usher Linder, and from what I hear, he almost never loses." I didn't tell her that French's motivation was strictly political and that Linder took the case to seek publicity.

"It doesn't matter," she stated stoically as she looked at the ceiling. "They're going to hang me no matter who defends me."

"They won't hang you if you tell your lawyers what they need to know," I pleaded. "You have to quit being defiant to the people who are trying to help you."

"You don't understand, Nathan! It's my destiny!"

"Destiny? Your destiny is to hang at the end of a rope?"

"Yes! Damn you! It is!" Tears started to well in her eyes, and she hid her face in her hands for a moment, then quickly regained her composure. "You wouldn't understand anyway."

"I'm trying to understand. But how can I understand if you don't tell me?"

She sighed then took a deep breath. "I saw a man hanged back in Kentucky when I was nine years old. His name was Will Davis. I'll never forget the name, because I see his pitiful eyes every night when I try to go to sleep. I heard that he slit a man's throat while stealing a hog. He was found guilty, and the whole town showed up for the hanging. It was one big shindig at the cutthroat's expense. But just before they dropped the rope, he looked directly into my eyes. I wanted to look away, but couldn't. It was if they were speaking to me. *This is your fate...You're going to be humiliated, scorned, and will die on the gallows, just like me.* Somehow, Will Davis was telling me to get ready. *They'll be coming for you some day...* They already have. They damn near got the job done in Palestine. I just wish they had finished it then. Now I have to go through it again." Betsey paused and began tracing the rope scars plainly visible on her neck.

"Let me get this straight," I interrupted. "You witnessed a hanging as a little girl, and right before the man died, his eyes told you that you were going to hang, too?

"I told you that you wouldn't understand. I don't know why I thought you were any different."

"I'm sorry, Betsey. I really want to understand. You have to admit that this isn't something a fellow hears every day. You're going to have to be patient with me. Please go on."

She seemed to accept my apology, and then closed her eyes as she continued. "I know that I've always been different. I've known that as long as I can remember. I used to go along with my father into the woods. We would gather bloodroot, wild ginger, snakeroot, lamb's ear, and sassafras to sell at the store. Pa was a healer, too, and he used the herbs for remedies when one of the neighbors got sick. He taught me everything he knew about tending the sick, but it was when he passed on his gift that things started to change.

"Pa was getting a bit feeble, and it became harder for him to go out into the woods, so I started to gather the roots on my own. One day when I returned, Ma and my brothers had gone to town, and Pa was waiting for me. He told me that he knew his health was failing and it was time to pass on his gift. That afternoon, he showed me how to blow fire, heal warts, stop bleeding, and blow the thrush out of babies. He told me it was my birthday gift. I didn't even realize that it was my birthday. When Ma came home, she got madder than a hornet. She was never that friendly to begin with, but from that day on, she hated me. That was the day I began to have premonitions. I started to see bad things happen before they actually happened. When I tried to warn people, they ignored me and called me a foolish child. When the calamity struck, they came back to me and called me a *witch* or a *devil*. Do you know what it's like to be declared a witch when you're nine years old?"

"It must have been difficult," I admitted.

"It was horrible! But the visions and premonitions got worse. At first, I only saw things that would happen to others, but it all changed on the day Will Davis was hanged. That's when I saw my future...my hanging."

"Maybe you saw the lynching in Palestine. The fact that you're still here means that the future can be changed." It felt illogical to give credence to what she was saying, but it was evident that she believed it.

"No, that was different from my vision. My hanging will take place during the daylight, and there will be thousands of people there to celebrate my demise. I will die alone and despised."

"So you're not going to help your lawyers because of a

vision you had when you were a little girl? That's ridiculous!"

"No, it's more than that," she continued. "I can see death. I can see it before it comes…and it's coming for me here."

"You can see death?" I was convinced that she was insane.

"Laugh if you want! It's true. Remember Green Baker? I didn't put a spell or curse on that boy. I just enlightened everyone as to what was about to happen. After he died, everyone said that it was all my fault. Betsey Reed, the wicked witch!"

I was trying to envision how I was going to explain this conversation to her lawyers. "So you're not going to help the men who are defending you?"

"What's the use? There's no reason to build my hope up. I know how this story ends: with the hanging of Betsey Reed."

What could I say? I called for Reverend Seed and walked to the cell door. "One thing before I go." I paused for a moment, not sure why I was asking the question. "Did you see death coming for Leonard?"

She seemed surprised. She paused, then smiled, "I didn't need the gift to see that Leonard was dying. Even a blind woman could see that."

As soon as Reverend Seed opened the door, Mrs. Hennissee rushed to Betsey's side, making sure I hadn't molested her. Convinced that her ward was not harmed, she opened her Bible and started reading a psalm out loud.

As we left the building, I shared my concerns with Reverend Seed that Betsey would almost surely hang if she didn't cooperate with her lawyers.

"She's a stubborn one, she is," he replied. "She feels she's beyond redemption."

"Has she mentioned anything about whether she killed her husband or not?" I asked, hoping for anything that might possibly help.

"Not a word. But then, I've never asked her. Man will judge her to be guilty or innocent; I'm only concerned about how she'll be judged when she stands before the white throne."

"Well, Reverend, if she does tell you something that might delay her arrival upstairs, will you let me know?"

"Of course I will," he winked as he replied. "Heaven will still be there."

Thirty-Four

The whiskey bottle shattered into pieces as it smashed against the brick wall. "I thought I was an obstinate sonofabitch," declared Usher Linder during his third tantrum of the day, "but Betsey Reed takes the cake."

I had arranged for Linder to use an empty room in the jail as his office during the trial. It was a small, windowless cube, furnished with an oak table, three rickety chairs, and an oil lamp. The doorway was barely six feet tall, so Linder, at six feet four inches, had to duck every time he entered. He made it crystal clear that he wasn't happy with the accommodations.

"I've tried to get her to talk about Leonard's death for the last few months," I explained, "All she says is that it doesn't matter because they're going to hang her no matter what she does."

"She's got that part right. If she doesn't change her demeanor, they'll hang her for certain. McCarter's testimony will give us some trouble, but I'll use it to muddy the water. I'll be able to countermand all of their witnesses except Eveline Deal. If she's believable, we'll be fighting an uphill battle. Mrs. Reed must get on the stand and defend herself. If she doesn't, she is doomed! Is there any chance at all that you can persuade her to change her mind?"

"I've tried everything," I said.

"What about the church woman, Mrs. Hennissee?" Linder opened up another bottle of whiskey and took an ample snort. "Can she talk to her?"

"She's only concerned with her soul. She refuses to speak about anything to do with the trial. Scripture and salvation; that's as far as it goes with her."

"It's a damn fine mess we find ourselves in, Mr. Crockett. Is there any news as to when Augustus French will be arriving?" He offered me a drink, but I passed after getting a whiff of his breath. Kerosene would smell like flowers compared to the hooch he was drinking.

"He's supposed to be here tomorrow morning." I was counting the minutes until his arrival, so Linder could focus his wrath on him instead of me.

Over five hundred people braved the rainy April weather just to get a chance to sit in the courtroom for the trial: *The State of Illinois versus Elizabeth "Betsey" Reed.* The room was just large enough to hold a hundred spectators, but over double that number had been allowed to enter. Tempers flared, and at least three fights erupted before the doors were opened. It seemed that everyone had an opinion as to the outcome of the trial. Most had already decided she was guilty, but a staunch few believed her to be innocent.

Usher Linder was relying on finding jurors who were sympathetic to Betsey's cause. Since Lawrenceville was only twenty miles south of Palestine, he was also counting on Augustus French to use his many acquaintances in Lawrence County to pick the jurors who were not prejudiced. But after interviewing only a few of the potential jurors, it was obvious that everyone had heard a version of the details of Leonard's death, not to mention the rumors of Betsey's wickedness. Instead of arguing before an impartial jury, they would face twelve men who already believed her to be guilty, while Aaron Shaw, the Lawrence County State's Attorney, would be preaching to the choir. After the defense and the prosecution agreed upon the jury, Augustus French bowed his head and said a quick prayer, his face void of color. Linder went out to find a new bottle of whiskey, while Aaron Shaw sat back with his hands behind his head, full of confidence. Arguments would begin in earnest the next morning.

The spectators in the courtroom fell silent when Sheriff Thorn escorted Betsey Reed to her seat. It was their first look at the green-eyed monster. She wore a simple gray flannel dress with her hair pulled tightly in a bun. If it wasn't for the fact that her legs were in irons, she looked as if she could be going to church. From my seat in the front row, directly behind the defense table, I could sense the animosity toward her. As soon as she took her seat between Linder and French, some of the spectators began to murmur.

"Scar-face! Murderer!" yelled a woman in the back of the courtroom.

"Burn in Hell!" cried another.

"Order in the courtroom!" shouted Judge William Wilson as he pounded his gavel. "I want order, and I want it now!" His voice boomed like a cannon shot, and the gallery became quiet once again. "I'll not tolerate any disruptions in my court room. A woman is on trial for her life, and if anyone wants to interfere with these proceedings, they can have thirty days in the county jail to think about it." Wilson was a huge, imposing man with a wide gait and a granite-like disposition. He had served as Chief Justice in the Illinois Supreme Court for twenty-seven years, so everyone knew there wouldn't be any appealing his decision. He glanced at the jury box to make sure the twelve jurors were situated and asked the foreman if he was ready for the trial to commence. The foreman nodded, and the judge ordered the clerk to read the indictment.

"The charges are as follows for the State of Illinois versus Elizabeth Reed: Elizabeth Reed, late of Crawford County and the State of Illinois, not having the fear of God before her eyes but being moved and seduced by the instigation of the Devil and of her own malice and forethought, on the date of August 19, 1844, did wickedly mix white arsenic poison into a half pint of sassafras tea and served it to her husband, Leonard Reed, causing his death; to wit, Elizabeth Reed is charged with the murder of Leonard Reed."

The judge turned his attention toward Betsey. "How does the defendant plead?"

Betsey, who had been staring blankly at the wall, refused to acknowledge the question, remaining silent and statuesque. After an uncomfortable pause, both Linder and French asked her to reply, but all she did was shrug and continue to stare at the wall. Red-faced and frustrated, Linder stood and adjusted his topcoat. "Mrs. Reed pleads not guilty, your honor."

Judge Wilson looked agitated by Betsey's irreverence, but said nothing and accepted the plea. "Mr. Shaw, you may begin your opening arguments."

"Gentlemen of the jury, you are about to hear a story of deceit and treachery that will haunt you for the rest of your lives. As we get into this trial, you will hear how Betsey Reed, a woman surely under the influence of the devil, placed enough poison to kill a team of horses into her poor, unsuspecting husband's sassafras tea. And after he finished the tea, she callously stood by and witched...I'm sorry; I mean watched him languish and agonize for hours until finally death mercifully took his soul...."

Aaron Shaw was an ambitious man who enjoyed confrontation and competition. He was a muscular six feet tall with coal black hair and a bald spot the size of a fist. He strutted like a prize rooster as he paced about the courtroom, keenly aware of his audience. He realized that public sentiment weighed heavily against Betsey Reed, and he hoped that sending her to the gallows would earn him the notoriety needed to launch his political career. And if he whipped Usher Linder in the process, all the better!

"...and in closing, I'm sure that all of you good citizens of Lawrence County will find there is only one conclusion as to what happened last August in that cabin at Heathsville. Elizabeth "Betsey" Reed murdered her husband, Leonard, in cold blood."

Usher Linder awkwardly stood and walked slowly toward the juror's box. "Leonard Reed was a sick man who had been in poor health for the last few years. He was dying of a stomach ailment, which can be verified by the prosecution's own witnesses. There was no need for Mrs. Reed to kill her husband, as he had one foot firmly planted in his grave at the time the murder supposedly took place. Even if she wanted her husband dead, there was no motive for her to act upon that desire. Leonard Reed was killed by his own decaying body. Nothing more. My worthy adversary will try to feed upon your fears and prejudices, portraying Mrs. Reed as a monster, a demon, or even a witch, but regardless of what you believe about the defendant, this trial is not a witch-hunt. Betsey Reed is not on trial for being a witch. She is on trial for the crime of murder, a crime that she had no motive to commit."

That afternoon, Aaron Shaw called Doc Logan and Doc Wynn to testify. Both men stated that it was their medical opinion that Leonard Reed died of arsenic poison. Both men also stated that they didn't come to this conclusion until they saw the piece of paper that had formerly contained two drachmas of arsenic. When asked if he was certain that the paper contained arsenic, Doc Logan stated he was not only sure, but he knew for a fact that the arsenic had come from his apothecary in Russellville.

When Linder cross-examined the doctors, both stated that Leonard had been in failing health for quite some time, and their opinion was that he did not have long to live at the time of his supposed poisoning. But it was Doc Logan's testimony he decided to scrutinize.

"Doctor Logan, did you consider arsenic poison to be the cause of Leonard Reed's illness before Eveline Deal made her accusations?" Linder stood next to the juror's box in order for him to speak directly to the jury.

"No, I didn't. I considered his stomach to be in a gangrenous state from natural causes."

"Surely a doctor of your experience would see evidence of poisoning?"

"Not necessarily," Logan replied without emotion.

"So if Miss Deal had never made her accusations, Leonard Reed would be dead and buried, and there wouldn't be a shred of doubt in your mind that he died of natural causes."

"I suppose so."

"Is it fair to say, Doctor Logan," Linder paused for effect, "that if it weren't for the accusations of Eveline Deal, we wouldn't be here today?"

"Objection!" shouted Aaron Shaw. "How would the doctor know whether we would be here?"

"Sustained," ruled Judge Wilson.

"Let me rephrase the question. Doctor Logan, Betsey Reed was indicted on your sworn testimony that Leonard died as a result of arsenic poisoning. If Eveline Deal had never made the accusations, you would have never testified against Mrs. Reed. Is that a fair and correct assumption on my part?"

Logan sighed. "Yes, that would be a fair assumption."

"So without your testimony, there would have never been an inquest, never have been a trial, and all these good people in the courtroom, including Mrs. Reed, would be home minding their own business."

"Objection!" shouted Shaw.

"Question withdrawn!" responded Linder. "I suppose we're fortunate that our renowned doctor had a teenage girl to assist in his diagnosis."

"Objection!"

"Sustained. Ask a question or take a seat, counselor," Judge Wilson ordered.

Linder shrugged his shoulders and sat down. He remained silent for about ten seconds, then shot out of his chair. He walked briskly back to the juror's box, pausing briefly as he made sure that he had everyone's attention. "You were a witness to Leonard Reed's final moments, were you not?"

"I was," responded Logan.

"Was Mr. Reed in a lot of pain?"

"Excruciating, I would have to say."

Linder paced before the jurors, gently massaging his chin. "After you administered opium for the pain, what else was done or could be done to ease his distress?"

Doc Logan took a deep breath and closed his eyes, attempting to recall the moment. "At that point, all that could be done was to massage his stomach with warm towels and keep cold towels on the rest of his body to deal with the fever."

"And you did this yourself?"

"No, I didn't," answered Doc Logan hesitantly.

"You mean you just allowed him to suffer?" Linder fired back in mock disgust.

"Of course not. Mrs. Reed was attending to her husband."

"Mrs. Reed? Do you mean Betsey Reed?"

"Of course."

Linder shook his head and ran his fingers through his hair. "Give me a moment to get my facts straight, Doctor Logan. If accusations were made claiming that Betsey Reed had poisoned her husband, why did you allow her to act as his nurse? Weren't you afraid she might do him in?"

"No, not at all." Doc Logan began to shift in his chair, as the tone of questioning made him seem a bit uncomfortable.

"May I ask why?" Linder prodded.

"Because Mrs. Reed was doing everything she possibly could to ease his pain."

"But according to you, she had just poisoned her husband, and now you're saying she was trying to ease his pain. I don't understand. Let me ask you this, Doctor Logan. Was she jovial while she was tending Mr. Reed?"

"No. She seemed distraught," Logan responded.

"Define distraught, Doctor...please."

"She was crying and weeping and seemed to be agonizing about her husband's condition."

Linder paced around the courtroom again to let the jury ponder Doc Logan's reply. "Crying and weeping. I've been involved in many murder trials, but I have yet to hear of any murderers who cried and wept over the victims while trying to ease their suffering. Doesn't that seem a bit strange to you, Doctor Logan?"

"Yes. I must admit that it does."

"Doctor, do you remember making a statement, moments before Leonard Reed's death, about your opinion of Mrs. Reed's guilt or innocence based on your observations of her bedside manner?"

Doc Logan paused for what seemed like an eternity. The

silence was deafening, and for the first time, Betsey stopped staring at the wall and turned to hear his answer. "I said that she was tender and loving toward him, that she seemed to be sincerely grieving over his condition, and that I was convinced that she was...innocent."

"You were convinced that she was innocent?"

"I was, at that time."

"What changed your mind, Doctor Logan?"

"It was when I studied the piece of paper that contained the arsenic. That's when I started to believe that she was guilty." Still acting unconcerned and emotionless, Betsey turned once again toward the wall.

"Based on Eveline Deal's word?" Linder asked.

"Objection," Aaron Shaw erupted. "Doctor Logan's already answered the question."

"Sustained," ruled Judge Wilson. "Move on, Mr. Linder."

Linder looked down at his fingers and seemed to be mumbling to himself. "I'm having trouble connecting the dots. Doctor Logan, you said that the arsenic came from your store. Did you sell the arsenic to Mrs. Reed?"

"Not to my knowledge."

"Did one of your employees sell the arsenic to Mrs. Reed?"

"One of them must have; how else did she get it? It came from my office."

"Is there an employee in your hire who will testify that he sold arsenic to Mrs. Reed?"

"No."

"So, as far as you know, anyone could have purchased the arsenic?"

"I guess so." Doc Logan wiped his forehead with a handkerchief, and for the first time, he looked unsure of himself.

"So what you're saying is there is no proof at all that Betsey Reed bought arsenic at your store, and yet you're willing to send a woman to the gallows based on your flawed logic and the word of a spiteful girl!"

"Objection!" shouted Shaw as the courtroom erupted in clamor.

"Question withdrawn!" Linder shouted. "I'm finished with the witness." Linder fumbled through his notes and took a seat, while Betsey remained oblivious to the proceedings.

Linder had managed to countermand both of the doctors' testimonies to the point where any reasonable man would have a measure of doubt as to the cause of Leonard Reed's death. While standing outside the courtroom, even Doc Logan admitted he was starting to doubt whether his diagnosis was correct. It was clear that Betsey Reed's fate would be determined by the credibility of Eveline Deal's testimony.

That afternoon, Harrison Reed testified that Eveline had given him the paper that had allegedly contained the arsenic. He stated that he suspected Betsey had been plotting to kill Leonard for some time. He went on to say that he had heard rumors that Betsey had a new lover from the Russellville area and that they were going to be married as soon as she got the title to the farm. Linder came out swinging with his cross-examination; within minutes, it was evident that Harrison despised Betsey and would say anything to see her hang. After a few more minutes of prodding, Harrison Reed admitted that it was actually he who started the rumor about Betsey's secret lover, and he left the witness chair, completely discredited.

The trial came to an abrupt halt when Aaron Shaw stated that John Herriman, the Reeds' neighbor, had failed to appear, and that his testimony was vital to the case. Judge Wilson adjourned court for the day and ordered Herriman to appear within 48 hours or be held in jail for contempt of court. As soon as the gavel dropped, Sheriff Thorn led Betsey back to her cell. She remained placid and indifferent, ignoring the taunts and jeers of the spectators, careful not to give any inkling of her vulnerability. Even though Usher Linder had battered all of the prosecution's witnesses that day, Betsey still believed her situation was hopeless.

Back in the dark defense office, Usher Linder's outlook

was a little more optimistic. "Shaw is worried," Linder said, as he opened up a new bottle of whiskey. "He's not going to call McCarter to the stand."

"Why in heaven not?" asked Augustus French, refusing a drink as Linder offered him the bottle. "The clause that gave Betsey ownership of the land if Leonard died before Halloween establishes motive. He'd be a fool if he didn't take advantage of it."

Linder took a huge swig, then wiped his mouth on his shirtsleeve. "He's no fool. He knows that if he introduces the plot into evidence, I'll be able to drag Eveline Deal through the mud for her involvement in the counterplot. After the jury learns that she had agreed to help McCarter foreclose on her uncle's farm for money, her testimony will be severely tainted. Just as I predicted, the entire trial will be decided by Eveline Deal's performance on the witness stand."

"What's keeping you from bringing up her involvement yourself?" French asked.

"I can't, because he'll bring up Betsey's motive and we'll be sunk like a rowboat full of milk cows. It's a Kentucky standoff. The entire plot helps both sides, but it hurts both sides, too. But in this case, whoever brings the matter up first is going to lose. Whatever good her testimony would do, it would be devastating during cross-examination."

"It definitely weakens their case if Shaw doesn't establish motive," said French.

"He's going to turn this into a witch-hunt. Good versus evil. Shaw seems absolutely certain that Eveline Deal's testimony will be enough for the jury to convict." Linder's confidence seemed to grow with each drink.

"You don't think she is up for the task?" asked French.

"Let's just say I like my chances." Linder leaned back in his chair, his feet on the desk with his head resting in his hands.

"Nathan, what do you think about Eveline's chances against our esteemed colleague?"

"Please, Nathan," added Linder. "After all, you almost

married the girl."

I had remained silent up to that point, feeling a bit uneasy about Linder's bravado. "I wouldn't underestimate Eveline's resolve. She's consumed with hatred for Betsey, and can be quite mercenary at times. She's had several months to prepare herself for this moment. She wants Betsey dead, and she is going to do whatever she has to do to make it happen."

"Hell hath no fury like a woman scorned, eh, Nathan?" laughed Linder. "Poppycock!"

That evening, after dinner, Augustus French and I visited Betsey in her jail cell. Mrs. Hennissee offered to leave us alone, but Augustus insisted that she hear what he had to say. Linder decided not to accompany us, fearing he might lose his patience and cause a scene.

"I'm going to be totally frank with you, Mrs. Reed," French pleaded. "Even though the trial is going well, we will be in dire straits if you don't testify tomorrow. To this point, all the testimony against you has been secondhand, but Eveline Deal claims she saw you put poison into Leonard's tea. If you don't dispute her claims, the jury will assume she is telling the truth. I need to know you will take the stand on your own behalf." French looked directly into Betsey's eyes. "Will you testify?"

"How many times have I told you? It doesn't matter what I say. They are not going to believe me. They'll never take my word over the word of that conniving little whore. I'm not going to give anyone the satisfaction of watching me beg for my life."

"That's suicide!" shouted French.

"That may be," said Betsey calmly," but it's the way things are going to be."

"Mrs. Hennissee, can't you talk some sense into her?" French implored.

"We've talked about the subject at great length, and I'm afraid she's made up her mind," admitted Mrs. Hennissee.

"Very well then. We'll just have to do the best we can." French said goodnight, then called for the deputy to open the door.

As soon as we were out of earshot, I asked French what he thought the odds were if she didn't testify. "I'm not as optimistic as Linder, but regardless, he'll make it most unpleasant for Miss Deal."

There seemed to be even more people in the courtroom than there were the day before. The spectators knew that Betsey Reed's fate would be determined that day, and everyone wanted to get a glimpse of history. At Linder's request, Betsey was allowed to enter the courtroom without wearing shackles. He felt that it unfairly prejudiced the jury, and Judge Wilson agreed. After John Herriman appeared, Aaron Shaw decided that his testimony wasn't needed, and notified the court that he planned to call his star witness instead: Eveline Deal McKinney.

As Eveline was being sworn in as a witness, the courtroom went completely silent in anticipation. I have to admit that I was stunned by her appearance. Her hair was pulled back tight and covered with a stylish, black wool hat adorned with a small yellow ribbon. Ringlets of curls were allowed to fall against each cheek, flaunting her youth, yet still within the bounds of proper courtroom decorum. She wore a style of conservative tailored dress that was popular among the wealthier families in the area, and looked more like the wife of a Presbyterian minister than the young bride of a poor dirt farmer.

As soon as she sat down in the witness chair, Eveline explained to the court that she had been married recently, and requested that she be addressed as Mrs. McKinney. Judge Wilson offered his congratulations and instructed the lawyers to honor her wishes.

After establishing the fact that Eveline was living with the Reeds, Shaw's questions shifted to the morning of Leonard's death. "Mrs. McKinney, please tell the court exactly what you witnessed on the morning of Leonard Reed's death."

Eveline was completely poised and answered each question in a sincere manner. Noticing that Betsey was staring in the opposite direction, Eveline spoke directly to the defense table, which made her statements seem more believable. "While I was cleaning the cabin, I noticed that Betsey took a small piece of paper from behind the dinner plates and emptied the contents into Uncle Leonard's tea. It was a white powder, and I assumed it was sugar or some kind of medicine."

"But then something made you suspicious, did it not?" asked Aaron Shaw.

"After she emptied the paper, instead of throwing it into the fireplace, she threw it out the door. But instead of falling to the ground, it got caught on the threshold. I could tell she thought I hadn't seen what she had done, so I continued with my cleaning. That's when she took the tea to Uncle Leonard. As soon as he swallowed the first bit of tea, he started to cough and choke, and then he fell to the ground, all doubled up. Betsey yelled at me to help get him into bed so she could tend to him. As soon as he was in bed, she put a towel in hot water and held it against Uncle Leonard's stomach. When she wasn't looking, I went to the door, found the piece of paper, and hid it in my apron. Then I reached behind the plates and found another piece of paper with more white powder still inside. I grabbed it and ran out of the house as fast as I could. I ran to Mr. Herriman's house and told him what had happened. He helped me saddle Uncle Leonard's horse, and I rode directly to Harrison Reed's for help."

"Why didn't you stay and help your uncle?" asked Shaw.

"I was afraid Betsey would kill me," Eveline answered

"Surely Mr. Herriman would have helped."

"Mr. Herriman was afraid she would kill him, too. People tend to end up dead if they cross Betsey Reed." Eveline sounded believable and her story sounded plausible, but anyone who knew her could see she was putting on an act. For the first time in the trial, Betsey seemed to be paying attention to the testimony. When Betsey started glaring at the witness stand, Eveline became a little less sure of herself. "Green Baker and Doyle Popplewell...both are dead because of her."

"Objection!" shouted Linder. "She's making up stories!"

"Overruled. You can dispute it during cross-examination," replied Judge Wilson.

"I'll rip her to shreds in cross-examination," whispered Linder to French. "All I need to do is catch her in one little lie and it will destroy her credibility."

"She almost killed Squire Logan," Eveline added. "Her first husband disappeared without a trace—"

"Objection!" cried Linder.

"—not to mention Uncle Leonard's two young boys. They both died while in her care," shouted Eveline over the voice of Linder.

Judge Wilson became visibly upset with the commotion and started pounding his gavel, frantically calling for order.

"Hang the witch," shouted a woman in the courtroom, followed by the jeers of countless others.

During the chaos, no one noticed that Betsey had crouched down and was ready to strike. Before anybody could react, she jumped over the table and ran to the witness stand. Eveline's eyes widened in horror as Betsey grabbed her by the hair and slammed her face into the rail at least a half dozen times before Sheriff Thorn managed to come to her aid. As he pulled her away, Betsey managed to rake her fingernails across Eveline's face, causing blood to flow from several wounds, not to mention the blood streaming from her obviously broken nose. Eveline collapsed like a broken doll and fell to the floor with a sickening thud. While running to his wife's aid, Thomas McKinney stopped to take a swing at me for old time's sake. He caught me squarely on the jaw, causing bells to sound in my head, jarring me to my core. I started to retaliate, but decided against it because of Eveline's condition.

Usher Linder and Augustus French watched in silent disbelief as a pair of deputies carried Eveline out of the courtroom. Both realized their case was doomed along with Betsey Reed's life.

Sam Thorn managed to get Betsey secured in a closet before a lynch mob could be organized. He deputized ten extra men and positioned them at both entrances to the jail, and then with the help of Reverend Seed, he escorted Betsey back to her cell. Judge Wilson called the attorneys back to his office. Linder told the judge that, under the circumstances, he wouldn't make Eveline Deal face cross-examination and would not be calling Betsey as a witness.

Later that afternoon, with Betsey back in her cell, both attorneys made the closing arguments in less than fifteen minutes. Judge Wilson sent the jury to deliberate until a unanimous verdict could be reached. Within an hour, the jury members returned with grim expressions on their faces. The gallery cheered when the foreman read the verdict: guilty. Judge Wilson adjourned the court until the next morning; at that time, he would announce Betsey's sentence.

That night, Augustus French was called home due to an illness in his family. I doubt anyone was actually sick, but it gave him an excuse to be absent when Judge Wilson passed judgment. Usher Linder passed out at his desk in the jailhouse office after a night of heavy drinking. Eveline Deal McKinney was recovering in bed at a local doctor's office. Julia Ann Hennissee read psalms by candlelight as Betsey sat silently on her bed.

I went to see Betsey in an attempt to get her to show remorse and throw herself on the mercy of the court, but she refused to acknowledge my presence. I ended up walking to the Yellow Banks Tavern, where I had rented an upstairs room to use during the trial. I met a reporter by the name of John Gimble who was covering the trial for the *New York Herald*. He said that, after the trial, he planned to write a book titled *The Legend of Elizabeth Reed*. He assured me it would become a bestseller. He then introduced me to a mountain of a man with long, unruly gray hair and matching beard, who was drinking the Blue Ruin straight from the jug. When he said his name was Isaac Fail, I hesitated a bit before shaking his hand. He was Betsey Reed's infamous big brother. He wanted to thank me for trying to help his sister, which I was relieved to hear. It would take a bullet to stop a man his size if he decided to start trouble.

"That girl was born under a dark cloud," he declared. "It's a wonder she's lived this long. She's always been as wild as an Indian, and she never learned to walk away from a fight. I've saved her so many times I can't even count, but she's got herself jammed up so good, there's nothing I can do to get her out of this mess. I'd break her out of the jail if I could, but it seems to be escape-proof."

"Maybe they'll send her to prison." I tried to offer him some hope.

He shook his head and patted me on the back. "You know as well as I do that after she busted up that little girl today, she doesn't have a snowball's chance in hell of avoiding a date with the hangman."

I shrugged and took a snort from his jug.

The courtroom was silent as Judge Wilson walked to his desk. Betsey was wearing a new set of shackles along with the same gray dress. Three deputies and Sheriff Thorn sat directly behind her, ready to pounce if she made a move. Amazingly, and against the doctor's instructions, Eveline was present with her face heavily bandaged and both eyes hideously blackened like a raccoon's. Nothing was going to cheat her out of her moment of victory. I noticed Isaac Fail standing in the corner of the courtroom with his back against the back wall. I hoped that someone had checked for concealed weapons at the door.

Judge Wilson shuffled some papers, then rapped the gavel and declared that court was in session. "First of all, is there anything the defendant would like to say before her sentence is read?"

Betsey looked at the judge and calmly spit on the floor, then turned away and looked at the wall. Usher Linder covered his face in shame.

"In that case, I have no choice," declared Judge Wilson as he put on a pair of gold-rimmed reading spectacles. "Elizabeth Reed, being found guilty of the murder of your late husband, Leonard Reed, it is the judgment of the law and of this court that you be taken from this courtroom to your place of confinement at the county jail. And on the twenty-third day of May, you will be taken from there to a convenient place within one mile of this courthouse and there be hanged by the neck until you are dead. The court also orders that Sheriff Thorn of Lawrence County, Illinois, execute this sentence." He paused a moment as he removed his spectacles. "And may the Lord have mercy on your soul."

The courtroom erupted in celebration as soon as the gavel dropped. Some ran outside to inform the hundreds of people waiting, while others cheered and hurled insults. Eveline Deal McKinney displayed a smile of satisfaction as she was carried back to her room above the doctor's office. Julia Ann Hennissee immediately started to weep. Betsey remained stoic and indifferent. Within minutes, the courtroom was empty with the exception of Isaac Fail, who was still lurking in the corner as the posse led Betsey back to her cell. I sat in my chair, silently pondering the irony of the situation, thinking how much better off things would have been if Betsey had died in the fire or been lynched by the mob in Palestine. Either way, Betsey Reed would have ended up dead. In essence, the trial allowed the citizens of Illinois to sleep at night knowing she received a fair trial before they killed her.

Two hours later, Usher Linder was on his way home to Charleston where he planned to appeal to Governor Ford. He was fairly optimistic that the Governor wouldn't want to have Betsey Reed's hanging as a blemish on his legacy and that a reprieve was a definite possibility. I agreed to remain in Lawrenceville and tend to Betsey's needs, and was authorized to act on her behalf in any way I saw fit.

That evening, Reverend Seed escorted me up the dark stairway to Betsey's cell. Julia Ann Hennissee was reading scripture as usual, but with a tinge of urgency in her voice. Betsey sat calmly on her bed, content with her company, unmindful of the fact that she was condemned to die in four weeks. She did request that I bring her stationery so she could write some letters, but other than that, she said she was quite content. As much as I wanted to, I refrained from asking her to confess what happened on the day Leonard died. Since she had already been found guilty, there wouldn't be any harm if she came clean, but I felt it would be too tawdry to ask at that time.

Thirty-Five

Governor Thomas Ford sat quietly in his executive office at Fifth and Adams in Springfield. He had always believed that decisive law and order was a necessity in a frontier state. An eye for an eye and a tooth for a tooth had worked for thousands of years. Who was he to change the due course of law? He had personally sent men to the gallows during his years as a state judge. Why was this any different? Why should this Reed woman not be put to death for murdering her husband? The law was executing the sentence, not him personally. But somehow, this case had become personal. His wife had made sure of that.

His charming and demure Francis had suddenly banished him to the guest bedroom. Under no circumstance would she sleep with a man who was about to murder a woman. When he explained that it was a jury of her peers who had condemned her to death, she asked, "How many women were on the jury?"

"Why…none, of course. Women don't serve on juries."

"Then it wasn't a jury of her peers," she rebutted. "If women were allowed to sit on juries, we would soon be missing a good number of pompous husbands, not to mention governors. There is only one man on this earth who can spare that woman's life, and that is you, Thomas Ford! You can do the right thing or go down as a modern-day Pontius Pilate."

The last thing Thomas Ford wanted was to be known as the man who washed his hands of the Elizabeth Reed situation. Someday, Illinois would execute a woman, but it wasn't going to happen on his watch. He called for his secretary. "Mrs. Agar, please take a letter and see that it gets to the Lawrence County Courthouse as quickly as possible."

The stern and steady Mrs. Agar copied the letter in

230

triplicate, placed the letter (titled "conditional reprieve") into a brown envelope, and sealed it with hot wax and the governor's stamp. She called for a courier and sent the life-sparing document on its way to Lawrenceville. Governor Ford would sleep in his own bed that night.

Judge William Wilson read the letter three times before throwing it on his roll-top desk in disgust. "What the hell does this mean? 'Please commute the sentence to life in prison as long as Mrs. Reed is contrite, showing the proper amount of remorse for her wrongdoing, and there is no chance for a civil uprising as a result of this potential act of clemency.' I've never seen such a load of political babble."

"Is it a stay of execution or not?" asked Sheriff Thorn.

"Well, it is, and it isn't," replied Judge Wilson. "Basically, what Governor Ford is saying is that as long as she says she's sorry, and it doesn't stir up too much of a fuss, he'd like to consider himself a bit of a humanitarian."

"So we don't have to hang her?"

"I don't think we'd have any problems getting her to say she felt remorse if it meant avoiding the noose, but it's the second condition I'm worried about." The judge reached into the bottom drawer of his desk and pulled out a bottle of O'Boyle's Finest.

"What do you mean?" Thorn was uneasy about Judge Wilson's tone of voice.

"It's the part about no civil uprising that has me concerned." He filled his glass and took a deep swallow. "Sam, go over to the window and tell me what you see."

Thorn walked over to the window and looked down on the public square. "Sure is a bunch of people down there."

"And why are there so many people here today?" asked the judge.

"I suppose they're here for the hanging," Thorn replied.

"Sam, there are over two thousand people in town for the execution, and it's still a week away. By the time next Friday gets here, there are likely to be ten thousand people looking for blood. They almost lynched her in Palestine last year. If we don't go ahead with the execution, they'll burn the jail down and do the job themselves."

"I'd never let that happen," Thorn said with a hint of defiance. "I'll deputize twenty good men and move them into the jail."

"You're a good man, Sam, but you're not a match for a mob of that size. Once vigilantism gets set into motion, you're likely to have the regulator and flathead skirmishes like they have down in Massac County." Judge Wilson finished his drink and wiped the glass carefully dry with his handkerchief. He placed it, along with the bottle, back into the same drawer in precisely the same spot. "No, Sam, I'm not going to put you in a situation where you and your deputies are in danger. Betsey Reed *has* to hang for the good of society. And I don't feel a damn bit good about it at all. And, Sam…" The judge hesitated as he looked out the window at the throng of activity. "…When you place the noose around her neck, make sure the knot is positioned directly behind her left ear. It will snap her neck and kill her instantly. If you don't, it could take up to ten minutes for her to strangle. Trust me…it isn't a pleasant sight."

Sam nodded solemnly to acknowledge the advice and then silently left the room. As soon as the door was closed behind him, he ran outside and found a spot behind a mulberry bush and became violently ill.

Betsey had never liked Fridays. She didn't have a logical reason for her dislike of the day, but bad things always seemed to happen on Fridays. As she looked out her cell window at the growing crowd below, she realized that her final Friday would be her worst. She had long since forgotten her childhood dream of becoming a preacher's wife and being the envy of her neighbors. That was a different life, a life where you could look forward to seeing the sunrise and hope for a better day. For the first time, she realized there wouldn't be any better days. She was the green-eyed monster getting what she deserved.

"Burn her at the stake, that's the proper death for a witch," taunted a woman out on the street. Betsey fell to the floor with a sharp pain to her stomach. Maybe she would die before they killed her. If she was going to spoil everyone's party, she would have to act quickly. She took the back end of her spoon and chipped away at the mortar with reckless abandon. It didn't matter if they caught her now. She would rather die a horrible death on her jail-room floor than allow herself to be humiliated in public.

She started eating the rocks and mortar pieces as soon as they hit the floor. She could feel the inside of her throat tearing apart as she tried to swallow. She crawled over to the water bucket and washed down what she could. Another sharp pain in her lower abdomen overwhelmed her as she sat up, resting her head on her knees. "Just let me die! I can't take any more!" For the first time in her adult life, Betsey Reed broke down and cried like a baby. She wailed and lamented for over an hour until she fell prostrate, exhausted but resolved to her fate.

When Mrs. Hennissee arrived and found her in such vulnerable condition, she realized that her work had not been in vain. She called for Reverend Seed, and Betsey, in her broken state, asked for forgiveness and redemption. After a short prayer, Reverend Seed declared that she was washed in the blood of the Lamb and was born again.

When Reverend Seed informed me of Betsey's salvation, I have to admit I was somewhat skeptical, but after meeting with her in her cell, I was convinced she was sincere. She cried and wept and praised the Lord and then cried and wept some more. She began confessing her life's work of evil deeds, begging for forgiveness after each act. I left before she was finished, as it was an extremely long list of sins. She never mentioned poisoning Leonard, however, which I considered to be odd.

Sheriff Thorn was impressed with the change also, and he informed me of the governor's conditional reprieve and Judge Wilson's response. I immediately sent letters by stagecoach to Usher Linder in Charleston and to Augustus French in Palestine, informing them of Governor Ford's reprieve and requesting immediate action. But with Betsey's execution date only a week away, I knew there wouldn't be time to get a request and response back from Springfield in time to save Betsey's life.

On Thursday morning, I received a short letter in my room at the Yellow Banks Tavern from Augustus French.

> My dear Nathan,
>
> In response to your letter, Linder and I were already aware of Governor Ford's conditional offer of clemency for Mrs. Reed and of Judge Wilson's decision not to issue a stay of execution. The reason given was fear of causing a public uprising. You remember how matters got out of control in Palestine; I could only imagine the riot that would break out with the horde that is now migrating to Lawrenceville. Governor Ford will not overrule Judge Wilson's decision. Mrs. Reed will be hanged on Friday. Please do what you can to make her last hours as comfortable as possible, and return home safely as soon as it is prudent.
>
> Sincerely yours,
>
> A.C. French

That's when I realized Betsey Reed was going to die in the morning. Even though she had been a condemned woman for a month, I had always believed her sentence would be reduced to life in prison. I thought that maybe the salvation of her soul would be reason enough for a reprieve, but then I realized there were quite a few conversions beneath the shadow of the gallows. Nevertheless, I was more than a little agitated that neither French nor Linder would be attending the hanging, leaving me to tend to the dirty business. Degrading jokes about unethical lawyers began to come to mind. *Did you hear the one about the two lawyers who were too busy to see their client hanged?*

As I walked to the jail that night, I had to navigate my way between hundreds of wagons that had recently appeared, forming a town-within-a-town as they encamped around the jail and courthouse in the public square. There were thousands of people, some from as far as one hundred miles away, who had made the journey to witness the hanging. I shook my head, contemplating the dark side of human nature.

When I arrived at the jail, I informed Sheriff Thorn about the letter from French and that there wouldn't be a pardon from the governor. His face went pale, and I realized he was dreading her hanging more than anybody. "I spent my day building the gallows down by the river, hoping I wouldn't have to use them. I tied a bag of sand to the rope and made three practice drops to make sure it would hold her weight. It worked perfectly all three times." Thorn started to choke up, but quickly regained his composure. "I tried to resign as sheriff today, but Judge Wilson wouldn't let me—and rightfully so. If I don't hang Betsey Reed, someone else will have to do it, and it won't be any easier on him. I still think the Crawford County Sheriff should have to be the executioner, though. After all, it's his murder in the first place."

"How's Betsey doing?" I asked.

"Other than the fact that she's vomiting blood, she's fine," replied Thorn, attempting gallows humor.

"Vomiting blood?" I couldn't tell if he was serious.

"It seems that Betsey wanted to do herself in. About a week ago, she started eating brick mortar and rocks in the hope that she would kill herself before we did. Then she got saved, but the rocks are still inside her. The doctor says she's torn up real bad. She'd probably bleed to death within a couple of weeks if we let her live that long. Maybe the hanging will save her from suffering. At least, that's what I try to tell myself."

"Is she in a lot of pain?" I asked.

"Not since they told her she could get baptized in the river tonight. It seemed to lift her spirits."

"Baptized? Has the judge lost his mind?"

"The judge doesn't know about it," Thorn admitted.

"Are you out of your mind? What if she escapes?" I had visions of Isaac Fail lurking in the shadows, waiting to save his little sister, killing anyone who got in his way.

"We'll wait till two in the morning, sneak her out the back door, throw her in a wagon, ride down to the river, dunk her under a couple of times, and have her back in her cell within thirty minutes."

"And Reverend Seed went for this scheme?"

"It was his idea," Thorn said. "Besides, I'll feel a lot better about killing her if she's saved and baptized. I'll be more like a conductor on a riverboat than her executioner. I'll just be punching her ticket and sending her upriver. The reason I'm telling you this is that she asked that you be present at the baptism."

"You've got to be joking. There's no way in hell that I'm going to be a part of breaking her out of jail. What if someone recognizes her? It could start a riot."

"You're supposed to be tending to her needs," he pleaded. "As far as I can tell, nobody's needed a baptizing worse than Betsey Reed. I sure hoped you'd be there, just in case somebody raised a fuss."

"That's exactly why I'm not going to be there," I said sternly. "Absolutely not! No! No! No!"

The Embarrass River was colder than I thought it would be. We had made the half mile journey down the hill without the benefit of a lantern or torch, hoping not to be noticed. Once we got beyond the campfires, it became increasingly hard to see; there was only a quarter moon, and it was about to be shrouded in clouds. That was probably a good thing, since the gallows was only a hundred yards downriver. Since the current was so strong, Reverend Seed recruited me to help steady Betsey as we walked out into the waist deep water, seeing as Sheriff Thorn conveniently forgot to say that he didn't know how to swim. As we put our arms behind Betsey's back, I could fell her tremble and sway, barely able to keep her balance. She crossed her arms tight against her chest as we submerged her beneath the water. *"In the name of the Father...the Son...and the Holy Ghost... "*

Cold and drenched, I reached my bed at the Yellow Banks Tavern at about two hours before dawn. I can't remember a time, before or since, when I have been so utterly exhausted. But no matter how hard I tried, I was unable to force myself to go to sleep. Thirty minutes after sunrise, I went downstairs and drank some steaming coffee. I tried to eat a plate of bacon and eggs, but as soon as it was served, I realized I had no appetite at all.

Thirty-Six

The Reverend John Seed walked solemnly down the jailhouse stairs, clutching his black preaching Bible in his left hand. Betsey Reed was following, wearing a snow-white cotton gown that looked amazingly like a Millerite ascension robe. She was carrying a bundle of letters and papers bound with a single piece of twine.

The Millerites were followers of William Miller, who predicted that the second coming of the Lord would occur on October 22, 1844. Many of his followers sold all their possessions and purchased white gowns in order to be properly dressed as they ascended to the pearly gates. After the date came and passed, October 22, 1844 became known as "The Great Disappointment." I guess someone had figured that Betsey's ascension seemed a bit more certain and purchased one of the unused robes for her.

Betsey wore her hair down on her shoulders without a bonnet or ribbon. She had brushed it for an hour that morning, creating a stark contrast as her dark brown hair glistened against the basic white robe. The countenance of her face was much different than when I saw her last. It was much softer, without sorrow. An accurate description would be that she had the glow of a bride on her wedding day. Her scar was barely noticeable. She looked absolutely beautiful. Her intimidating, cat-like green eyes had changed to be innocent and loving. The looming gallows might have been the motivation for her conversion, but the midnight baptism in the Embarrass River had truly changed her. The green-eyed monster was now a child of God. She said good-bye to the jailers and asked for their forgiveness, which was immediately given.

Betsey walked over and handed me the bundle of papers. "The answers are all there, Nathan," she said. "It's everything you wanted to know. I figured you would be the only one who might want to set the record straight. The only condition is that you can't read the letters until after I'm gone."

"Sure, Betsey, whatever you say."

"There's one more thing," Betsey added. "Sheriff Thorn, is it all right if I have a minute alone with Nathan? It will be my last request."

"I don't see how that would be a problem; why don't you use my office." He pulled out a ring of keys and unlocked the door.

I closed the door behind us and sat on the sheriff's oversized desk. I looked to see if there were any weapons lying around, just to be on the safe side. There weren't.

"Please, Nathan, just listen to me and don't say a word. I know that you've been trying to help me, and I'm grateful, I truly am. But I realize now that this is my destiny. I've done horrible things in my life, and this is my punishment. But as Reverend Seed says, I'm now washed in the blood of the Lamb. As soon as I leave this body, I'll be with Jesus for eternity. I don't deserve salvation, but the Lord has given it to me anyway. I am ready to leave this world and start all over in heaven. But before I go, I wanted to ask your forgiveness. You were always kind to me, even when I hurt you. I guess that's why I'm trying to tell you that I fell in love with you on the day we met. I was jealous when you came home with Eveline, and did everything possible to make sure you two wouldn't stay together. It was a horrible thing to do, and I've cost you your chance at being happy with her. I've only told you this because I hope that someday you'll find a way in your heart to forgive me for my evildoing. I still love you, and I ask forgiveness for feeling this way, but I wanted you to know how I felt."

"I forgave you on that Christmas night when you saved the Fuller baby. That was my first glimpse of the woman I see now."

Tears started to well up in her eyes. "Thank you so much. It means everything to me to hear you say that. If I could, though, I'd like to ask you one last thing, and if you don't want to...I'll understand." She hesitated and stared at the floor.

"What is it, Betsey? I'll do whatever I can."

"I was wondering if you would hold me in your arms for a minute and let me pretend that you loved me, too. It would give me a memory to help me get through these last few minutes."

At first, I started to back away, thinking of Liddy, but then I concluded it was very little to ask of me. I took her in my arms and held her tight against me. I could feel her tremble and then sob as we stood alone in silence. I was filled with several emotions all at once. I felt guilt, pity, regret, shame, and even some measure of love toward Betsey. It wasn't a love of want or desire, but rather a reciprocal love in response to her confession. The embrace was intense and sincere, but the clock was ticking, and I became aware that we had gone past our allotted time. I didn't know how to break the embrace, so I gently lifted her face and softly kissed her lips.

"Thank you, Nathan," she said, wiping the tears from her eyes with the sleeve of her robe. "I'm ready to go now." She walked directly over to the sheriff and held out her hands to be put into handcuffs.

Sheriff Thorn placed the shackles on her wrists and opened the door. Betsey stepped back when she saw the magnitude of the crowd. Thousands of people pushed close to get a look at the convicted murderess. The mob parted as a deputy walked with a pair of huge brown oxen pulling a farm cart toward the jail door. Betsey gasped when she saw the rough pine casket resting in the back of the cart. Sheriff Thorn lifted her onto the cart, and she took her seat on her own coffin. Mrs. Hennissee, outraged by the humiliating act of making her ride to her death in such a horrible way, climbed into the cart, took a seat next to Betsey and clutched her hand tightly.

The crowd began to roar the usual insults as the cart slowly began to inch down the hill.

"Hang the witch!" a woman yelled, igniting the wrath of the onlookers.

"Hanging's too good for her! Burn her!"

"Lord, give me strength," Betsey whispered, as she clutched Julia Ann's hand as tight as she could. She looked toward the sky, afraid to make eye contact with anyone.

Reverend Seed, anticipating that things might get ugly, had recruited two dozen men from his congregation to walk next to the cart. On his command, they started singing at the top of their lungs:

"Rock of ages, cleft for me,
Let me hide myself in Thee."

Betsey joined in, and about half of the crowd followed along. The others, who I assumed were not of the church-going type, cursed even louder, demanding blood and a pound of flesh.

Sheriff Thorn walked silently behind the cart, feeling ill in his stomach. "If we make it through the day without getting anyone else killed, it will be a miracle," he mumbled to himself. He looked up and caught a glimpse of Judge Wilson watching the proceedings from the safety of his office. He was right about the mob and its need for justice, but he thought the judge was wrong for not granting clemency. They could have moved her out in the middle of the night and avoided this whole event. They couldn't lynch her if they couldn't find her.

Betsey seemed to be energized by the hymn and even stood up in the cart with her hands lifted toward the sky. This made her a better target, and some boys started throwing dirt clods at her as she passed by. One hit her squarely in the side of the head and dazed her momentarily, causing her to fall down on the casket. She quickly gained her composure and stood up again. "Praise be to Jesus," she yelled to the mob, stirring the people into even more of a frenzy.

Someone threw another clod that missed Betsey and hit Sheriff Thorn. He immediately jumped in the back of the cart and fired his rifle into the air. The crowd became completely silent. "If I see anyone interfering with the progress of this cart again, I'm going to make sure that person spends the next thirty days in jail. Do I make myself clear?" People dropped their clods and rocks and gave the cart plenty of room as it passed by. Reverend Seed started singing again and was soon joined by the faithful.

The cart turned onto Second Street, heading toward a grove of sugar maples at the water's edge of the Embarrass River. Betsey looked around and seemed startled by the number of people sitting on the hillside of the natural amphitheater. No less than twenty thousand people had gathered to witness her execution. It was the largest crowd that has ever been assembled in the State of Illinois.

Mrs. Hennissee sensed that she was overwhelmed by the size of the crowd and steadied her as they rounded the corner. She almost fainted when the single braced beam gallows came into sight. The deputy pulled the wagon next to the platform, which was held in place by a rope that was tied to a spike in the ground. Betsey refused to look at the noose, which dangled ominously only a few feet away.

Eveline Deal McKinney was seated in a chair next to her husband and Harrison Reed. She didn't try to hide her animosity toward Betsey as she glared at her with burning contempt, far beyond any hope of forgiveness. I couldn't help but notice that Eveline had aged in the last month; her eyes had dulled and lost their sparkle of youth. She was starting to swell, as she was now two months pregnant, and was pale from an earlier bout of morning sickness. She looked at me and then turned away quickly. She was angry and felt betrayed by the fact that I had tried to stop the hanging. I felt guilty for not taking her away from this mess when I had the chance. The girl who had been so full of love and hope for the future had replaced that love with a soul-consuming hatred for Betsey, a hatred so strong that it would not be quenched even with the destruction of her nemesis.

Reverend Seed stepped up on the ox-cart as people pushed closer to the gallows. Children climbed on the shoulders of the adults, while others filled the limbs of the surrounding trees. Everyone was trying to get a look at the Green-Eyed Monster. Sheriff Thorn fired his rifle in the air to quiet the crowd once again, and Reverend Seed started to speak in a booming voice.

"Today is a day of rejoicing! For Sister Elizabeth Reed is washed in the blood of the Lamb, baptized, sealed up, and bound for glory."

"Amen!" yelled Betsey loud enough so that everyone within a quarter mile could hear her.

The crowd remained silent. They were there to see the notorious Betsey Reed get what she deserved for killing her poor husband, not the rapture of one of the chosen saints. The mob remained silent and a bit confused. No one had ever seen a woman hung before, so this was new territory for everyone. Never one to miss an opportunity to spread the Gospel, Reverend Seed started into a sermon that seemed to pull thunder down from the sky. The public hanging of Betsey Reed had turned into the world's largest revival meeting.

Reverend Seed exhorted the masses for over an hour, and even offered an altar call, which was answered by dozens. Betsey seemed to be enjoying the whole spectacle, and shouted, "Glory, Hallelujah, and Amen," through the entire sermon. To say that the Lord works in mysterious ways would be a colossal understatement.

When the discourse was over, Reverend Seed walked over to Betsey and told her to be brave. In a few minutes, she would be with her Savior, who was also executed in public and was jeered at by a mob.

Betsey smiled and simply said, "I'm ready."

Reverend Seed jumped down from the cart and helped Mrs. Hennissee to the ground, where she took a spot beside him.

Sheriff Thorn climbed into the wagon and unlocked the shackles from Betsey's wrists, then took a thick piece of twine and tied her hands behind her back He tried to inflict as little pain as possible. He positioned her on the platform and asked her if she had any last words. She shook her head no and closed her eyes. He took a black bag made out of a rough sackcloth and placed it over her head, then secured the heavy hemp noose around her neck, being careful to position the knot behind her left ear as per the judge's instructions. The black hood of the condemned murderess stood out in contrast to the snow-white choir robe, symbolizing how paradoxical the entire execution had become.

Reverend Seed, along with some of his congregation, fell to his knees in prayer while Mrs. Hennissee collapsed in a heap on the ground. Eveline Deal McKinney clenched her teeth together in anticipation. I stood in the background, pretending this was all a bad dream.

Sheriff Thorn climbed out of the wagon, grabbed his newly sharpened axe, and circled slowly toward the gallows. A deputy pulled the cart away while another deputy steadied Betsey's legs, making sure she didn't lose her balance and hang herself by accident. Betsey stood still as a statue and never made a sound.

The sheriff pulled a court document from his vest pocket and began to read the court order:

And now, on this day, the prisoner and defendant in custody comes to receive the sentence of the court, whereupon the court pronounced the following sentence. The Judgment of the Law and the Court Pronounces it, that you, Elizabeth Reed, be taken from hence to the place of your confinement, and that on the twenty-third day of May, you are to be taken from thence to some convenient place within one mile of this courthouse and there be hanged by the neck until you are dead, and the sheriff shall execute this sentence. And may the Lord have mercy on your soul. Honorable William Wilson, Judge."

Sheriff Thorn neatly folded the court order and placed it carefully back into his pocket. He grabbed his axe and took a deep breath. "Lord, make my aim true," he prayed. As he lifted the axe over his head, a thunderous crack and boom came from the grove of maple trees. Spectators had overloaded a branch, causing it to snap, sending its inhabitants tumbling to the ground. Thorn thought about waiting to see if anyone was hurt, but decided to continue while he still had the nerve. While much of the crowd was watching the commotion by the maple tree, he struck the rope dead center, causing the platform to fall under the pressure of Betsey's weight.

She fell approximately two feet until the slack was gone, causing a violent stop to her freefall. Her neck snapped immediately and her body started to twirl clockwise as if she were dancing. Some cried, some cheered, and others watched in silence as Betsey's lifeless body spiraled in the afternoon sun next to the river.

Eveline walked over to Betsey's body and touched her hand to confirm she was actually dead. Once convinced of her demise, she walked away, wishing they could have done more to punish her. Her death had been too humane, she thought. She had wanted Betsey Reed to suffer. Eveline wouldn't have been satisfied with anything short of boiling or burning, the standard methods of eradicating witches.

Within minutes, the vast gathering of twenty thousand began to disperse. Many of the women spoke of how hard and cold she looked on the way to the gallows, while many of the men spoke softly about how beautiful she appeared to be in her white gown. "Good riddance!" shouted the women. "What a waste of a good-looking female," whispered the men.

Sheriff Thorn leaned against a tree several feet from the gallows, contemplating the proper amount of time to leave the body hanging. He had heard of cases where they had cut the body down too soon only to find the prisoner still alive. The last thing he wanted to do was hang her again, so he decided that twenty minutes would be enough.

William Hennissee helped his wife walk back up the hill toward their home, assuring her that Betsey was in a better place. Reverend Seed gave final instructions to the undertaker to take Betsey's coffin over to the cemetery and bury her in the area set aside for the Methodist Church. Later in the afternoon, he would go over to the gravesite and say a few words over her. He would go alone, as she requested.

Isaac Fail watched silently from the top of the hill, then left for the Yellow Banks Tavern and started to drink heavily.

Judge William Wilson watched from the courthouse as the people quietly left the hanging with their bloodlust satisfied. He looked at Governor Ford's pardon letter one last time, then threw it into the fireplace and burned it as if it had never existed.

John Gimble, the reporter for the *New York Herald*, rushed back to catch the stage coach to Vincennes. In two weeks, he would be back in New York City to file his report.

I walked slowly back to the Yellow Banks Tavern, carrying the bundle of papers Betsey had given me. I was anxious to read what she had to say, but couldn't bring myself to look at them. The vision of her twirling around at the end of the rope was too fresh in my mind.

Betsey Reed, The Green-Eyed Monster, The Wicked Witch of the Dark Bend, was dead.

Thirty-Seven

Even in death, Betsey managed to stir up a fuss. After the crowd was gone and she was placed in her casket, the undertaker loaded her in his new funeral carriage and made his way toward the city cemetery, which was about a mile west of the gallows. Instead of taking the river road, which would have been more discreet, he decided to drive back up the hill past the courthouse where he was sure to cause a commotion. Any publicity was good for business, and he wasn't going to miss any opportunity to promote himself.

Unfortunately, some people became outraged when they realized she was headed toward the cemetery. "That's hallowed ground. It's reserved for God-fearing Christians!"

A few of the more self-righteous of the mob actually blocked the entrance to the cemetery and started to assault the undertaker's carriage, intending to throw Betsey's body into the Embarrass River.

Reverend Seed got word of what was happening and came riding at break-neck speed, waving his Bible as if it were a sword. He jumped from his mount and literally beat them over the head with the Word of God until they backed away from the carriage. Many of the churchgoers who were not part of the Methodist congregation remained steadfast and refused to allow Betsey entry. As a compromise, the mob consented to allow Betsey to be laid to rest beneath an oak tree just outside of the cemetery.

As dozens of people watched, two young gravediggers lowered Betsey Reed into a shallow grave beside the entry gates. Satisfied that they had protected holy ground, the mob quietly went home.

However, two overzealous medical students, who were serving apprenticeships with a local doctor named Lowell, saw an opportunity for an advanced lesson in the female anatomy. Shortly after sundown, they quietly exhumed Betsey's body, wrapped it in a blanket, took the back streets to a barn behind Dr. Lowell's office, and began to perform an autopsy.

As they cut into her bowels, they were surprised to find almost five pounds of stones and brick mortar. They concluded that Betsey must have swallowed them in a suicide attempt to avoid the humiliation of public execution.

Unfortunately for the interns, that's as far as they got. A caretaker at the cemetery who was acquainted with Isaac Fail witnessed the two men rob the grave. Afraid to confront the men himself, he knew Isaac was at the Yellow Banks Tavern and went to find him at once.

Isaac left the tavern, throwing chairs out of his way as he stormed out the door. As soon as I discovered what had transpired, I was right behind him. By the time I got to the barn he was beating both of the young men with a wooden beam. One was covered in blood, and the other was dazed and on the floor. I pulled him away, trying to convince him there had been enough killing. He took a swing at me and missed by inches. I grabbed his arm and used his momentum to pin him against the wall. After a few tense moments, he agreed. He kicked the interns one last time to get the last of the hostility out of his system and ordered them to sew Betsey up just as she had been before.

The distress of the day's incidents had left her body almost beyond recognition. She was no longer Isaac's little sister, but rather a twisted bag of bones that simply needed to be put to rest. He began to well up with emotion again, and I thought we were headed for more violence when he turned and asked me if I could bury Betsey next to Leonard. I told him I didn't think the neighborhood folks would mind, but I suggested that we bury her the next night, in secret, to be on the safe side. I have always found it easier to ask for forgiveness instead of permission.

I accompanied Isaac Fail along with his wife and children as they hauled the pine casket northeast to Heathsville. We arrived at Baker Cemetery around midnight, and by the light of hickory branch torches, we quietly buried Betsey next to Leonard.

A few folks started to raise a fuss about Betsey tainting the cemetery, but Hannah Fuller came to Betsey's defense, reminding everyone of the fact that Betsey had saved her and her baby on Christmas Day, and that one good deed alone ought to be reason enough to allow her to rest in peace. No one could argue with such an impassioned plea, so Betsey was allowed to stay next to Leonard for eternity.

A few weeks later, a wooden marker appeared over their graves with the simple inscription:

Leonard Reed
Died August 19, 1844
Death By Murder

Elizabeth "Betsey" Reed
Died May 23, 1845
Death By Hanging

It remains a mystery as to who donated the grave marker. For some odd reason, the donor never took credit for the gift. In a ghoulish way, Leonard's and Betsey's graves became a popular tourist attraction. Everyone who stopped with the stagecoach at The Heath Inn wanted to see the grave of the infamous murderess. For a small fee, Rennick would take the curious travelers to the cemetery and give his ever-changing account of the Reeds' untimely demise.

As time goes by, Leonard seems to get more righteous, and Betsey becomes more sinister. But regardless of the truth, the saga of Leonard and Betsey Reed has always fascinated people and probably always will. In reality, there were no winners in this tragedy. Only losers. Betsey Reed's name will live on in infamy as the first and only woman to be hanged in the State of Illinois, a convicted murderess who gave her husband a little extra sweetening in his sassafras tea.

However, the story doesn't end with Betsey's death.

After Betsey was buried, I tried to get back to my life as best I could. I wanted to forget about the last few months and pretend that everything had been a bad dream, but it was no use; there were too many unanswered questions. With all of the commotion that surrounded Betsey's burial, I realized I had forgotten the bundle of papers she had given me prior to her execution. I had left them with the owner of the Yellow Banks Tavern in Lawrenceville, intending to retrieve them on my way home. At first, I decided to leave Betsey Reed in the past, but then I remembered her words: *"The answers are all there...It's everything that you wanted to know."*

Liddy wasn't due back for a couple of weeks, so I saddled Newton and headed south toward Lawrenceville, hoping the bundle would still be there. Miraculously, it was exactly where I had left it, completely undisturbed. Being careful not to divulge the contents of my package, I thanked the tavern keeper for his diligence and honesty. I left immediately and looked for a quiet place where I could finally learn what happened on that infamous August day.

I found a shady spot beneath a sugar maple tree on the southern shore of the Embarrass River, near the location of Betsey's hanging. I could see the remnants of the gallows and the spot where Betsey had been baptized over a month ago. I considered it to be an appropriate place to read her manuscript. As I searched though the stack, I found journal entries detailing the sins and adventures of her youth, including the demise of two evil men in the Dark Bend. She included a brief history of her adult years along with a lecture on the proper use of the healing arts. She recorded many of her random thoughts during her final days, but it was a single-page letter, hastily written on parchment, which completed her story.

May 23, 1845

Dear Nathan,

As the sun is starting to rise on my last morning, I find it hard to steady my hand to write this letter. I'm as prepared as one can possibly be for departure, but I must admit that I am horribly frightened, and pray that I am able to die with some measure of dignity. I am confident that I am washed in the blood of the Lamb and will be with the Lord at day's end, and only wish that I could have come to know this peace earlier. Even though God's judgment is the only one that matters, I would like to set the record straight as to what transpired on the day of Leonard's death. I hate to burden you again, but you are the only one who I trust to tell my story. Even if you don't believe what I have to say, I will go to my grave knowing that at least one person has heard the truth.

Did I poison Leonard? The answer, I'm ashamed to say, is...yes. Did I kill Leonard? The answer to that question is...no. Most of what Eveline said at the trial was true. I did stir arsenic into Leonard's tea in the hope of killing him. The part of Eveline's testimony that wasn't true was that it all happened over a year before Leonard's death, shortly before your trip to Springfield. Leonard became violently ill, but recovered after two days of bed rest. When Eveline became suspicious and accused me of trying to kill him, I knew that if anything happened to Leonard, I would be blamed. From that moment on, I did everything within my power to keep Leonard alive.

The most ironic part of this tragedy is that, on the morning of his death, Leonard actually asked me to end his misery. I refused, but I suspect that Eveline overheard the conversation. I'm sure that's where she got the idea to combine the facts and get rid of me in the process. It would have been pointless to defend myself by telling the truth, because it would only incriminate me for the earlier act. Besides, I doubt that anyone was going to believe the wicked witch of the Dark Bend.

But it doesn't matter now. My soul is at peace, as I have been born again. I wish that things were different, but I realize I was never suited for this world. Thank you for attending my baptism, as it did mean a lot to me to have you there. I've not done right by you over the past few years, and I ask that you find it in your heart to forgive me. I hope to see you one last time before the trip to the gallows. There are some things I'd like to tell you in person, but if it doesn't come about, I want to wish you a long and happy life. Use this letter as you see fit, as I trust your judgment completely.

In Christian love,

Betsey

I read the letter several times before placing it back in the bundle and then into my saddlebag. If what she said was true, then Eveline Deal had murdered Betsey with a lie. The ramifications would be devastating if the information became public. I considered giving the letter to the sheriff or to Augustus French, but decided it would be an act of futility. It would only open up old wounds and divide the community all over again.

After a week of mulling over my options, I filled a jug with sassafras tea and walked two miles until I reached the bluff above Doe Run Creek, which now goes by the name of Baker Cemetery. I walked to the southwest corner and stood directly over the graves of Leonard and Betsey Reed. I pulled the cork out with my teeth and took a healthy slug of tea, then divided the rest by pouring an equal amount over husband and wife. I popped the cork back into the empty bottle and took Betsey's letter and placed it on the dirt directly over her grave. With the flick of a match, the parchment disappeared in a small consuming flame.

"You'll have to trust my judgment," I told her in an apologetic voice. After giving her a chance to respond, I walked back to my cabin on the Wabash, and with Newton, Ole Hickory, and Kate the Cat, I waited for Liddy to return.

Epilogue

In 1846, Augustus C. French was elected as the ninth governor of Illinois. In 1848, he became the first governor ever to be re-elected in the state's history. After retirement, he moved back to Maplewood, his country home south of Palestine. But after two years he became bored, so when the opportunity presented itself, he accepted the offer to start a law school at McKendree College in Lebanon, Illinois.

In 1857, Jesse K. Dubois was elected Illinois State Auditor, and he moved to Springfield where he bought a house next door to his good friend, Abraham Lincoln. He assisted Lincoln with his presidential campaign and was at his side on election night. Jessie became bitter, though, when he didn't receive a patronage position during Lincoln's first administration. Jesse became even more resentful when James Harlan was chosen as Secretary of the Interior due to the fact that he was a Methodist and Dubois was a Catholic. The two men did reconcile their differences at the end of the war, and Jessie served as a pallbearer at Lincoln's funeral. Jessie and Adelia's son, Fred Dubois, went on to serve two terms as senator for the State of Idaho.

Judge William Wilson retired as Illinois Supreme Court Chief Justice in 1848 and practiced law in Carmi, Illinois until his death in 1857. His twenty-four years as an Illinois Supreme Court Justice is still the longest term of service in the history of the state.

State's attorney Aaron Shaw went on to become a circuit judge, and served as a member of the Illinois State House of Representatives. Shaw was also elected as a member of the United States Congress on two separate occasions, after which he retired and resumed his law practice in Olney, Illinois.

Usher Linder, the once young and promising Attorney

General, never did reach his political potential as a result of his obsessive drinking and foul language. He moved to Chicago, where he became one of the most powerful attorneys in the city. He authored a book of biographical sketches about the early judges and lawyers of Illinois, which is still considered an important work of history. He died of a liver disorder in Chicago as a very wealthy man.

Governor Thomas Ford left office at the end of his term in 1846 and moved back home to Peoria. He believed that a man shouldn't profit from public service, and he left his family penniless at the time of his death in 1850. Some years later, his sons were convicted of horse thievery in Kansas and were hanged by the neck until dead. The Governor of Kansas refused to grant them a pardon.

General Othneil Looker delivered a rousing speech on the necessity of freedom at the Independence Day celebration in Palestine in 1845. He died three weeks later at the age of ninety-two. He was buried in Palestine at Kitchell Cemetery next to his granddaughter, Clarissa, who had died during childbirth a few years earlier. Clarissa was Augustus French's first wife.

Reverend John Seed continued to preach and spread the gospel for the rest of his days. At his funeral, the entire town of Lawrenceville came out to pay their respects. It was said to be the largest public gathering in the history of Lawrence County with the exception of the hanging of Betsey Reed.

Sheriff Sam Thorn finished out his term and did not seek re-election. Soured by Betsey's execution, he moved to Bridgeport, Illinois, and opened the village's first grocery store.

Rennick Heath continued to act as hub of the community, and later gained a measure of regional fame as the creator of the Heath Cling Peach. It should be mentioned that his nephew, L.S. Heath, later made a name for himself in the chocolate industry. Rennick and Malinda are buried at the center of Baker Cemetery, thirty yards from Leonard and Betsey Reed.

Harrison Reed, humiliated by the trial, sold his farm and

moved out west. He was never heard from again.

Eveline Deal McKinney lived on a farm near New Hebron with her husband, Thomas, and their two small children. Eveline died while giving birth to her third child at the age of twenty-four. Thomas McKinney remarried within a year and had three more children. His second wife's name was Emiline.

Leonard and Betsey Reed remain side by side beneath a giant maple tree in the southwest corner of Baker Cemetery. Shortly after Betsey's death, the gravesite became a popular site for impromptu picnics and tea parties. The tradition is still practiced today, and from what I can tell, Leonard and Betsey don't mind at all.

As for me, I passed the Illinois State Bar Exam on July 1, 1845. Liddy and I were married the next evening at the Dubois Tavern in Palestine. The wedding was supposed to be a small, intimate affair, but Adelia Dubois had secretly invited over a hundred people who were all in attendance that night. The party was said to have lasted all night long, but we weren't around to see it end. As soon as our vows were exchanged, we jumped into our new carriage, a wedding gift from the Dubois Family, and ordered Newton to take us to our new home beneath the Five Sisters.

After remaining silent on the subject for so many years, I decided that I owed it to Betsey to set the record straight and tell her story. She was a complex woman, wild and untamed, and was full of hatred and love. She was hurtful to some and a healer to others. She could be passionate and vicious at the same time. To use Betsey's words, she was really never suited for this world. Hopefully, she's found the hereafter more to her liking. As the years go by, the Legend of Betsey Reed seems to grow with each rendition. Everyone remembers the arsenic in the tea and the jail burning, along with the trial and the massive crowd at her hanging. But few remember that Betsey found redemption in the end, which proves that there is hope for all of us.

Author's Note

The reader of any historical novel is entitled to know who among the characters are real and who are fictional. The following people are real: Elizabeth "Betsey" Reed; Leonard Reed; Harrison Reed; Eveline Deal; Rennick and Malinda Heath; Jesse and Adelia Dubois; Augustus French; Usher Linder; Aaron Shaw; Thomas McKinney; Judge William Wilson; Sheriff Sam Thorn; Sheriff Leonard Cullom; Othneil Looker; Dr. John Logan; Dr. Josiah Wynn; John Herriman; Abraham Fail; Eli Adams; Major Gaines; Governor Thomas Ford; Reverend John Seed; Julia Ann Hennissee; Father Augustus Bessonies; and everyone at the Palestine Christmas celebration. Green Baker was a real person who was killed while participating in a race for the jug shortly before Leonard Reed's death.

Hannah Fuller was not real; however, there were several Fuller families living in the Heathsville vicinity in 1845. Likewise, Sam McCarter was not real; however, a man named McCarter did loan Leonard Reed money shortly before he died. McCarter claimed to have witnessed Betsey mixing a mysterious powder into Leonard's squirrel stew.

All of the bad guys, Will Davis, Alfred Dean, Jesse Scott, Doyle Popplewell, and Eli Napier, are fictional.

Liddy Parker and Charlotte Campbell are fictional, which is a shame since they're both great gals.

Nathan Crockett is also a fictional character. *Nathan* is in tribute to a grandfather on my mother's side of the family, Nathan Berry Farmer, who was killed as a union soldier during the Battle of Shiloh in 1862. *Crockett* is in tribute to a grandfather on my father's side of the family, David Crockett, grandfather to Davy.

With the exception of the cabin beneath the Five Sisters, all locations are historical.

I owe a debt of gratitude to Teri Nash for her countless hours of research and to Terry Gillies Fear, "a real straight shooter," for editing my assault on the English language.

I would also like to thank Mark Weber (the historian, not the lawyer), whose previous work on the subject of Betsey Reed made this book possible.

I would also like to give an honorable mention to Tom Compton, who suggested a fictional character as the storyteller. Nathan thanks you, too.

Kudos to the librarians at The Abraham Lincoln Presidential Library, Palestine Public Library, Lawrenceville Public Library, Robinson Public Library, The Merom Public Library and The Susie Wesley Memorial Library in Flat Rock. Bless them all!

And finally, thanks to Anna, Ben, and Beth, whose love and support inspired me to persevere.

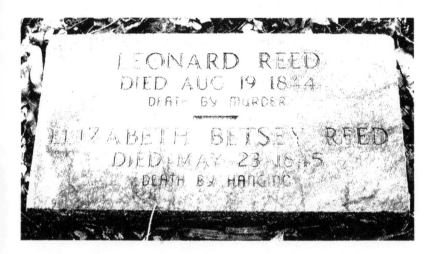

14345741R00162

Made in the USA
San Bernardino, CA
23 August 2014